PROSE FICTION

PROSE FICTION

UEA MA
Creative Writing Anthologies
2020

CONTENTS

RACHEL CUSK	Foreword	IX
PHILIP LANGESKOV & NAOMI WOOD	Introduction	XIII
EMMA BAMFORD	These Yellow Sands	2
TANYA BANERJEE	Somewhere In Between	8
PHILIP BRENNAN	Concrete Beaches	16
CHRISTABELLE DILKS	Flotsam	22
JOHN DIMITROFF	Total	28
DREW EVANS	Trap House	36
ALICE FRANKLIN	Life Hacks for an Alien	42
ELAINE FROST	Natural Selection	48
YAN GE	The Little House	54
CARA GEORGE	Fight, Flight, Freeze, Comply, Film (FFFCF)	62
LINDEN HIBBERT	Daphne	70
DELWAR HUSSAIN	All The Man That I Need	76
MAIRÉAD KIERNAN	A Million Pop Rocks	82
PEGGY LEE	Goodbye Happiness	88
JOSEPHINE LISTER	Little Yellow Teeth	96
MARGARET MEYER	The Cleftwater Poppet	102
LAUREN MOONEY	Tank	108
HANNAH MURPHY	Galatea of Gretton Road	114
ZAINAB OMAKI	I Promise These Many Fights Will Make Us	120
JYOTI PATEL	Six of One	126
ABHISHEK PRASAD	Bloody Child	132
LUCIEN ROSS	How to Survive a Fairy Tale	138
REX ROWLEY	Untitled	144
LILY SHAHMOON	Pas de Deux	150
ELEANOR SHEEHAN	Ghostwriter	156
ELLISON SKINNER	The Teakettler	160
ROBERT F W SMITH	Halcyon Days	166
REBECCA SOLLOM	The Fireman	172
STEPHANIE Y TAM	An Inheritance of Flight	178

OMER TENNENHAUS	The Sticking Point	184
RAJASREE VARIYAR	The Wanted Girl	190
J H L WAI	Tysami	196
DANIEL WILES	A Black Country Parable	202
BROCK ZAWILA	A Dome Within Falling Domes	208

    Acknowledgements   215

RACHEL CUSK
Foreword

It may be that this period – the spring and early summer of 2020 – is looked back on as anomalous or is half-forgotten, but it is nonetheless the case that for the past two months the confinement and isolation that are the private conditions of creativity have been curiously expanded to make a shared public reality. We are living for now in a society-wide simulation of the writer's life. Those people for whom this represents normality may have had cause to reflect, therefore, on what they do, since their terrain has been made, as it were, open to the public. Whatever else the crisis has done, it has exposed the creative space – or moment, or opportunity – in the lives of large numbers of people for whom that space is generally unavailable or concealed.

One response to that exposure has doubtless been to recoil from it, finding the suspension of normal life unacceptable. The idea that that social reality is not invincible is deeply disillusioning for those who rely on and believe in the values of the real. What the withdrawal of this reality can seem to have exposed is simply a blank. I have seen and heard numerous writers and artists say that they themselves have been unable to create under these conditions, as though the seclusion in which they customarily perform their activities needs to run counter to, or constitute their own withdrawal from, normal life. The choice to be alone is an exercise of freedom; the obligation to be is not. There is often a note of shame, even of anger, in these admissions. Given uninterrupted time and space, the creative artist 'ought' to be able to create. The selfsame need that drove him or her to seek the public identity of artist has now brought about a kind of exposé of something that perhaps feels, at bottom, fraudulent.

But many non-artists might indeed find in social isolation an opportunity for a reunion with a long-lost part of themselves; this could be an additional cause of irritation for people who have dared to stake a great deal on retaining that part and giving it utterance in daily life. Yet in that same sense, there has been a chance in these weeks for the writer or artist to revisit the site of their own original impulse to create, and to examine when and where – if indeed they do exist – these feelings of fraudulence came into being. In the early days of a writer's career, it might seem that the impulse is almost entirely internalised, to the point of being half-unconscious. It springs from a need, not from a blank; or rather, it is continuous with rather than blocked off from the self. The activity of writing seems and is both legitimate and illegitimate in equal parts, legitimate in its internal reality, inadmissible or invisible as a public act. Publication legitimises the whole thing: one is entitled to be – and call oneself – a writer. Yet the suspicion later on that in the course of that exposure the internal reality was bruised or neglected is easily entertained, and can keep growing. The very thing that had once seemed irreducibly authentic, to have been the only entirely necessary part of the process, can sometimes feel relegated to a corner, to be glanced at occasionally with guilt. The questions – do I write simply to get published? would I still write if I weren't paid to do it, or if I knew I would never be published again? – aren't just private manifestations of these feelings of guilt or impostor-hood: they are asked of writers in public with extraordinary frequency. What they signify is not a culture-wide mistrust of writers, but a suspicion about the self, entertained privately and spoken aloud. The person who asks the question asks it in a condition of personal doubt about the value and meaning of their own creativity, and about whether that creativity has been lost or betrayed; and if so, what the moral status of the betrayal is.

Creative writers are people endeavouring to maintain or reforge their links to their original selves. Part of that endeavour lies in the struggle to serve and find meaning in reality, and ultimately to align oneself to it sufficiently to offer an authoritative interpretation of what one sees. It is an attempt to understand and represent the world while remaining in it as a vulnerable and fallible living thing. Yet the nature of reality is to upset this balance and offer challenges to the sense of self: art – whether one's own or other people's – can appear casually swept away by the instability of our environment, just as a child's game can be scattered and ruined by someone carelessly interrupting it. What I remember from the years I spent learning to be a writer was the difficulty of bringing these two opposites – the burning importance of the play-world and the utter indifference of the actual world – into sufficient balance for the work to be done. It remains, in fact, the central difficulty of creative work, one that is always presenting itself anew.

This period, for me, has represented a kind of armistice in that conflict: since the actual world has broken down, play can at the very least command the field for a period. I have enjoyed the return, as it were, to my roots, and have found myself far less fettered in the conception and composition of my work. Most of all I have been sustained by it, absorbed by and interested in it for its own sake, in much the same way I was as an unpublished writer. Perhaps when the actual world went away, it took the criticisms and the caveats and the possibilities of mockery and abuse with it. For the emerging writer, the fear will be that no one is listening. My advice to the writers of this volume, and to my younger self, is to enjoy the silence while it lasts and to use it well.

PHILIP LANGESKOV AND NAOMI WOOD
Introduction

J M Coetzee's novel, *Elizabeth Costello*, begins with a short discourse on the problem of beginning, of getting us from where we are – 'as yet, nowhere' – to where we need to be: 'the far bank'. 'It is,' the narrator tells us, 'a simple bridging problem, a problem of knocking together a bridge.' As any writer can tell you, beginning anything – a book, a story, a career, a foreword to an anthology – is rarely as simple as it might sound. And yet, Coetzee's analogy feels consoling: we can do this, it seems to be saying; people do this kind of thing, solve this kind of problem, all the time.

In some ways, a creative writing course is its own bridging problem. Each year we have to find a way to get a new cohort of writers from the beginning to the end. Each year the bridge is a little different – and carries writers of different kinds – but each bridge unfolds in broadly the same fashion. Not this year.

Back in September we welcomed some thirty writers who had made the journey from their various parts of the world – Canada, America, Nigeria, India, Hong Kong, Israel, France, Australia, China, Ireland – to the city of Norwich. Among them were realists and fantasists, short story writers and novelists, utopianists and apocalyptics, writers of the grand sweeping vision and the delicate intimate gesture. Each came with their own dream for their work and what might happen in the year that then lay ahead. In all these imaginaries, surely none anticipated what has transpired since.

As we write, the world is in the grip of a pandemic. Countries across the globe are in lockdown. Hundreds of thousands have died of an illness that didn't even have a name back in September. In very recent days – yesterday, the day before – cities across America have been gripped by riots and protests against a deep legacy of racial injustice that is particular to that country, but that is far too present in many other countries, including this one. The mood, almost everywhere, is tense, uncertain and fearful.

In this context, the fate of thirty-odd writers in a university city in the east of England is relatively small beer. Even so, for the last year we have worked with these writers very closely. We have seen their excitement when their work has broken new ground; we have seen their frustration when it has become stuck. And so, we have been conscious these past few months that they have not had the experience they were expecting, the experience for which many of them made considerable sacrifices. Prevented from coming to campus, denied conventional social interaction and uprooted from the communities they were in the process of forming. In addition, they have had to experience – as so many have around the world – the peculiar and particular burden of living in this strange, as yet unfinished moment.

In the circumstances, we can only commend them for their forbearance: for keeping going, for preserving their communities and helping one another through; for bringing the same energy and commitment to their digital workshops as they did IRL; for continuing, goddammit, to write. It is possible, in the end, that all this disorder and confusion will prove some of the best teaching these writers will ever receive. As we say in more normal times, there is no such thing as a perfect condition for writing. This cohort of writers will perhaps have a better grasp on that than any before.

Nobody knows what the future will bring – what will happen to our politics, to our societies, to our systems of living. We might like to be hopeful, might even be able to identify sources of hope. If hope is too much to hope for, however, perhaps we can find sources of consolation, or at least relief. Early in the pandemic, Maggie Nelson, writing in the *New Yorker,* delivered an essay that while short on hope proves long on consolation. An account of the pleasure of rereading Natalia Ginzburg's *Winter in the Abruzzi,* Nelson concluded with a passage of such biting luminosity that it still seems possible to see by its light:

> 'I only mean to say that, for those steeped in the belief that great calamity should not, cannot, be our lot—or that, if we work hard enough or try hard enough or hope hard enough or are good or inventive enough, we might be able to outfox it—it can be a relief to admit our folly and rejoin the species, which is defined, as are all forms of life, by a terrible and precious precarity, to which some bodies need no reintroduction.'

On that note, of neither hope nor despair, we commend to you the writers in this volume. As the opening of Coetzee's novel continues: 'Let us assume that, however it may have been done, it is done. Let us take it that the bridge is built and crossed, that we can put it out of our mind. We have left behind the territory in which we were. We are in the far territory, where we want to be.'

Philip Langeskov & Naomi Wood
June 2020

This diverse anthology showcases the work of prose writers graduating from UEA's renowned Creative Writing MA and MFA courses in 2020.

EMMA BAMFORD

Emma Bamford is a journalist who has worked for the *Independent* and *BOAT International* and the author of the travel memoirs *Casting Off* and *Untie the Lines* (Bloomsbury, 2014 and 2016). *These Yellow Sands*, her first novel, was shortlisted for the Wilbur Smith Adventure Writing Prize for Best Unpublished Manuscript in 2019.

emma@emmabamford.com

These Yellow Sands
The opening chapter of a novel

CHAPTER ONE

When you spend as much time at the mercy of the sea as I have, your soul forgets how to rest. As a seafarer, your life, and the lives of others, depend on your ability to react to the slightest changes in the environment, both internally, in the structure and seaworthiness of your vessel, and externally, in the conditions of the ocean and sky that surround it. And the one person who must always be most attuned to every creak of a bulkhead, every slam of the hull, every change in the cadence of the engines or the howl of the wind, is the captain.

Even on my off-watch, lying asleep in my narrow bunk, my soul is always alert. So that night I was already waking up before my First Officer had finished the resounding rap of his knuckles against the steel of my cabin door, was swinging my bare soles to the cool lino by the time he had turned the handle, was rubbing the sleep from my eyes as he entered and saluted me.

'Sorry to disturb you, captain.' He had his feet planted wide, to counter the pitch of the ship in the waves. There was a near-gale outside – the forerunner of a monsoon come early.

'What is it, Yusuf?'

'Flares sighted, sir.'

'Flares?' We were in the middle of the Indian Ocean, nearly a thousand nautical miles from land – Africa, Sri Lanka, Sumatra – and even further from our home port. There were no shipping lanes nearby. 'Are you sure?'

'Yes, sir.'

I reached into my locker for tomorrow's shirt. Pulled on my uniform trousers. 'How many?'

'Two. Both red parachutes. Umar saw the first one as it arced down. We waited two minutes, then a second went up.'

A gap of two minutes between the first and second. Red parachute flares. Done by the book. I slipped on my shoes. 'Any vessels showing on AIS?' My voice was squashed thin as I bent to tie the laces.

'No, sir. We think we're picking something up on radar, seven nautical miles east-south-east, but we're not sure if it's just a rain shadow.'

I strode to the door. Yusuf followed, keeping pace along the crimson-lit corridor and up the stairs to the bridge. The steel lattice reverberated beneath the soles of our government-issued shoes.

The bridge launched an immediate assault on my senses. The overhead lights were searing after the soft dimness of the corridor, and rap music blared from a phone. The air was spiked with spice and oil, and the spoor led to an illicit samosa wrapper by the bin. I decided to ignore the transgressions.

Ensign Umar was hunched over the radar, examining the screen where the range rings glowed, green leaching into black. Rainclouds and the growing sea state created ghosts on the screen, coming, going, vanishing, reappearing, changing shape with every revolution of the radar antenna. I glanced at the windshield. The wipers were set to maximum speed, and past the reach of their curves the glass was greasy with salt. Beyond, all was black.

I turned back to the radar screen. 'Where's the object?'

'Here,' said Umar, omitting the 'sir.' I suspected the rap music was his fault – his ringtone was KL Sneak's *Hit Me Up*; a lot of my men were just kampong boys, really. Umar tapped the screen at the five o'clock position. I watched the blip for a few seconds, trying to discern a pattern in the jigging pixels, to find the constancy that would tell me there was a boat out there.

The rapper was still raging. '*Chigga, you wanna know the truth, feel the truth, be the truth, but the truth is, the truth ain't ready for you.*'

It was hard to concentrate through the noise. Music was banned while on watch. Whenever I was on board, I switched off my personal phone and left it in my locker. Besides, even when we were within signal range, there was no one left to call me.

I blinked. 'Ensign Mohammed Umar bin Rayyan. Turn that off!'

'Yes, captain.' He scrambled across the bridge to the electronics panel, where his phone was on charge. He constantly had it with him, was always polishing the glass, checking it was still tucked safe in its protective case.

After he muted the music, there was a moment of blissful silence. And then I heard it. The radio.

'...day, mayday... –ver—'

'Umar!' I barked. 'The VHF.'

He was already there, reaching for the fist mic with one hand and turning up the volume on the transceiver with the other. Static filled the bridge, invading my ears like the roar of water a drowning person must hear.

The voice came through the radio again. 'May—, —day, may—ay.' Everyone stilled. '—t Santa Maria, Sailing ya—aria, Sailing yacht Sant—Ma—ia.'

'That's a woman,' Umar said.

I glared at him, straining to hear, wanting to confirm she'd said Maria. He shut up.

'—edical emergency. Require immediate assist—' the woman said, in English. When she added what I thought was 'Over,' I took the mic from Umar and replied, also in English.

'*Santa Maria*, this is Royal Malaysian Navy patrol vessel *Patusan*, over.'

There was a crunch of interference, and I wondered if my transmission had failed to reach her. I waited, my finger hovering over the transmit button. Felt Umar's and Yusuf's eyes on me. Mine were on the radar screen. Santa Maria.

'Oh my God,' she said, breathing distortion into her mic. 'Is there somebody there? There's somebody there!' She sounded British, white.

'Hello,' she said, into the radio again. 'I thought you might be a mirage.' She let out a noise, and I couldn't tell if she was laughing or crying. 'I've been calling for days. Then I saw you on my screen. This is *Santa Maria*. I mean Mayday, I mean over.'

'Ma'am,' I said, as clearly as I could. 'I understand you require assistance. I need to know the location of your vessel, and the nature of your distress.'

The connection was clearer as she read out her lat and long. She repeated it twice more, without my having to prompt her. Umar wrote down the co-ordinates, plotted the position and nodded at me to indicate it corresponded with the blip on the radar.

'Please come, please hurry,' she said, and her voice broke. 'My husband. He's badly injured. Very badly.'

'We are on our way, ma'am,' I said. Yusuf had already changed our course. 'Our ETA is...'

'Two eight minutes,' Yusuf said.

'Twenty-eight minutes,' I relayed in English.

'Oh God.'

The tremor in her words made me reach past Yusuf's shoulder to nudge the throttle forwards. Seawater exploded against the portlights. I couldn't take us any faster in this sea state.

'Ma'am,' I said, clicking down. 'What happened? To your boat? To your husband?' There was just the soft crrr of white noise. Maybe she hadn't heard me. I tried again, depressed the transmit button. 'Ma'am? Can you tell me what has happened? With *Santa Maria*?' I released my finger, listened. Again, nothing but CMB. I wondered if I was sensing reluctance, or whether I was reading too much into an unsteady radio link. Perhaps she was just out of reach of the radio, tending to her husband.

Depress. 'Ma'am,' I tried again. My voice swelled with professionalism – my ability to switch off the personal had proved a blessing in recent years. 'We are coming to you.' Release. Although perhaps 'benefit' was a better term, since I no longer believed in blessings. Depress. 'My officers are trained in first aid.' Release. I wanted – needed – to keep her on the line. Depress. 'Ma'am, what is your name?' Depress, release, transmit, receive.

A crackle. 'Virginie.'

'Virginie. I am Captain Danial Tengku.'

'Help us.' She was crying.

Often when I think of Maria, I wish someone had been there with her.

'Virginie. Listen to me. We will be with you as soon as we can. It is now,' I checked the bridge clock, 'twenty-six minutes.' She was quiet. 'Can you hear me?'

'Yes.'

'Good.'

I let thirty seconds pass. 'Virginie, are you there?'

She answered immediately. 'Yes.'

'Now our ETA is twenty-five minutes.'

While we steamed towards *Santa Maria*, I kept on calling her every thirty seconds, using her name each time, both to calm her, so that she would know she wasn't alone, and to build a connection, trust, and she told me yes, the word choked each time, as if it were tangled in a fisherman's net. Ten, twenty, fifty, fifty-two times I asked her this. Fifty-two – the number of weeks in a year, the number of cards in a deck, the number of Penangites lost that fateful day.

'Virginie, are you there?'

'Yes.'

Eventually, the drone of the engines lowered as Yusuf took all way off, and we slowed, braked by the waves. The *Patusan* bucked. I grabbed the flashlight and threw open the door to the deck. It was slippery, and I needed to hold on with one hand as I swept the churning black ocean with the beam. Nothing.

Then – boom! – the thick night was detonated, the sky lit white as day, and there, off our starboard bow, against a backdrop of star-censoring clouds, a sailing yacht was silhouetted, its sails and rigging flickering like a phantom in the guttering pyrotechnics of a dying flare.

Maria. My wife's name.

I did then something I hadn't done for years. I crossed myself.

TANYA BANERJEE

Tanya Banerjee was born in India and moved to the US when she was four. She studied Psychology and Communication at Rutgers University, New Brunswick. Her stories explore the intersecting themes of interculturality, ethnicity, gender, mental illness, and trauma through characters of colour. She writes for both adult and young adult audiences.

tb475@rutgers.edu

Somewhere In Between
An extract from the opening of a novel

PROLOGUE

May 2018

They stood outside the crematorium.

It was on the other side of town. In all their years living in Nissin, they had passed it just a few times. They had noticed it even less.

All of them had heard, but not believed, the stories that suggested sad days were just like any other day. As they stood outside the crematorium, they were surprised to find that those stories were true. There was nothing different about today – blue skies with stray clouds, a pleasant breeze, swaying trees in the distance. The world remained the same, yet everything had changed.

They made their way to the car.

Sparrows chirped to one another in the trees. Squirrels fought on the branches.

The ashes, they were told, would be ready to be collected in a few days.

There were two short clicks as the car doors unlocked. A dog barked loudly in the distance. A leaf fell onto the windshield. Several white, cotton-like balls floated through the air.

They got into the car. Once inside, nobody moved. They all just sat there, breathing and thinking their own thoughts.

CHAPTER ONE

Pradeep – July 2002

In the taxi, Pradeep bristled with nervous excitement, refusing to think about all the things he hadn't told his family. The palms of his hands were damp and his shirt stuck to his back. The summer here was a pale comparison to the Indian heat. Of course, it wasn't hot everywhere in India, contrary to popular American belief.

He patted his hair down, not that it needed a patting-down; he had generously applied coconut oil on it this morning to make sure he looked as neat and clean as possible. Ironed shirt and pants, trimmed nails, and shiny black shoes.

After almost a year, Pradeep was going to see his wife and children.

Over the past many months, he had only heard their voices on costly phone calls and occasionally seen their faces in the photographs Sarthika sent with her handwritten letters. Recently, Pradeep had received a picture of the three of them at the local park. Beta and Anji, now twelve and five years old, both looked taller than he remembered. All three looked thinner. They were smiling, but Pradeep knew it was only for the picture. He had wished he could be there in the photograph too, but it didn't matter now. They would make new memories together in this new country, the four of them.

He was running late. Their flight had landed a half hour ago. Even so, he knew there would be a long line at Immigration, like there had been for him. He prayed everything would go smoothly. After all, they weren't breaking the law.

Yesterday, Pradeep had called Sarthika to go over the questions she might be asked. He spoke in English to mimic the actual scenario.

'Why are you here?'

'To live with my husband, who has been studying in America for a year now. My children and I, we are his dependants.'

'How long will you stay?'

'Until his visa expires. That's when ours will, too.'

'*Na*, Sarthika. Remember, specific.'

'One year.'

'Where will you stay?'

'In New Jersey.'

'Specific. Address?'

'Six Willow Lane, Issin, New Jersey. Don't ask me the PIN code, I won't remember.'

'They call it "zip code" here. It's *Nissin*, not "Issin".'

You have one minute remaining.

'Yes, yes, I know what it is.'

'What is your occupation?'

'I don't work.'

'*Na.*'

'Oh! Housewife. I am a housewife.'

'OK,' he said, switching to Bengali, 'I will see you soon.' He paused, thinking about how everything had become harder since the attacks, but he knew mentioning this would only make Sarthika more worried. She knew anyway, even if she didn't talk about it. 'Remember each answer.'

'Why do I have to bring so many things? Blankets, pillowcases, curtains?'

'Have a safe journey, OK? You will be fine. I will be at the airport, waiting to see you and our children again.'

'Nothing's fitting in the suitcases! Our flight's in no time, and I'm still putting the tarpaulin over everything. Blue everywhere in our flat. I don't want to leave it like this. My parents' pictures – I can't cover them up, but then they'll catch dust. I can't leave everything.'

Beep. Ten seconds.

'Sarthika, be safe. You will be OK.'

'I can't even bring the things I want to. Babu's toys. Ani's colouring books. Not even our wedding album.'

'Beta and Anji will find new things here. Don't worry. Bye, Sarthika. I'll see you soon.'

'I've never been on a plane before! Pradeep—'

The line clicked.

He and Sarthika had gone over those questions and others like times tables. Pradeep knew she was well-prepared, but there was no telling what Immigration would be like.

'Can you go a bit faster, please?' he asked the driver. They were well under the highway speed limit, inching along a barely occupied lane.

The taxi seemed to go even slower after that. Pradeep looked out the window. Trees passed them for many miles. Soon, the trees gave way to some run-down buildings that he knew were close to Newark International Airport. He was almost there.

The traffic thickened. Pradeep found it hard to swallow. He was beyond joyous to see his family again, but there were things Sarthika didn't know. Partly because their short phone conversations never allowed him time to tell her those things, but more so because he couldn't say them.

As the yellow signs pointing to different terminals appeared, he tried pushing out of his mind the question he'd been suppressing the last few weeks, but it was no use. Would they be happy living here? He put a hand to his forehead. All the other questions tumbled in. Would they be angry with him? What would Sarthika say? What kind of husband was he? Was he a bad father too?

'Terminal?'

'B.'

The taxi turned, and in what seemed like a few seconds, they pulled in front of Terminal B. Pradeep reached inside his pocket for his wallet, a gift from his older brother. He handed the driver a fifty-dollar bill. He would have to pay back his housemate, Akash, soon.

The driver looked expectantly at Pradeep.

Pradeep understood that the man wanted a tip, but he just didn't have enough money. 'Thank you,' Pradeep said, reaching for the car handle. He had hardly stepped out of the taxi when it sped away.

People were hurrying about. As he made for the sliding doors, a family with far too many suitcases walked in the opposite direction. A couple with backpacks ran hand in hand. Several taxis were waiting in a line. Pradeep was thankful that his other housemate, Sanjeev, would be picking them up, so he didn't need to worry about getting another taxi.

He reached the doors, remembering when he had walked out of them last August. A new land – a new life – had awaited him. America, where everyone goes. America, where dreams come true. America, where lives truly begin. He had been excited to embark on that journey. A year later, that excitement had deflated, replaced by a will to make things work the way they were supposed to. Some would call it desperation; he called it determination.

A blast of semi-cool air greeted him as he entered. Cooler than outside, but not enough to dry his sweat and unstick his shirt from his back. People were hurrying inside the airport too. Security guards were spread throughout.

The arrivals hall was on the left. He took a step forward and somebody crashed into him from behind.

Fixing his glasses and rubbing his shoulder, Pradeep heard the man, who shoved past him, say, 'Can't you see where you're going?' He was holding *The Star-Ledger* in one hand and a cup of Starbucks coffee in another.

Pradeep looked at his coffee-splattered shoes. No matter. He wasn't supposed to argue with Americans. Pradeep moved on, towards the waiting area as if the collision hadn't taken place, as if he wasn't angry and didn't smell like coffee. He felt the eyes of security guards on him as he walked.

Most of the seats were occupied, so he stood by them. The people, almost all Indian, were either young couples expecting a child or husbands and wives already with their baby in a pram. No doubt they were waiting for their parents or in-laws from India to help them out for a few months. Sarthika had said to him once that nobody went to America at their age.

These Indian couples were no older than thirty, many of them younger. He was nearing forty.

Passengers were trickling through the doors opposite the waiting area. Every time someone exited, Pradeep's heart leapt. It had been an hour now since the flight had landed.

Bending down to wipe his shoes with some napkins he kept in his pocket, his anxiety returned. He forced himself not to think about what Sarthika would say once she found out all the things he hadn't told her, and focused instead on the moment he'd see her, Beta and Anji. What would be the first thing he'd say to them? What would they all say to *him*?

He straightened up, praying again that everything was all right with them at Immigration. There would be no reason for the officers to give them grief, surely? It was what came before that mattered the most, the visa process, which they'd successfully completed. All the forms were in place, all the documents.

Amidst the loud chatter, Pradeep heard a familiar voice speaking in Bengali. He looked over at the other end of the seats, where three people with two large, bulging suitcases were just sitting down. It was them! They must've exited right when he was cleaning his shoes.

He couldn't help himself. He ran towards them, sidestepping the suitcases strewn in his path, a grin breaking across his face.

'Babu, here, eat the remaining sandwich,' Sarthika was saying.

As his son reached for the sandwich, he caught sight of Pradeep. Even as Beta's sandwich fell to the floor, Pradeep continued to smile.

'Baba!' Beta exclaimed, his face lighting up.

Pradeep walked forward, as calmly as possible. Sarthika turned around.

'Eyi, Pradeep!'

In a few seconds, his family was around him again. He picked up Beta, who had grown taller but also thinner. He didn't look like someone who would be starting secondary school. Sarthika had lost weight too. Her collarbone stuck out. She had her dupatta over her hair, framing her sunken cheeks.

Pradeep crouched in front of Anji, skinny as well. She wasn't smiling as much as he'd expected her to. He made to pick her up, but she wriggled out of his hands. She stared at him.

'Ani, it's Baba,' Sarthika whispered, nudging her forward.

Pradeep extended a hand towards her. He was still the happiest man in the world, but he felt afraid of Anji's reaction. Had she forgotten him already?

He exhaled as Anji cautiously wrapped her small fingers around his thumb and smiled shyly. Laughing, Pradeep swung his daughter in the air.

He transferred her to one arm and picked up Beta again in the other. Beta put an arm around his neck.

Sarthika smiled at him, dark circles under her eyes. 'We had a long flight,' she said. 'It didn't treat Babu well.'

'Meaning?'

'Babu vomited several times. That sandwich,' she said, pointing to the mess on the floor, 'was going to be the first bit of food he'd have kept down since we left home.'

'Eh-heh,' Pradeep said, nodding his head from side to side. He would probably have just enough money in his wallet to get something, but airport food was expensive. 'OK, don't worry, Sanjeev will be here to pick us up soon. Then we'll head home and have food.'

'Sounds so strange,' Sarthika said. 'Home.'

'I know,' he said, 'but we'll all get used to it. This is our life now.'

PHILIP BRENNAN

Philip Brennan is a writer from Reading whose work has been published by Sea Post Press, The Thrown Gauntlet Festival, *Push Magazine* and others. He is working on a novel.

philipbrenn@hotmail.com

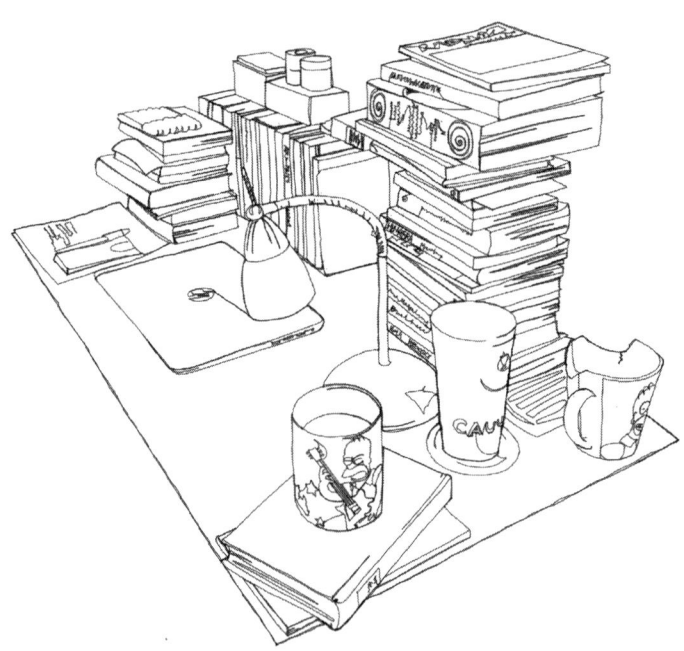

Concrete Beaches
The opening of a novel

I didn't see you doing it so soon after your birthday. You told me it was the best birthday of your life, and I could tell you meant it because you were drunk. You always told the truth when you were drunk. Case in question/famous lines: 'I love you', 'I hate myself', 'I want to die'.

—

After university I moved back to Woodley. I slept in past eleven every day through June until Jem McAllister, of all people, broke into my house. I hadn't seen him in years.

My parents were out. They'd left the back door open. Jem must have come straight up into my bedroom and carried me out on his shoulder. I was deep in a dream of mountains, snow, and a town like somewhere in Switzerland. I didn't wake until Jem set me down on the front lawn, in the dew. The fresh air came up my nose like a knife. I recognised him instantly.

'Jem? What the fuck?'

He laughed. 'You sleep deeply.' He pulled me up and shushed me. 'Listen. Listen!' My neighbour had a carpenter in. 'Hear that? That sound, it's like. . .' He bit his tongue. 'It's like two different sounds screaming over each other. You know? As if something's being born.' He was always odd like that. He was describing the razor-high pitch of a buzz saw. His face wrinkled, as if he could see his effort to impress me had failed.

'Jem, what the fuck are you on about?' I laughed.

'Never mind, Mikey. I was walking by. Thought I'd say hello again.'

We hugged hard. I could feel his bones through his jacket. He smelt of denim and dead cigarettes. He looked dead too, his eye sockets deep and yellow. His spidery hands gripped my forearms strong, and his eyes burned with a dark grey flame.

'What are you up to tonight?' he said.

That evening he kicked down a mesh panel fence and took me onto the old industrial estate. 'I want to show you something, for a laugh.'

It was still warm. Frozen machinery stood at ease, digger arms bent and pointed at the fading sky. Their initial work was done, razing two square kilometres of warehouse into rubble. Jem pointed to a mound towering in the centre. 'This is it,' he said, spreading his arm out. It must have been fifty foot high. He scrambled up it, pulling me with him. 'This is the highest point in Woodley. Isn't that mad?'

We stood for a moment and then we sat. Jem hugged his knees. He wanted to talk about the old days, each question framed the same. Remember? Remember?

'What have you been up to all this time?' I said.

'It's been a few years hasn't it?' He laughed and scratched his neck. Jem didn't go to university. That's when we drifted apart. 'Fuck man. I couldn't begin to tell you what I've been up to.' He looked at the sky, darkening in streaks. 'What's good with you man? Fill me in.'

I rambled for a while. I talked about home, my parents, university, and then I stumbled on to Katy. I had to swallow. I had to dig my fingers into the rubble. And then I told Jem how she died. 'Fuck man. Fuck,' he said. 'Out of the blue?'

'Yes and no.'

Dusk arrived, the sunset dead behind the houses. I asked Jem if he was working. He didn't answer. He was gazing intently at the sky.

'Are you still living with your mum?' I said.

'I'm here and there.'

He got fidgety. He stood up and asked me about K-man, a friend of ours he fell out with. Was I in contact with him? I said yeah, quite a bit actually. K-man had also gone to university. He'd just graduated too. He'd be moving back to Woodley any day now.

'Well that's good for you. You'll have someone around.'

'He's just got a girlfriend now. I think they're pretty serious.'

'Well I'll be here,' Jem said. 'If you get bored. If you wanna smoke some zoots or something.'

We watched the car lights wash along the road and slope around the borders of the industrial estate. One car every five or six minutes. Brake lights winked at the roundabout, and then the cars turned off out of sight. The giant blue door of Storage King was visible, and the tops of the terraced houses off east towards Tesco. To the north more houses, packed in, semi-detached, indistinguishable below their roofs. We weren't high enough to see our old school, or Sandford Park, or Ashenbury. Only the spiralling expanse of homes, and the dull yellow of exhausted street lights. They set a glow above the town, blocking out any stars that might have been.

'I'm sick of this,' Jem said. 'Let's go.'

Bits of rubble broke off as he skidded down the hill. I followed coughing in the dust. He pulled out bricks and chunks of concrete as he went and lobbed them at the diggers. He couldn't aim for shit. When we reached the bottom he was grazed and exhilarated. His eyes flashed as he dashed towards a digger. He had us searching for unlocked doors, hidden keys in the wheel arches. We got around five diggers with no luck before a van pulled in, its lights swooping across us, and we legged it all the way to Ashenbury. We sucked in air by the tennis courts. Jem pulled out a small baggie of weed. 'How about by the lake?'

I closed his hands around it.

'I need to be home.'

'Don't be kidding.'

'Jem, it's late. I need sleep.'

He looked at me like he read something new in my face. Maybe he thought I was thinking about Katy. He smiled. 'All right then.' As I turned to go he grabbed me by the shoulders and kissed me flat on the lips.

'Don't waste yourself here. I always thought you'd do something special.'

I laughed. 'And you look after yourself. Let's hang tomorrow.'

'You've got my number?'

In the morning I rang him twice. He didn't pick up. I drove to his mum's. She lived in the same terraced house she always had, on the east side of Woodley. The lawn was mud, churned right down to the guts of the earth and a network of roots. She opened the door in a dressing gown. Her face quivered.

'What do you want from me?'

She clutched her dressing gown at her throat.

'Sue, is Jem here?'

She laughed. 'That boy's a cunt, of course not.'

'What?'

'Please,' she said softly, 'I haven't seen him in years. Don't fuck me around.'

I woke up the next day paralysed by the sky framed in the window. It was like one of those raw mornings just after Katy died. I rang Jem again. He didn't pick up. I tried to come up with reasons. This was just part of who he was. Unpredictable. Unreliable. He'd be OK. He would call.

When my phone did ring it was K-man. He was finally back in Woodley. He told me he'd take me to the football. Fifteen minutes later he was outside blasting a vuvuzela through the sunroof of his car.

After the game we went to the pub. I heard plenty about his girlfriend, Sally. Then we talked shit about the prospect of a job. We imagined interviewers wrinkling their noses at the quality of our handshakes, clearing their throats at our lack of experience, smiling through our answers overstuffed with enthusiasm and empty of sense. We'd both been rejected from grad schemes over the winter. I mentioned Jem in passing. That I'd seem him. That he'd now disappeared.

'It's what he does,' K-man said. 'He fucks you around.'

'I don't know, K. There was something up with him this time.'

'There's never not been something up with him.'

K-man cupped my hands and massaged them, like the blood had frozen. 'Don't go looking for him. I've always said it. One day that guy is going to kill someone.'

The next day was punctuated by showers. I sat in my room watching the trees bend under the rain. Dusted spray flew off from the roof and gusted into the window. At the sound of the letterbox I went downstairs. A postcard drenched in rain. The ink had run, but I could still read the message.

    Sorry, taking myself off for a while
    Jem X

I ran to the window and he was out in the road, laughing under the rain. A car screeched around him. I ran outside and he was gone. The road empty. 'Jem! Jem!' I shouted. But there was no reply, only the rake of the rain slashing through the trees, clawing at the road. I took Mum's car and drove it all over Woodley, blasting the horn around every corner. I didn't see him anywhere, and the rain kept falling.

Christabelle Dilks honed her story-telling instincts at the BBC and Channel 4, where she developed and script-edited many award-winning television dramas, some of which she also wrote. Her novel-in-progress, *The Real Guide to the Argentine*, is a love story about retrieving the life you might have led.

christabelleddilks@gmail.com

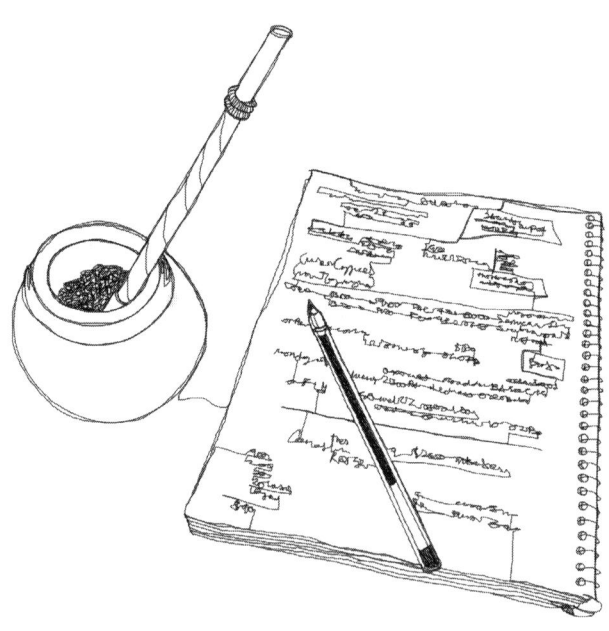

Flotsam
An extract from a novel

Ricardo disappears into a dense gloom which is charged with life. In the darkness, illuminated here and there by dim torchlight, are half-human shapes, hundreds of them, discernible only at the very last moment, so that I have to duck and swerve to avoid being hit, since this human tide is carrying on its back furniture and bundled sheets, small children, and dogs. Men stagger under televisions, hobble under rolled-up rugs, skew their bodies to shoulder armchairs and bicycles. And this is not a quiet coming, but a clamorous surge, because aside from the constant sloshing of water against legs is the tumult of their voices, crying and yelling to one another, Patri! Where are you? Pancho! Stay close! Vale! Are you there? Come on! Don't stop! Keep going!

What if she passes and I miss her?

Then, unexpectedly, nothing. The crowd is sparse and the quality of the darkness has changed. Water now swills around my knees, splashes my thighs. Before me is a vast lake of stinking, pitch-black water. For a moment, a hush.

Out of the darkness they emerge, sound first. A rhythmic wash pushed by trudging feet; the slow tread of exhausted legs. Then voices, carried across the water from people unseen; carried so clearly, it seems the voices have come unaccompanied. Ghosts: all that remains. Their shapes are indistinct at first: a mere thickening of darkness which gradually takes human form, is found by the beam of a torch, and becomes a man, carrying a mattress on his shoulders, dropping his cargo into welcoming arms. For now I see that, waiting at the margin of this lake, there is a line of people. Some hold large lamps, whose beams skim the oily surface and pick out a glint, here and there, of animate life.

Now comes a beast with three heads, a wailing monster, whose movement is so slow that for minutes at a time it seems not to be moving at all. Then the bright ray finds him, and it is a man, holding something high on each shoulder, wading unevenly under the weight. What can it be that he needed so urgently to save? As he comes closer I see he carries two small children. Now the waiting people throng around him and in the brief glare of torchlight, the children have eyes like saucers, while the man stands heroic. He hands each child to the waiting rescuers, then buckles. A flash of white, and a doctor comes to him, embraces him like a friend.

Then silence falls and in it a new cadence of sobs comes skimming. Slowly a figure appears, moving uncertainly from side to side. Then a spark – just a momentary spark – of what might be an earring. It is a woman. A woman limping. My breath quickens. Oh but this would be too good, too perfect. And yet. I move forward. She would never expect this. Perhaps, in an unguarded moment, she would embrace me out of sheer relief. But now the sobs are accompanied by breathless words in Spanish. And as the narrow shaft of light catches her, a man rushes to her and she sinks to her knees and cries out, '*Gracias a Dios, gracias a Dios,*' and the man picks her up from the deep water. That cry speaks of terror. Suddenly it is impossible to imagine Sophia enduring such discomfort. She who would always sit rather than stand. Take a taxi rather than walk four blocks.

The army's amphibian vehicles arrive so swiftly, it is as if the channel has changed to a wartime drama. Three trucks send a great surge of water before them as they push into the flood. In their searchlights, soldiers unload inflatable boats from the roof, and work as a chain to pass boxes and blankets, and stow them in the boats.

An ambulance pulls up and several white jackets join the mêlée of bodies and shouts, giving instructions, pulling on life jackets, distributing metal cases which shine in the shadows. The first of the boats roars off. Then another. I move among them, and see that three more boats are being readied to depart. Something savage seizes me and I wade towards the waiting Zodiacs.

'I'm a doctor,' I tell the soldier who is holding the nearest boat. I try to send authoritative. 'Ricardo told me to help with the evacuation of the hospital.' I step over the wide bulwark without checking his response, and pick up a life vest. Two soldiers come over and pass me blankets, and two heavy trunks. Adopting a professional air, I stow the blankets under the benches running along the sides, and busy myself placing the trunks with care in the bow, careful to keep my face turned away from the soldiers. Then the boat rocks as two people step in, one rips the outboard cord, and we speed off. Behind us there are shouts, and the roaring of more motors, and I feel sure someone has spotted that the wrong doctor has slipped into one of the Zodiacs. Guilt sticks in my gut. What I am doing is insane.

At first the houses rise tall on either side, and the river is recognisable as a street. Behind me the men discuss in loud voices which is the best way to go. The soldier shines a torch ahead, catching street signs and saplings up to their armpits in water. Then the boat turns abruptly left, and we enter a street so narrow I could reach out and pluck a plant from the window box.

The torch goes off. Now there is just the chug of the motor and the wash against the buildings. The men, too, are silenced. Here the darkness is so complete, it seems we are pressing into solid matter, swallowed without trace. Though my eyes are wide open, I see nothing. I feel the wet air on my cheeks and sense fantastical shapes which my mind projects before my unseeing eyes. And yet this solid night is not soundless, as a dream might be, but filled with noises in all directions, which give the darkness three-dimensional space, at odds with the prickling closeness of the night air pressing on my skin. There are shouts, some way off, and then there is conversation to my right, very close. Two men are talking in gentle tones, as one might by the bedside of a sleeping relative.

'Evening,' calls the doctor on my boat, cordially.

'Have you got any cigarettes?' one of the men asks, apparently not surprised to hear a boat in the night.

'Sorry,' replies the doctor – I assume it is the doctor, since the soldier must be at the tiller.

'*Bueno. Chau. Suerte.*'

The soft murmur continues as our boat moves on. And other voices jump up from the dark. There are people on many of the rooftops we pass. Some hold candles in jars, and the wavering light illuminates makeshift shelters: sheets of tarpaulin held up with sticks, a discarded door leaning on a water tower. The dull red glow of a brazier.

A young woman's voice calls from ahead, sharp with desperation, 'Have you got any food? We need food here.'

The doctor shouts up to her, searching with his torch. Its shaft falls on a group of maybe seven people standing on a flat roof, waving their arms. Among them is a tall woman holding a baby.

'We haven't got anything left to eat,' she shouts, as our boat comes level.

'I'm sorry,' the doctor calls. 'We have no food here. We're on our way to rescue children from the hospital.'

'And what about my children?'

'I am really sorry.'

'You don't care, you officials. You have no idea. The kids came to our house with guns. They fired shots. They took our last piece of bread.'

The doctor stretches his arms wide in a gesture of helplessness.

The boat moves on, but this woman's need has pierced me. It is terrible, to leave her like this.

'God. This country,' says the doctor.

At the corner the boat slows and the motor churns the water. My companions, it seems, are discussing the route. In this impasse, a sharp crack cuts the air, loud as gunshot.

'Oouf,' says the doctor.

'Crazies,' says the soldier.

Another crack rings out. It *is* gunshot. I realise I am shaking.

'Are you OK?' asks the doctor.

'It gave me a shock,' I say. I have nothing to lose now.

He murmurs something, kind and consoling. There is something familiar in his voice.

'Why don't they leave their roofs?' I ask.

'They are afraid. Afraid there will be nothing left when they go back. Those kids will take everything.'

What kind of a choice is that, I think, to risk one's life for a drowned house?

'*Che,* what is your specialism, exactly?' asks the doctor. My silence in the darkness says what I cannot.

'I'm not a doctor. I'm a journalist.' There is an uncomfortable pause.

'From London,' says the doctor. It is Ricardo.

'I have been sent from the BBC to interview an English woman who is trapped in the floods.'

'Argentine people not interesting enough for you?' says Ricardo.

'This woman has been missing a long time.'

'Ah, a missing person. Half our city is under water. Nobody can find anybody. Seventy thousand people have been evacuated, and thirty thousand of them will *never* go back to their homes. And the government *knew* this was going to happen. Sooner or later, the Salado would break its banks. It was completely predictable. But our government here did nothing. *Nada.* This is what you should report to the BBC.'

The rest of Ricardo's words are obliterated by a helicopter, hammering the air above our heads. The whole scene is instantly flooded with very bright light and there, to my right, is the unmistakeable structure of a football stadium. The concrete uprights, and stairwells now filled with water. This was the backdrop to the shot. She was here.

'*Cancha* Colón,' Ricardo points out, in the ironic tone of a tour guide.

But the houses next to the stadium are no longer visible. Only water towers perching on their roofs catch the glare. In the violent noise, it is hard to think, but it seems the river has risen and the people have been evacuated. I feel my heart dropping inside me. She has gone.

JOHN DIMITROFF

John Dimitroff grew up in London, and received a BFA in Film Production and Comparative Literature from New York University. He worked in film production before beginning his MA at UEA. He is writing a novel.

john.m.dimitroff@gmail.com

Total
An excerpt from a novel

[*Page breaks have been replaced by dashes to meet the formatting requirements of this anthology.*]

was there something I could have done, or not done, that, if I had or hadn't done it, then she [Ana] might not have left? Do they know somehow [Noodle and Mary]? Could she [mother] still be down there, alive? These were the preoccupations between which I'd been alternating, from the one to the other, from the other to the next, from the next back to the one, or vice versa, and so on in my head, in the swivel chair behind the desk, in the near darkness of the foyer at the Buffo, with the skull-rattling trucks convulsing the room so tremendously as they passed that every other day all its furniture had to be reshifted into place, as always on the one hand, and with the soporificity of the screensaver's neon meteors vermiculating in a pattern I knew by now by heart, as always on the other, as always conspiring to suspend me in a nauseating half-sleep, and with my vision inwardly dilating, a darkening at the edges slowly constricting towards a central pinpoint, so that before long everything looked like I was looking at it through a judas hole, or the wrong end of a telescope, on the night on which what resulted in my leaving there and never going back again, happened the night, namely, of Henry's, I've remembered, arrival

—

on my way there'd been no hint in the sky, burning cloudlessly, of the torrential downpour, without which, later on, there'd likely have been no good reason for his stopping there, on his way wherever it was he presumably was going to or away from – unlikely any of it would have taken place there, at the motel, and maybe nowhere else either. And whether it would or wouldn't have happened somewhere else anyway, in neither case would that have had anything to do with me. But because it happened where it did, there, at the motel, it came to have everything to do with me.

There was nothing afterwards having to do with me, who'd had nothing to do with it, that remained unaffected

—

nor any hint of it during the hour or more before nightfall, seated in the swivel chair swivelled to face the far side of the room and watching while the sun sank lower down the window, through the red clear sky, behind the leafless trees beyond the parking lot, over which the shadow of the still-unilluminated gas station sign, in outline looking vaguely like a headstone, or like a piece of toast, orbited and lengthened, before merging finally with the asphalt in the darkness

—

Klo-no-pin. Shaping the two open-mid back rounded vowels half-silently. Like the enunciation, or its hearing, rather than its ingestion, is what triggers the analgesia, I thought, half-numb now to the swivel chair, as though afloat

sedation motor impairment aggression psychomotor agitation loss of libido hallucinations anterograde amnesia dysphoria thrombocytopenia seizures ataxia psychosis incontinence liver damage rage

not clairvoyance though, I don't think

growing too small to read them all before the glare yielded to the screensaver, and soon afterwards was when the rain started, which even then when it was still just incipient speckles had a glitch-like repetitiveness, like notches at the end of a record rotating under the needle

—

could I have paralysed myself? I wondered for some reason. Since I hadn't yet tried and failed to do anything. Then my hand moved towards a Post-it note I must at some point have crumpled up into a ball next to the keyboard, and flicked it, sending the pale yellow, jagged orb through the dim air, which seemed less like the bodily fulfilment of a mental intention than a coincidence but everything you might imagine someone might be likely to imagine and to worry about when considering whether or not to stay at a motel, thinking it'd be better to keep on driving, better to risk falling asleep at the wheel than to take the innumerable imaginable and unimaginable risks inevitably associated with staying overnight at a motel, before deciding, in the end, to pull off the highway for the night after all, having dismissed everything they'd imagined and imagined they'd failed to imagine as only paranoid inventions, all of course derived from the cliches of the cinema – everything anyone would inevitably suspect before dismissing their suspicions as merely paranoiac fantasies turns out here, at the Buffo, to actually be the case, I thought while walking back down the already constricting hallway, away from Roberto's room, passing the ice machine, and the vending machine, and the for now still empty leak bucket, and the quarter-operated stale gumball dispenser, tripping again on one of the pothole-sized pockmarks in the grungy colourless carpet where

—

because before any of this I'd gone into Roberto's room and taken a whole bunch of his pills, something I'd been doing with increasing frequency, though more this time, how much exactly I don't know, a whole fistful, several multiples at least of what I'd ever taken all at once previously, having waited until after one in the morning, since, when I'd arrived earlier I'd seen that the key to the room next to his was missing, meaning that going in there much before then would be more likely than not to result in my seeing something I'd rather not have to try to erase, and in the intervening hours alternating in the swivel chair among the above mentioned preoccupations while

—

some time later a sound, not unlike the sound of a mosquito, or of a singing saw, or of the slow escape, from a punctured balloon, of air, began to waver into hearing, as if out of a distance that far exceeded the limits of the small room, where by this point it could only be said in a loose, or in a strictly literal sense, that I still was sitting, in the near darkness, in the swivel chair, and where despite my eyes having remained shut, the image of the plant on the windowsill, and of the shadows of the rainwater wriggling down the faces of its leaves, seeped gradually, as if in close-up, as though the lens had been switched, into view, prompting the inference that it was from them that the balloon sound had been slowly swelling, articulated by their multiplicity of voices that seemed somehow to be modulating the rain, like they were weeping, so that

—

which was the first thing, It's a little wet out there, that Henry said, in ironic understatement, when stepping into the room. Or had it been hyperbole, It's like it's the end of the world out there. Something to do with the weather. About the fact that it was raining. Nothing, in other words, in a way that made it sound like his voice was coming out of an old radio, or on the other end of a phone call with a bad connection – at a remove mediated by a telephonic apparatus of one kind or another that, to the extent that it failed – in transmitting not just his voice, but the faint sounds of the other place from which he spoke, or else in adding them to his words during their conveyance itself – to make the mediation imperceptible, was obsolete, or else defective. Which, once the door finished closing behind him, I recognised had been the effect of the rain

—

and so it seems it was the plant that had known beforehand, or its leaves that told me, in their dolorous balloon voices, that amplified and subsided with the oscillating violence of the rain, whether anything about his imminent arrival was explicitly verbalised, or whether it was an only inarticulate wailing that didn't say per se anything about what had provoked it, what would provoke it, which I myself inferred as having been in reference to him, once he appeared there shortly afterwards, and to what he would only later do but that I knew about as soon as he came in, on account of something to do with his disposition, I suppose, and on account of their wailing, deducing that this near-coincidence of their wailing with his arrival wasn't arbitrary but that they stood in a relation to one another that was causal

—

he wore a hat that he lifted as he said this, intending it, it seemed, as a greeting that he abandoned, however, midway through, having realised that the gesture was as ludicrous and archaic as the misshapen, rain-sodden fedora, or pork pie, maybe, was, itself, attempting to make it look like it had instead been in order to scrape the sparse strings, briefly revealed, back into place over his scalp, which he did now with his other hand before replacing it with the one, and not just his hat but his whole outfit in general looked like a composite of hand-me-downs, the effect of which, combined with the tone-deaf benevolence of his way of speaking, patronising in its hollowness, was that it was as if I'd been confronted at after four a.m. with something like a Jimmy Stewart impersonator-impersonator, who sank now, along with the rest of the room, out of view, in what must have been a disdain, or drug, or disdain-and-drug-induced oculogyric episode, so that for some unknown period of time I imagine I'd been staring out at him from the swivel chair with what must have looked like half-shut boiled eggs for eyes

—

thinking what, if not what must be the suicide who's shown up here more or less right after they started wailing, could this wailing be in reference to, here, in the salle d'attente of the Buffo, where, but for him, and for the unusual violence of the rain for this time of year at least I suppose as well, everything has been precisely identical to how it always is

—

but how could I have come to learn his name, since introductions wouldn't seem to be accommodated, would if anything be more or less prohibited by the conventions governing impersonal non-encounters such as this one

so that it seems more likely than not that I fabricated Henry, catachrestically, with no plausible explanation for how I might've learnt that that had been his name, which, even if he'd said so, might only have been a nickname, or a plain lie

and what difference would it make anyway, whether I knew what his name had been or not. I know nothing of a man, by knowing that his name is Jacob

—

and yet we know what we know, in the end whatever we might try to tell ourselves to the contrary there's no getting around this conviction, however far afield, whatever our scepticism or our reason in general might say otherwise, and no matter how convenient or preferable it would be for us to instead be unconvinced of what we're convinced of, when discrediting the prognosticatory significance of the rain shadows on the plant's leaves' multiplicity of balloon-voiced ululations, despite recognising the impossibility of such a boundless grief arising from an only imaginary disaster, for example, would obviate the need to account for why we did nothing to prevent what they'd said would happen, which we'd known, and still know, they'd said with an authority not subject to question, when dismissing the credibility of the knowledge they'd imparted but that we'd refrained from acting upon would absolve us of responsibility for this inertia, which we know unavoidably to be indistinguishable, in light of its consequence and in light of the fact that we'd known its consequence in advance, from our murderousness, when this dismissal would mean that we'd no longer be required to answer for this murderous inertia which is no different from an act however passive of inertial murder, for why we'd allowed this stranger, about whom we'd known not even so much as what

DREW EVANS

Drew Evans grew up in Toronto, Canada and has a BFA in Writing from the University of Victoria. His work has been longlisted twice by *The Fiddlehead*'s Annual Literary Contest. He is currently working on *Trap House*, a gritty urban novel told in a fragmented style, which explores relationships, isolation, and power dynamics on the fringes of society.

evans.andrew.da@gmail.com

Trap House
The opening of a novel

The dead live on in the memories of those who loved them. Charlie is told this at his parents' funeral, years earlier than where we are, were, will start from.

An abandoned house at the end of a cul-de-sac in a Toronto subdivision. Its gutters loose, stuffed with pine needles and empty nests. All the entrances and windows boarded. A mess of weeds and grass hiding old tires and other refuse dumped on evenings like this.

Any stray passers-by, which are rare, scoff at the eyesore. They wonder why no one does anything about it. Ages ago a divorce and an accident left its ownership in limbo. And the neighbours, well, they keep to themselves. The old promise of community is gone, backyard barbeques and Tupperware parties traded for second jobs, night shifts, and paranoia. The faceless folks grinding to stay afloat. But aren't we all? Grasping at whatever's available to keep our rafts intact? We can't, couldn't, won't go back to nothing.

The group converges most nights. Supply in the house and deals at the baseball diamond, through the woods at the back of the lot. It all goes so smoothly. It feels like a game we can win. The night in question is no different, other than the inclement weather. Three wait for the rest to arrive at the Trap. But maybe it's more than that. Maybe it's a home and we are born there. Maybe we never leave.

CHAPTER ONE

A faint beam from the skylight pierced the darkness of the living room. Outside rain pounded against the siding. Charlie ripped at the shag carpet with his toes. Sasha and Russell were late, and the fibres felt reassuring under Charlie's feet. He could barely see anything in the room, apart from vague shapes of the mismatched furniture they'd salvaged from roadsides. Dylan sat in the armchair, and Kirk was on the sofa, illuminated by the glow of his phone. The portable speaker by Dylan's chair pushed forth the bounce of an old school instrumental.

Charlie needed to get one of the lamps because shit, they couldn't count cash by the light of Dylan's cigarettes. Though if Dylan kept loose-gripping them into the carpet they'd have a real blaze. Charlie paced. It was odd, Sasha usually got to the house first. Sometimes she even slept upstairs in that room with the slanted ceiling and the bare mattress. Charlie shivered. More than a few times he'd slept there with her, though she had never let him hold her. Always both of them on their backs, a breath between them. Good times. But the present situation was probably for the best.

Somehow the darkness amplified the mould stench, even with Dylan's tobacco. The house was a rancid sweat lodge. But who needed white picketing? They had each other. They had customers. They had cash in bags on the coffee table they'd made out of an old door and milk crates. Once Russell and Sasha added their pitch, it would be a mountain of cash. And in a few hours when the new contact came through, they would be serious players. No more nickel and dime. Charlie stopped at the front window. Its plywood pane had a slight crack near the bottom, and he knelt to scan the street beyond.

From behind him, Kirk spoke, 'I spy?'

'Dead as,' said Charlie. 'Just rain.' He leaned against the plywood and squinted. 'Couple of glows near the intersection. Porch lights probably.'

'Something, ah.' Dylan stood and danced an awkward bob around the room. 'Something, purple.'

'Might need to open your eyes, Genius.' Kirk spread his legs wide and took a joint from behind his ear. 'We can't look inside your head, Dylan. Who would want to?'

'Chill,' said Charlie.

Kirk put the joint between his lips.

'You,' said Dylan, 'going to guess?'

'I'm going to find that lamp,' said Charlie. 'I can barely see as is.'

'Who needs to see when we have Gonzo here.' Kirk lit his joint. 'You heard from Russ or Sasha? Don't want to leave this too late. These guys don't clown.'

Charlie pinched the bridge of his nose and stalked from the room. Kirk had been difficult since he linked up with Sergei and the Russians from the West End. Constant reminders of the hierarchy. So they weren't shot callers yet, but God damn!

Charlie groped his way along the kitchen wall to the sink and pulled a lamp from the cupboard. He clicked it on and placed it in the middle of the room. Then he pulled out his phone and texted Russell, Where you at?

—

Terrific, thought Russell. Rain rain rain. It was all so obtuse, the weather never behaving as it should. Always, Hello, it's me, Mother Gaia. Thanks but no thanks. The city buses were already such a pain. A car, that would be the first splurge. Maybe a Miata? No, a Celica.

Russell's phone vibrated in his pocket, but he ignored it, readjusted his grasp on the handrail by the back exit, and noticed flecks of dirt under his index nail. He tried to scrape it clean with his thumb, but that just caused his satchel to slip from his shoulder. He hop-jostled the strap back into position as if performing some weird high school dance move. Resettled, he ran a hand across his hair, flattening the rogue strands. Could the day have gotten any worse? No no no. That train led to the *bad place*. Thoughts were just an aftermath of emotion, and if emotional reservoirs were drained of all the gunk and sediment that had people like, Fuck off, Don't look at me, then one would be right as – lame. Russell rolled his eyes to himself. Fog laced the bus's windows, but Russell still made out the sickly glow of the Steer In Burgers sign. Who was on time anyways? Better to be fashionable. The bus slowed at yet another stop, and a figure on a bike flashed past the window Russell faced. A bicycle, in this weather?

Charlie had texted everyone earlier in the day, Be there at twelve. Russell imagined now that it continued, Bring your stash, kiddies. It's time to make moves.

Make moves. God, as if they did anything else. Move move move. Meet at the baseball diamond. Meet at YC Karaoke. Meet at The Acropolis, that restaurant on the Danforth with the horribly outdated decor. Sometimes Charlie's conceit was sickening. Though what else was *family* if not slightly sickening, in a *haha so cringe* kind of way that spread warmth through the heart.

—

Bull, thought Sasha, as she muscled the pedals to pass a slowing bus. Like, total absolute bull. Rain skunked up her backside from the rear wheel and waterfalled from the cuffs of her jeans. Why go out in a storm, Pumpkin? Come and watch TV with us, Princess. As if she could survive another night of reality shows with her parents. As if another second of chiselled jaws or bleached hair wouldn't have had her digging eyes out with her butterfly knife. She had waited for the rain to stop like a total imbecile, and it had only gotten worse. Complete unmistakable undeniable bull. She leaned a hard right and had to turtle her head to avoid a signpost.

The best thing parents could do was die. Honestly, look at Charlie. He was grand, well adjusted, didn't even freak when she broke it off, just business as usual, like no brakes on that train. Charlie had a certain – what did they call it? Disposition. And great hair, not like her straw. Absolute bull! She hated her hair. Maybe she shouldn't have broken it off. Given him a chance. Here comes the groom down the steps of city hall, licence in hand. No, that was weird. They were too close, like some Sid and Nancy wannabes. Maybe they could all get married and live happily ever after as some polygamous cult, carving out a space like Manson's brood. But with a different symbol for their foreheads. Or none at all. That was way too group-think. But tattoos could be cool, like loosely connected ones, and it certainly wouldn't impress Mother. Mother was always like, Princess, why'd so-and-so put ugly ink on her beautiful skin? Yeah, tattoos would be killer.

Half a block ahead a puddle, check that, a small pond, bloomed around a sewer grate. Sasha stood on the pedals and steered a drift around it. Perfect. Flawless. Where was the cameraman when you needed him so she could show Charlie, Dylan, Russ, and even Kirk when she got to the house? She needed a GoPro. No, that was being too full of oneself.

Overhead, a street light flickered and went out as she flew past. It had been like that back when her family lived on Shaker Street. It would flicker and go out, and then a few minutes later come back on. So absolutely like the city never to fix anything. They just collected taxes and had their catered meetings and got nothing done. No one that needed help ever got it. Bullying in schools, no big deal. Gentrifying the local shops out of existence, who cares? Slashing social programmes, get fucked! All they had was each other. Yeah, she'd made the right decision in breaking it off with Charlie. If it had gone on any longer it might have fractured the crew. And that was a huge *yikes*, because then she'd have nothing but her nosey It's-just-because-we-love-you parents.

Sasha cut through an alley and then coasted down Shaker Street. The block was dead. Though half the households were on graveyards or split shifts and were rarely seen outside anyways. But that was a good thing. It made the abandoned house all the better to sell from. Sasha stopped on the street, picked up her bike, and carried it through the long grass to the side of the house, where she tucked it behind the stack of loose boards and debris by the side entrance. She pulled back the unnailed corner of the plywood over the doorway, and a faint beat and bassline leaked out in counterpoint to the rain.

Kirk and Dylan were obviously having one of their East Coast versus West Coast debates. She lifted her head to the sky and let a few drops fall onto her face, then shimmied through the gap between plywood and frame.

She shook like a wet dog. Sprayed flecks of water across the mudroom. A light glimmered on the kitchen floor. Not the best look, since the place was supposed to be abandoned and all. But with the windows boarded it was probably fine.

In the living room, Kirk bobbed on the sofa to the music and Charlie stood in the corner, curling his barbell. She raised her eyebrows at him, and something passed between the two that felt deeper than a general hello. Dylan was slumped in the La-Z-Boy, a cigarette dangling from his lower lip as if glued there.

'Looks like you're the big winner tonight, Kirk,' she said.

'Hell yeah, Tupac over Biggie any day of the week.'

Sasha straddled one of Dylan's outstretched legs. 'How long has he been like this?'

'He was dancing a few minutes ago.' The weights rattled as Charlie set them down.

'K-holed,' said Kirk. 'Dude is getting to be a liability.'

'His parents are separating,' said Charlie. He took a step towards Kirk, his pectorals clearly flexed under his shirt.

'Childish,' said Sasha. She leaned forward and peeled the cigarette from Dylan's lip. The skin stretched and rebounded against his gums with a plunk. Sasha took a drag. 'Isn't it ironic?' She stretched one of Dylan's eyes open with two fingers and exhaled. 'That he's technically *the smart one*?'

Dylan winced from the smoke and blinked, then pushed Sasha off his leg to the floor. 'Hey, Sash,' he said, readjusting in the seat and closing his eyes again. The rest of them burst into laughter.

ALICE FRANKLIN

Alice Franklin is a prize-winning writer from London. Her writing has appeared in various literary magazines and newspapers, and she was the 2019 recipient of the Kowitz scholarship. She is at work on her first novel, *Life Hacks for an Alien*, a fictionalised account of her experience growing up autistic.

alicenfranklin@gmail.com
www.alicefranklin.co.uk

Life Hacks for an Alien
The opening of a novel

You are sat on the living room floor, spooning strawberry yoghurt onto the carpet. On the carpet, an insect crawls. Your mum asks what you're doing even though it's obvious what you're doing: you're spooning strawberry yoghurt onto the carpet where an insect crawls.

'What are you doing?' your mum asks. Her question is rhetorical but you don't know the meaning of rhetorical, let alone how to identify something rhetorical.

'I'm dying a spider,' you say.

You are three years old and these are your first words. Your mum doesn't react. Your mum doesn't react even though you're three years old and these are your first words. She doesn't look pleased or surprised. She doesn't run to tell your dad. Instead, she gets up from the sofa and leaves the room, thinking about a book she bought, a book entitled *So Your Child Is A Psychopath*. She is worried. You have worried your mum. Did you know you've worried your mum? Your first ever sentence was a catastrophe. Did you know your first ever sentence was a catastrophe?

Let me explain. Firstly, that's not a spider, the insect on the carpet is a beetle. Not all insects are spiders. Calling a beetle 'spider' is a silly mistake. However, I can probably let this go. After all, this kind of thing is common in the early stages of language acquisition. Children might call every insect 'spider', every female 'Mum' and every spherical fruit 'orange'. This phenomenon is called overextending.[1] Overextending is just one of the reasons children are funny. And by funny, I mean strange and a little bit dim.

I don't know if I can forgive your verb choice, though. Dying, in this context, is an intransitive verb which cannot be followed by a direct object such as spider. The verb you're looking for is kill. You were supposed to say: 'I'm killing a spider which is actually a beetle.'

---

[1] Underextending happens too. Sometimes kids think the only orange in the world is the one they have just eaten and are baffled when there is more fruit by the same name.

But is killing even the right word here? This beetle won't necessarily be killed by the yoghurt globs. It'll be maimed for sure, but killed? It might have been more apt to have said: 'I am trying to kill this spider which is actually a beetle but maybe I'll just maim it instead.'

That said, I imagine your mum isn't that worried by you overextending the odd noun or messing up the odd verb. I imagine she's just worried you're a psychopath. Like many parents, she places undue weight on her child's first words. She considers them a Very Significant Event. Your brother's first word was 'moon'. This pleased her. She thought it was very significant. She thought it meant he would become a well-paid astrophysicist.[2]

But now your mum is flicking through *So Your Child Is A Psychopath* and all she imagines for you is a short career as a vandal followed by a long stretch behind bars. Don't worry too much. Parents are funny. And by funny, I mean strange and a little bit dim.

As it happens, I am not dim. Instead, I am a linguist, and as a very smart linguist, I can say your mum is right to be worried. There is something wrong with you. I know this for certain. Something is wrong with you. Something is wrong with you right now as you sit on the carpet still holding the yoghurt pot. The yoghurt pot is empty and the beetle still.

You are contemplating the beetle which is still. Stop contemplating the beetle. The beetle is so still, it is unlikely it will ever move again.

Look at me. I know you understand. Your vocabulary is enormous, or to be precise, your passive vocabulary is enormous and your active vocabulary is shite. Listen. I know having something wrong with you sounds scary, but don't worry about it. At least, not for the time being. Don't be sad. Stop crying. I am going to help you. Climb up here, little alien. Sit next to me. I will tell you about life on this planet. I will tell you how it goes.

Further reading: So Your Child Is A Psychopath

It goes like this. You won't be normal. Aliens can't be normal. You'll be normal enough, though. And by this, I mean you'll have just enough normal to seem normal without actually being normal.

Let me explain. Like normal human children, you'll disregard every grammatical irregularity that comes your way. You'll say things like: 'I goed to school with my brother', or 'I eated the orange', or 'colouring in is funner than skipping'.

---

2 Your brother's first word was not a Very Significant Event. He won't be an astrophysicist or an astro-anything. He's not so bright, that kid.

I would have once lambasted you for these flagrant overregularisations. I would have once waged a war against these egregious mistakes. I used to be a prescriptivist, you see.[3] I am not any more. I am a different person now. I'm a descriptivist.[4] And as a descriptivist, I applaud you. 'Goed' is more logical than 'went'. 'Eated' is more logical than 'eaten'. 'Funner' is more logical than 'more fun' and it's a funner expression to boot. Well done, these assertions would chime with the internal grammars of many small humans. You're blending in. Well done.

But you're still wrong. 'Goed' and 'eated' and 'funner' aren't words. You won't find them in reputable or even disreputable dictionaries. They're wrong. You're wrong. You're wrong all the time and you can't help it.

Let me explain. On your first day of school, you look cute in your tiny, stripy tie. You go into the classroom, looking cute, holding your dad's hand, which is also cute. When he lets go of your hand, you cling on to his elbow. When he shakes his elbow free, you wrap your entire body around his legs. When he wriggles you off him, he disappears out the door and you panic.

You are panicked. You don't know what to do. There are other children. The other children are busy. The other children are doing random activities. You wonder if you should join in with the random activities, but you don't know which activity to choose. Do you Play-Do or colour in? Do you sandpit or clay? Do you Jenga or glockenspiel?

All these questions – or perhaps the absence of any answers to these questions – make your throat feel weird and your eyes well up. You're upset. This is what happens when you're upset. You don't know that yet, though. Your little body is still a mystery to you.

The teacher comes over, but only at a leisurely speed. For a human, she is not in very good condition. She is old and creaks when she walks. Slowly, she eases herself down to your level until her head is at your height. She asks if you're OK.

'Are you OK?' she asks.

You don't know if you're OK because you don't know what 'OK' means in this context. You don't currently have any unmet physiological needs. You don't need to eat or sleep or drink or pee. Does that mean you're OK?

'Do you want to play with Henry?' the teacher asks.

---

3 Prescriptivists are people who wince at aspirated aitches, rage against unsightly neologisms and 'correct' people's grammar in the comments section of YouTube.
4 Descriptivists embrace the unrelenting sea of language change as neither a sign of progress nor a sign of decay. Some of us wear our aspirated aitches like a badge of honour.

You wipe your nose on your sleeve. 'Henry' is just another word you do not understand.

'Let's go find Henry.'

The teacher prods you gently in the direction of outside. When you get outside, she prods you in the direction of the sandpit. When you get to the edge of the sandpit, she prods you until you step into the sandpit.

'Here's Henry,' the teacher says.

In the sandpit, there are three boys. One has red hair, one has brown hair and one is blond. One of these boys must be Henry, but the teacher doesn't tell you which one. The three boys stare at you. You wonder if you have a Cheerio stuck on your forehead. You ate Cheerios that morning and it wouldn't be the first time one of them got stuck on your forehead, it would be the second. You rub your forehead. There is no Cheerio.

The teacher tells you she's going to leave you with Henry now.

'I'm going to leave you with Henry now,' the teacher says. 'Don't throw anything. If sand gets into anyone's eye, they'll have to go to hospital.'

When the teacher's gone, you stand with your arms at your sides while you sway, wondering if 'Henry' is the collective noun for a group of feral children.

At some point, the boy with red hair speaks.

'Why isn't she joining in?' he asks. 'Why is she swaying like that?'

Ten minutes later, you are covered in sand in the teacher's office. Your teacher is looking at you through her glasses. The glasses have a magnifying quality. They make her look like one of those animals with massive eyes.[5]

The teacher is talking to you about being nice. She is saying 'it's nice to be nice' and 'we don't attack each other with sand in this classroom.' You do not dignify this crap with a nod, let alone a verbal response.

The teacher then tells you she is going to call your dad. She tells you this twice, and twice you do not care.

'I'm going to call your dad,' she says.

When your dad answers, the teacher changes her tone of voice. What was once a nasal drone is now a breathy sing-song. This makes her sound manically chipper, as if she's determined to have a really good time despite life being despicable.

'Your daughter is not saying anything… We didn't know she was… We really need to know… We need to know if children don't… No, she's not speaking at all… She also just attacked several other children… Sand…'

You're pissed off when your dad arrives. You know this because you feel

---

5 Bush babies.

like frowning. You look at your dad, frowning. Your dad looks at you. He's not frowning. He doesn't say anything. He just starts walking you home. While he's walking you home, you want to ask him what on earth he was thinking, sending you to a school where they don't even teach you how to read. But then he asks you if you want pizza for tea.

'Do you want pizza for tea?' he asks.

You nod. Even though you eated pizza yesterday, another pizza can't hurt.

'What do you say?'

In most families, when an adult asks a child 'what do you say?,' it means 'don't be a little shit, say please' or 'say thank you, you little shit.' In your family, however, it just means you are required to speak.

'Yes,' you say.

'What do you say?'

'Yes, please.'

Further reading: Is Homeschooling Right for Your Child?; An Introduction to Literacy for Illiterate Kids; Bush Babies: Why the Massive Eyes?

ELAINE FROST

Elaine Frost is a fashion designer working for a sustainable clothing brand. She writes thrillers centred on strong yet flawed female protagonists. Current works-in-progress include futuristic eco-thriller *Natural Selection,* and *Silent Disco,* a crime thriller. Her completed first novel, *Smoke and Broken Mirrors,* is set in the fashion industry.

elainefrost@icloud.com

Natural Selection
The opening of a novel

PROLOGUE – SUFFOCATION

A farmer left the clearing and entered the rainforest, chasing a species of wild Brazilian pig he hadn't seen since the fires of 2029, almost fifty years ago. He ran further into the dense trees and vines, until the pig was out of sight. Exhausted and sweating, the farmer stopped and turned on the spot, rotating three hundred and sixty degrees, not sure from which direction he'd come. He tapped his wrist, but his Holocomm had no signal. The sun was hidden by the thick canopy of trees, and the river was no longer in sight. All he could do was pick a direction and hope to reach home before nightfall.

He started to walk away, but there was a tug on his left foot, and then his right. The forest floor clasped his ankles, gripping them tight, and rooted him to the spot. He yanked and pulled, fell forwards and back, before standing up again. The vines climbed his thighs growing thicker and stronger, winding themselves around his chest, and pinning his arms to his sides. They reached his neck, curling around his throat like a noose. With his last breath he screamed as the vines entered his mouth, silencing him forever.

—

In the deep sea beside the submerged Galápagos Islands, an egg sac which had lain dormant on the barren ocean floor hatched.

Above it, an amphibious vehicle drilled a large hole into the volcanic rock, reaching half a mile into the submerged island, until it hit the vein of rare cryolite it had been searching for. The two men inside the vehicle high-fived each other.

As the baby shark grew and the mining continued, it swam unnoticed amongst the seaweed and jellyfish, around the mine scaffolding, initialled RNUP.

Property of the Republic of New United Pangea.

By four months old, the shark had grown, and learned stealth as well as survival. The RNUP miner swimming in the usually empty water, felt a tug on his leg and a bloom of agony as the shark's teeth sunk into his flesh. The shark dragged the miner to the sea floor, drowning him first before swallowing him in six huge bites.

CHAPTER ONE – HAIL

Saira was woken by pounding on her roof and tornado sirens howling on the docks of London Bay. What sounded like handfuls of rocks being thrown at her Pyraboat proved to be hailstones the size of eyeballs, ricocheting off the sloping walls and exploding into the surrounding murky water. The clouds were slate grey, and lightning split the sky into bright fissures. Deafening thunder put every nerve on high alert.

Jumping out of bed, Saira landed on a wet floor. A slimy green film formed around her feet, and everything smelled like a bog. The violent storms of late had given the solar panels a bashing, and the power had failed during the night. No power meant no pump, and no pump meant a leak.

Outside on the deck, Delta was trying to drag the planters inside, and in the process was being assaulted by the giant hail.

'Go inside! I'll do that,' shouted Saira. Delta was an old model but being brave and protective was hardwired into her. Replacing her with a more robust humanoid had been suggested by the engineers, but she had belonged to her mother.

'It's no problem,' said Delta in her steady voice, programmed always to stay the same. 'We must shelter the plants and the bees or the RNUP—'

'I know. But let me do it before you get damaged. I need you to unblock the pipe. We've flooded again. It'll be another jellyfish in there.'

Delta walked inside, her smooth surface dimpled with pockmarks, like bullet-blasted tin.

'You've been hit pretty hard,' said Saira. 'Just be careful your skin doesn't split, or you'll malfunction.'

The sirens were drowned out by the roar of the approaching tornado, a combination of a thousand freight trains and crackling electrical cables. The sky was dark although it was 6am on what would usually have been a bright, late spring morning.

'Wear my waterproofs until it's dry inside. And pass me my helmet please?' asked Saira.

Delta handed Saira her helmet which was still attached to the top of her sub-suit. She put it on and rushed out to the garden deck. Through the protective bubble, the hail sounded like gunshots at close range. The wind dragged her in all directions, pulling her with invisible arms, while any exposed parts of her body were hammered by icy rocks.

On the horizon, a funnel cloud formed, and dipped its spout into the water like a mother's elbow testing the temperature of her baby's bathwater. Saira zipped over the cover of the hive, full of agitated bees and pulled it inside before going out again to drag in the planters.

The tornado disappeared back into the sky for a moment, before reforming, wider and stronger, and heading straight for the community. She pulled in the last of the planters, slid the door shut, and removed her helmet. Even inside, the noise was like a battlefield, and the Pyraboat jerked. Saira swayed and stumbled as if she was drunk.

Delta sat with her body half-inside the sewage hatch. A planter rolled across the floor and hit her in the back. She fell to the side and slumped over.

'Damn it Delta! Don't malfunction now, please.' Delta's eyes were blank. Saira heaved her on to the dry sofa, before more water could find its way into the humanoid.

Saira waded through the basement to check the tethers through the porthole windows. Long tendrils of a passing jellyfish pulsed by, slipping past the algae and the chains that permanently anchored the Pyraboat to the drowned City of London below. All four tethers tugged and jerked in the currents, but through the cloudy water she could see the chains were firmly anchored to the algae-furred walls. She prayed they were secure enough to withstand the storm above. Pyraboats were built to withstand most extreme weather events, and while one had never sunk in London Bay, Saira was afraid hers would be the first. This storm seemed even stronger than the last.

She grabbed anything she could from the basement and carried it up the dripping steps. Concentrating on not falling, she didn't notice the figure standing by the door in full sub-suit, dripping more water and slime onto the floor.

A wave slammed the boat, and she saved herself from falling by grabbing the kitchen bench and dropping everything she was carrying.

'What the—?' she shrieked, as a blast of lightning lit up the intruder removing its helmet. In New Pangea, most citizens had their heads regulation-shaved, but this intruder had dark hair falling below their neck, and the skin on their forehead and cheeks was sun-weathered. Only Free People looked like this. Saira picked up a knife from the kitchen drawer.

'Who are you?' shouted Saira.

The intruder raised their hand. 'I'm sorry, I didn't mean to scare you. My name is Gala.'

'What do you want?'

'I'm not here to hurt you.'

Saira exhaled.

'How did you even get here?' She nodded to outside, as the tornado clipped the edge of the Pyra community. Hail, rain, algae, all slammed against the glass.

'With these,' said Gala pointing to the sub-propellers attached to her thighs. 'Excuse me,' she added, before opening the sliding door and throwing up. A blast of wind and debris hurled indoors; a jellyfish landed on the ceiling, then fell to the floor in a quivering heap. Saira grabbed hold of Gala's arm and pulled her back inside and forced the door shut again. This person may have been one of the Free, but she didn't want to be responsible for a human's death, unless it was in self-defence.

'You can't open the door, it's not safe,' said Saira. 'If you're going to be sick, you'd better use the sink.'

Gala immediately threw up again. In her white silicon sub-suit, she looked like a giant shimmering squid, albeit one puking in the kitchen sink.

She wiped her mouth with the back of her arm. 'Sorry. It's rough out there, even underwater. I'm not usually seasick.' She swallowed and paused. 'Kahn sent me.'

'Kahn?'

'Kahn Tas—'

'Yes, Kahn Tasman? What for? Isn't he in the Galápagos?'

'He, I mean, we, need your help.'

'You've come all that way? Couldn't he have just sent a message?'

'He's back, and for now in Gravesend. He needs to see you.' Gala was retching over the sink again.

Typical, thought Saira. No word from Kahn in over a year, and now he was sending some rebel to scare her half to death in the middle of a tornado? She'd moved on since he'd left and had no intention of going back to him.

'Whatever it is, you can tell Kahn I'm not interested. I'm sorry you've had a wasted trip.'

'I've put myself in danger to come here. I can't accept that. You've got to hear me out.'

'Then what's so important?' said Saira. Although she wasn't going to give Kahn the time of day, she decided to listen to Gala.

'It's the RNUP. They're dangerous.'

'Don't be absurd. Dangerous? Without the RNUP, the world would be in chaos.' Saira wanted to laugh at the absurdity. 'What has Kahn got to do with this anyway?'

'They are mining for cryolite in the Galápagos, for a start.'

'Ridiculous. Mining was banned by them fifteen years ago,' said Saira. 'What purpose would they be mining for?'

'They're rebuilding Mars Colony.'

'So we're going to Mars. Is that it?'

'They're only taking three hundred people.'

'I tell you what. I'll talk to my boss about it when I get to The Centre,' said Saira. 'She'll know.'

'No! Don't do that. Look around the databases if you like, but you won't have access to the ones you need. And don't get caught. They tried to kill Kahn.'

The wind had dropped, and the boat started to settle. Gala looked outside.

'Look. I'm sorry, I've got to go, but Kahn said to tell you there is a way to reverse our decline without going to Mars. Also, he wants you to know there was a shark spotted off Darwin Island.'

'A shark? I would be the first to know that. It's my speciality at The Centre.'

'That's one of the reasons we need you. Kahn couldn't message you, or he'd have put you in danger too.' She looked outside again at the brightening sky. 'Listen, I'm sorry, but I really do have to go now. You need to come to Gravesend as soon as you can. We'll be moving on tomorrow morning.'

Gravesend was a Free ghetto. Seedy, dirty and where the dregs of RNUP society washed up: drug addicts, murderers, mercenaries and rebels like Gala, and Pickers. It was full of rusting ships, foul waste and toxic men like Kahn. Not somewhere she wanted to go in a hurry.

'Kahn says you have the skills we need to survive, and you are vital to our survival as a species, as well as the sharks. Do not let anyone follow you, but you need to come to Gravesend to see the evidence. Tonight.'

Saira said nothing as she watched Gala replace her helmet, slide open the door and dive back into the choppy water like a fish released from a hook.

YAN GE

Yan Ge is a fiction writer in both Chinese and English. She is the author of thirteen books in Chinese, including six novels. Yan Ge started to write in English in 2016. Since then, her writing has been published in *The New York Times*, *The Times Literary Supplement*, *Brick* and elsewhere.

yange.may@gmail.com

The Little House
An extract from a short story

Outside the Little House, Old Stone was talking about geese.

'Their intestines. That's the best part,' he said. 'The best goose intestines come from White Family Town, do you know why?'

'No idea,' I said.

'The women there have strong and slender fingers. The perfect kind of fingers for plunging into the goose's asshole and yanking out the entrails while it's still alive. They do it with precision and determination. They do this in a flash to preserve its tenderness.'

'I'm a vegetarian.'

He shook his head. 'Why?'

I thought about how to reply.

'That's no good,' he said. 'Plus, I don't think I've seen you eating since you came here.'

'I don't feel hungry,' I said.

He turned around to the table next to us and shouted, 'Small Bamboo! Can you talk some sense into this girl?'

Small Bamboo had fallen asleep in his chair. It was almost 3 a.m.

'Anyway,' he said, turning back to me, 'guess which part of the cow the yellow throat comes from?'

'Its throat?'

'Ha!' He reached for his beer and took a long pull. 'I've asked more than a hundred people this question. Nobody's got it right. It comes from the cow's coronary artery. And it has to be the right one. Because the right one's thinner than the left one so it gets cooked very quickly in the hot pot. Do you know how many seconds it takes to cook the yellow throat?'

'Uh-uh.'

'Eight seconds. Lots of people overcook it. That's why you should never throw a piece of yellow throat into the pot. Hold it with chopsticks and dip it into the soup. Count to eight and take it out. Only this way will it be crispy and chewy.'

'I need to go to bed now,' I said.

'Sure. You go.' He took another mouthful from his beer bottle.

'Aren't you going to sleep?'

'Ah no no, I'm fine. When you are old you don't need to sleep. I'll just get another beer.'

He stood up and walked into the Little House. The light was still on. Sister Du was curled up on a booth seat, snoring. I watched through the window as Old Stone went behind the bar, grabbed a Tsingtao and returned.

'I'll ask her to put it on my tab in the morning.' He slumped back into his chair.

'I'm going now. Good night.' I stood up and walked back into the tent I shared with Vertical.

Small Bamboo had brought me to the Little House three days earlier. When he bumped into me, I was sitting on a bench outside my apartment compound, reading a book.

'Hey, Pigeon,' he said, coming swiftly across the street towards me. 'What are you doing here?'

'Just reading,' I said, waving my book at him. 'To kill some time.'

He tilted his head and read: '*The Plague*. I didn't know you kids still read Camus.'

'Some of us do.'

'Where are you staying these days?' he asked.

'I'm camping in the courtyard, with my neighbours.' I pointed back over my head.

'That's no fun,' Small Bamboo said. 'Why don't you come with me to the Little House? We're all staying there in the square: Old Stone, Young Li, Six Times, Vertical, Chilly and lots of other poets.'

'But I don't write poems,' I said.

He grinned. 'It doesn't matter. Just come with me.'

We walked to the Little House. The buses hadn't been running since the 12th and there were no taxis. Small Bamboo had smoked three cigarettes by the time he finally remembered to offer me one. I told him I didn't smoke.

'You're sensible. Cigarettes kill you.' He nodded, taking out another one and lighting it up.

We went across the Second Ring Road and turned into Ping'an Square.

'Wow,' I said.

The sunken square was brimming with tents of various sizes and spectacular styles, their colours ranging the full visible spectrum. Small Bamboo pointed at the building at the far end of the square and told me the Little House was on that corner. We descended into the square and wove our way through it. The tents were clustered closely together and cast shadows over one another. People sat outside, eating, chatting, bartering. Vendors elbowed past with their baskets, selling food, magazines, T-shirts and cosmetics. Kids chased each other, laughing. We steered through, Small Bamboo nodding at acquaintances and friends. Ahead of us, I saw a gigantic scarlet tent. It looked like a castle.

'That's Young Li's,' Small Bamboo said. 'One big living room and three bedrooms for him, his wife and two kids. There's even a kitchen inside. God knows where that prawn got it from!'

It was a warm late May afternoon. The air was stale and humid. We walked from the sunken square up the steps and arrived at a rundown pub. Above, three big white characters hung, which said: The Little House. A dot in the first character was missing. A large group of men and women – the poets – sat outside, drinking beer. Small Bamboo introduced me. 'This is Pigeon.'

'Pigeon!' they called out together, like a choir singing.

'I've heard about you,' one of them, a man in his forties, said. 'You're the kid who writes fiction.'

A middle-aged woman in a red floral dress looked me up and down. 'You seem like a smart kid,' she said. 'You should write poems.'

'Ignore these old drunks,' Small Bamboo said apologetically. 'You go sit with Vertical.' He pointed me to a table on the side, at which a young woman and two men in their twenties sat. They waved at me gleefully.

Later I realised they were all in varying degrees of drunkenness. Some had been drinking since Monday; some had started on the evening of the 12th. Sister Du, the owner of the Little House and Small Bamboo's cousin, had driven her mini truck to the wholesale market outside the city three times to restock beer. The supermarkets nearby had nothing left.

'And all of these rats here, they don't even bother to pay,' Sister Du said. '"Put it on the tab" they say – but nobody ever opened a tab!'

'I'll have a tea please,' I said, taking out my wallet.

'Ah come 'n take a beer,' she said and opened a Tsingtao for me. 'I'll put it on the tab.'

I took the bottle, walked outside and sat down at the table with Vertical, her boyfriend Chilly, and Six Times. A woman with a basket approached, wondering if any of us would like to buy some turtles. She lifted up the lid, revealing the little turtles inside. They were luminous, as white as pearls.

We were admiring the turtles when the alarm rang out in the sky.

'Always this time of day,' the woman said. She covered her basket and went away.

That night I washed my face for the first time since the 12th and slept in Vertical's tent. There was moaning coming, off and on, from different directions. Someone sang until the small hours. Eventually, I slept like a dead person and did not dream of anything.

It was 2008. My father had passed away six years ago. My grandfather had died in 2000 after having a stroke outside a convenience store. My first aunt, she'd lost her life in 1998 due to a haemorrhoid removal operation. My uncle had broken his neck in the summer of 1990, when going for a dive in the river with his friends.

'Both of my parents died in 1989,' Small Bamboo said. 'My mother at the beginning of the year because of diabetes; my father at the end of the year, in prison.'

'My girlfriend has been dead for ten years now,' Old Stone said. 'She struggled with anorexia for years and killed herself in the winter of 1998.'

'You prawns!' Young Li puffed out a mouthful of smoke. 'Can we talk about something else? Haven't we had enough of dead people?'

'Shall we have a game of mahjong?' Old Stone suggested.

After they left the table, I took out my book and began to read. The TV was on in the next room, and Sister Du and the waitresses were watching the news. They wept.

Six Times wandered over and sat down beside me. 'What are you reading?'

I showed him the book.

'Camus,' he said. 'Interesting. Do you like him?'

'He's all right,' I said.

'You should read Márquez,' he said. '*Love in The Time of Cholera* is a better choice.'

I put down the book and looked at him. 'What are you getting at?'

He smiled shyly. 'Vertical and Chilly are having sex in my tent. Shall we go to Vertical's tent and have sex as well?'

I thought about his proposal for a while. 'OK,' I said.

We walked into Vertical's tent and removed our clothes. He touched me briefly before entering. We hugged and moved towards and away from each other repeatedly. I felt cold the whole time because I was lying on the ground. He cried when he came.

Afterwards, we sat outside the tent, sharing a cigarette.

'Four days ago I was a non-smoker,' I said.

'Five days ago I had no idea there'd be an earthquake,' he said. 'What were you doing?'

'I was giving my cat a bath,' I said. 'And you?'

'I was trying to fix my laptop,' he said. 'How's your cat?'

'She ran away wet. Hope she's dry now. How's your laptop?'

'Dead,' he said.

'I heard earlier on TV,' I said, 'that the number of casualties is now two hundred and sixty-two thousand, three hundred and fifty-seven.'

He took the cigarette and smoked. 'You have a good memory,' he said.

The alarm rang again. It rang sharply across the city.

Sister Du rushed out of the Little House and shouted: 'Another one is coming! The news just said there's a big aftershock tonight! A 7.8 to 8 magnitude one. The government is telling us to seek shelter.'

'Relax, cousin,' Small Bamboo said, half-turning from the mahjong table. 'We are already in a shelter.'

That night, nobody could sleep. We went into Young Li's tent and sat down in the living room. It was surreally spacious, furnished with a pair of ivory four-seater leather sofas, one white armchair and a cream chaise longue. There was even a bookshelf.

Small Bamboo sat down in the armchair. 'Bloody hell,' he said, slapping his thigh. 'This is a palace.' Young Li and Six Times walked in, carrying a square table. They put it down and flipped up four curved extensions. An enormous round table emerged.

We all stared at it. 'Bloody hell,' Small Bamboo said.

'Old Stone asked me to get a big table for dinner,' Young Li said.

'If this is the table we're sitting at, I'll need a telescope to see the dishes,' said Chilly.

'When the aftershock comes, we can hide underneath it,' Six Times said, knocking the tabletop.

While Old Stone was busy cooking in the kitchen with Calm – Young Li's wife – and Sister Du helping out, we talked about him. Apparently, after his girlfriend died, Old Stone immersed himself in the study of how to make the perfect twice-cooked pork. From there, taking it dish by dish, he had become a chef and a reputable food critic. He had published three books: *Love and Lust in Sichuan Cuisine*, *The Pepper Corn Empire* and *The Night We Ate Armadillos*. The last one was a collection of poems.

'I actually have the books here.' Young Li stood up and searched on the bookshelf. 'Here.' He took a book out, leaned on the bookshelf and started to read: '"When language becomes corrupt, we need to talk about fish. Are fish happy? someone asked, a long time ago. You have no idea because you're not a fish. If a tomato knows a fish well..."'

'Is this the poetry book?' I asked.

'No, it's his cookbook,' Young Li said and pushed it back.

CARA GEORGE

Cara George is a fiction writer. She studied fine art at The Ruskin in Oxford and goldsmithing at the Royal College of Art in London. Cara was longlisted for the National Poetry Competition in 2017 and was awarded The Sir Malcolm Bradbury Memorial Scholarship at UEA in 2019.

mailcarag@gmail.com

Fight, Flight, Freeze, Comply, Film (FFFCF)
A short story

The birds were where they always were. In the trees or nests or flittering around in the fallen leaves or stabbing the earth for worms. The rest were in the air, between places.

Then all the birds flew straight up. Every bird that could fly, flew. They went higher than the scientists thought they could. To ice-making altitudes and then beyond. Shooting skywards in one immediate motion. They left.

There was a global call to take shelter as it was predicted solid carcasses would rain down, killing instantly upon impact. People locked out hated spouses and unwanted pets in the hope that they would be crushed by a frozen blackbird. Nothing fell back to Earth.

The scientists could not explain where the birds went. Atomised, some said. Realm shifted, said others.

People filmed The Great Flight. People everywhere because there was not a place on Earth free from the sudden flight of the birds. And apparently there was nowhere on Earth free from cameras.

Footage even came out of a patch of Amazon rainforest that still stood. Scarlet macaws, plum-throated cotingas, speckled owls, yellow-crowned caracaras, vultures and cobalt kingfishers lifted themselves from the canopies forever. The treetops quivered and bounced back, lightened of their load.

The rainforest videos amazed anthropologists more than ornithologists but no one was more surprised than the telecommunications people.

In places that it was daytime and cloudless, the full shape of the sky, usually so empty, could be seen. Replete with birds, the sky was noted by some to look quite small. The revelation about the size of the sky could only be witnessed for a few minutes before the sun was blotted out. Day became feather-clogged. In the places that it was nighttime, the stars and moon were ghosted away.

Hundreds of planes crashed as unceasing waves of birds missiled into their engines. Feathered corpses, avian and human, landed on houses and roads and killed the many who came out to watch. A video of a dismembered, charred leg that landed and bounced on a trampoline was uploaded online. The bouncing leg clip had been looped to *Jump Around* by House of Pain. The footage was removed several times before all video channels were temporarily disabled. If people couldn't be tasteful and sensitive, the government said, then liberty for all must be paused.

Captive birds hurled themselves into the rafters of the barns and the bars of the cages they were kept in with deathly determination. Squads of Avian Clean Up Teams (ACUT) were assembled. Forensic scientists, the army and birdwatchers were called upon to assist.

The air pressure changed, they told us later. Millions of wings pushing down like that. People said they felt instantly depressed. Even the happiest of people reported feeling heavily sad. There were videos of spontaneous, collective suicide, so rapid it looked joyous.

The videos were taken down from one online platform only to emerge on another, haunting the internet with liquid ease. There were rumours of 'avian suicide' being contagious. People started to prepare. Do Not Resuscitate forms were given out at pharmacies. At first, the government boosted funding for the Samaritans and similar charities. Later the funding was channelled into building emergency morgues.

International efforts were made. Large investments were funnelled into incubation labs. All eggs were seized, wild or otherwise. Nothing hatched.

Scientists tried to create birds, harvesting DNA from the swathes of feathers that rained down during The Great Flight. Great Flight Replication Centres were set up to simulate the event and determine the cause. The hope was a reversal could be triggered. The centres were quietly dismantled after a few years.

Google reported a surge in searches for collective nouns to describe gatherings of different bird species. Top searches included hummingbirds (a bouquet, charm, hover, glittering, shimmer, tune) and woodpeckers (a descent, drumming, fall, gatling). The most popular online search was for birds that prefer solitude.

CCTV from zoos went viral. A flamboyance of flamingos in China flew repeatedly into the expanse of netting that enclosed them. Eventually the flamingos dislodged the mesh but became ensnared. They managed to get airborne. A tangle of flapping pink panic ascended. A peacock in London Zoo who couldn't escape plucked all its feathers out. People videoed pet budgies slamming into their cage roofs. Many people filmed all the way to the end, zooming in to capture the lifeless feathery mess of blood. Fight, flight, freeze, comply. Disaster psychologists added 'film' to the list after studying hours of footage that surfaced online.

The flightless birds all stopped singing. Then stopped eating. Like fasting mystics, they vanished too but more slowly. The government developed Benevolent Avian Assisted Suicide Scheme (BAASS) because the public were becoming distressed at the sight of rotting, skeletal sparrows and blue tits littering their gardens. Defunct chicken farms were repurposed into industrial avian incinerators. Some of the birdwatchers refused to help with the round-up but most agreed it was the kindest plan of action.

All the eggs in the world sold out within 27 hours of The Great Flight. There was a national Memorial Omelette Day. People cooked their last eggs in the shapes of crosses and wore black at breakfast.

NASA said there was no evidence that the birds made it as far as the Earth's atmosphere. On the anniversary of The Great Flight, astronauts recorded a flash of colour around Earth. The colour changed every year but no method to capture the event succeeded. The scientists called it spectrum resistance. The faithful called it God's promise. The sceptics didn't believe the phenomenon happened at all.

In the weeks immediately afterwards, children and probably some adults, drew bird wings on windows. People started to wear beak masks. There was a touch of the plague about everything.

People changed their ringtones to birdsong. Shopping centres and supermarkets swapped music for the dawn chorus. The government commissioned civil engineers to create speakers that could be hidden in parks and green spaces. Birdsong flooded the cities. People in rural locations complained that they had to travel to urban places or shops to hear the birds sing again. A radio station that exclusively played birdsong was introduced to the airwaves.

At the beginning, people remembered how to hunt. Forests and hedgerows teemed with humans clambering into trees, shaking branches to release any nests and abandoned eggs. No one managed to rear a new bird. Children buried the last of the unhatched in eggbox coffins.

The bioengineers tried to artificially inseminate platypuses, hoping their eggs could be hijacked and repurposed to birth birds. The platypuses crushed any eggs that emerged. The scientists created contraptions to prevent the mammals destroying their eggs. The eggs were empty anyway.

People hacked up paving stones splattered in bird excrement and sold them in chunks for huge sums, much like the Berlin Wall was siphoned off.

'Plumage' started to be used in conversation to mean a rare or unlikely event. *Fat plumage he'll be faithful.*

Tinned Confit de Canard was sold for its weight in gold.

A craze for 'nest' hairstyles took off. Plaits woven into circular coils. Extensions for those who wanted to partake but had been disthatched of their own crop. Shaven depressions into full heads of hair. Hairbands scattered with tiny plastic birds. For a few years it felt like a continual Easter bonnet competition.

People bought T-shirts with phrases on like Avian Flew, On a Wing & Prayer, and FeatherLite.

Musicians staged a global farewell concert. A little late some said. Orchestras in every time zone played a symphony at daybreak and dusk. The choruses of their native birdsong for the start and end of the day. Nightingales and cockerels.

For a while, chocolate manufacturers stopped making bars and only produced confectionery in the shape of eggs and feathers. Kinder Egg sales rocketed and then plummeted.

The Pope prayed in private. Then he prayed harder in public, on his weak knees, for forty days. And then again for forty nights. Finally, he lay prostrate on the ground and begged Saint Francis to intercede and talk the birds back. *Solo una colomba*. Not even a pigeon returned.

David Attenborough said I told you so.

Chris Packham tweeted to say this was just the beginning.

The last of the goose down duvets and pillows were bought in one multibillion-dollar transaction by an anonymous private buyer. The middle-poor cleared mortgages by selling their feather-filled bed linen to the middle-rich. The price of synthetic bedding tripled overnight as it was no longer the cheaper option. Some nests were feathered, some beds became colder.

People gave their children new names. The most popular name for a boy was Eagle and for a girl, Dove. Dodo, Ostrich and Albatross were also common.

Tattoos of feathers started to emerge on backs and necks. Little trendy angel wings tucked behind ears. A flutter of quills on smooth juvenile wrists.

There was an RSPB RIP event.

The MP in charge of social control systems and promotional messages of hope (and warning) was publicly shamed after a drone-camera filmed her PA stockpiling free-range eggs during the aftermath.

A homing pigeon champion said he tried to warn everyone. They were flitty, he said, the day before they all flew away. Wouldn't leave the coop. Like they were afraid or preparing.

Cats went mad for a while; with nothing to hunt they started to torment each other. Cat-on-cat crime went up. Gradually they stopped wanting to breed. Chris Packham said I told you so. David Attenborough retired.

Legislation was changed to give the police more power. Avian Related Hate Speech (ARHS) was a crime that carried an instant hefty fine. All profits, the government promised, went into funding Bird Replacement Research Programmes.

There were riots. The police patrolled the streets to split up the meat eaters from the climateers. Chicken shops were double targets. Raided for the last of the chicken nuggets and torched for being the cause. WE TOLD YOU THEY HAD FEELINGS AND WINGS was sprayed across KFC shops in a nationally synced vegan graffiti protest.

The government said we had to Keep Calm And Carry On. The Queen said we've done it before, we can do it again.

The campaign was quickly changed to Keep Calm And Move On. 'Carry On' was thought to be too similar to 'carrion' and so moving on was firmly encouraged. Carrying on as normal was no longer spoken of. Panic had to be avoided. People complained about the buses emblazoned with the old motto triggering anxiety attacks.

Someone found an unreleased Prince song called *The Day The Birds Left*. An international vigil was held as the song played for the first time on the radio. Fans waved feathers aloft instead of candles and painted PRINCE WAS A PROPHET across their glittered cheeks.

There were reports of birds flying over the polar icecaps but they were found to be fake and the teenage hackers involved were charged with the crime of Inciting Avian Related False Hope (IARFH) and then enlisted to help at the Bird Replacement Research Programmes.

People started to worry that all winged creatures would leave. They tried to build netting systems around areas of outstanding natural beauty. To keep the bees and butterflies safe, they said. To keep them trapped, others said. Move on, move on.

'Ghosting' was replaced by 'birding'. The lover who vanishes.

LINDEN HIBBERT

Linden Hibbert worked in advertising in New York and runs a pop-up art gallery in rural Suffolk. Her first novel was longlisted for the *Mslexia* Novel competition and received an Escalator award. Her current novel, *Daphne*, explores the connection between time and memory, particularly traumatic memory, and art.

lindenhibbert@gmail.com

Daphne
An extract from the opening of a novel

Today I am working alabaster. Spanish alabaster. A piece from Alonso's quarry in Zaragoza. I blow dust from my hands. Dust gets everywhere when I polish – on the tips of my fingers and the lines of my palm holding the emery pad, the webbing and knuckles of my hands, the hairs up my forearms. It's on my face too, I can taste it: alabaster dust, known to some as plaster of Paris. One of the many reasons I love this stone is how it froths as I work it, like the foam of a wave. Most people wouldn't even think of it as stone, this dust I sweep into pots and label, and keep in the storeroom for making good – covering cracks, that kind of thing – but also because each is a link to a piece of work; most of which I'm unlikely to touch again.

I shift towards the window to get the best of the light. On warm summer evenings like this they come into their own, more doors than windows, great sheets of glass on runners where the old barn used to open out onto the farmyard. This glorious brick and oak barn has stood in the shadow of the old manor, here on my family's farm, for five hundred years; a staggering thought, but a drop in the ocean compared to the little bits of life stuck in stone.

Now the doors are shut to keep out the midges already swarming thickly above the old boundary wall. I lift the finished piece to catch the last of the light. How it glows. All stone has shade and texture, but only alabaster holds light like this. In this one piece are memories of many others, particularly the first piece of alabaster I fell in love with as a student straight out of the Slade. Hadley and I were backpacking from Barcelona through Aragon to Madrid and were waylaid near Zaragoza. I met a stonemason and his daughter who took us round a local quarry the next day. I'd never before seen stone freshly hewn from the ground like that – cut to order, considerably softer and more porous than aged stone. We were introduced to Alonso the quarry manager. Dear Alonso and his family, my friends now for twenty years. But back then he offered to take us round, delighted, he said, to have the opportunity to show the stone he cut, which meant nothing to Hadley, who made no effort to hide her boredom. Where they hew the stone, there were off-cuts all over the floor like builder's debris. Such a glut of stone. I picked up a piece while Alonso talked, the way I often pocket a flint on a walk, choosing it, holding it until it was warm in my hand all without noticing what I did, because of the comfort of holding something precisely the right size and weight for my hand. My palms were damp as I brushed my thumb absently across the alabaster, smearing a little window on the surface, just the way you'd rub the steam in the shower to see through the glass. It caught my eye and I held the piece of alabaster to the bright Spanish sun. It's hard to put into words what this glimpse into the heart of the stone did to me. Alonso must have noticed because he called over to me. 'You can have that bit if you want. It's just waste.' I carried it home in my rucksack wrapped in clothes.

—

I yawn. It's time to stop. To admit I'm finished and pack up the piece. I hate this part. Smothering it in bubble wrap, snipping and taping it until it's safely trussed. My mind drifts. I thought I was finished with birds after Bittern. Not that it looks like a bird. All my pieces are about memory, which seems to come from the very stone, as if the stone speaks to me and tells me: this is what I am. All stones have whispers if you listen.

When I started on Bittern, years ago now, it took an age for the stone to speak or, more likely, for me to take note. The memory from that stone is this: I'm fifteen and a boy called Watson thinks he can stick his tongue down my throat and poke his hand up my skirt because I'm a girl who stares at people. My friend Henry drags Watson off me, almost breaks this boy's nose. But then he turns to me, as if it's my fault, demanding, *What did you think would happen if you stared at him like tha*t? I start to believe it *is* my fault, and worse, that to appear normal I might have to change. Then I hear a Bittern call out from the reeds. No one else appears to notice it, just me, and in that moment I start to understand myself. I hear Bitterns. I stare too much. So be it. It's who I am.

With the piece in the crate, I pour myself a gin and print out the paperwork for the courier company. While my printer labours, I check my email. It's been weeks, clearly. My inbox has hundreds of unopened messages, mostly junk, but a few requests for me to speak about my work. Scrolling down I see one from the curator at the Borghese in Rome. I read: out of many works they have been considering, my work has been selected. To exhibit at the Borghese! Surely this compensates a little for the courier taking away my sculpture? My head is so dizzy I almost miss the line towards the end asking me to be in Rome next week to meet Dr Vanetti, the museum's head curator.

—

The Borghese Galleries, Rome. I am here as requested the following Friday, waiting at the staff entrance, as the email stipulated. The security guard finds my name on the list and ticks it off. Then he clicks his fingers at my bag.

'Show me.'

I open the clasp wide for inspection. He peers inside and stirs the contents before nodding and stepping back. Before he sends me on, he says, in English, 'We can't be too careful. These pieces are priceless.'

It bothers me deeply when a public place for art seems to have forgotten its purpose: to enable art to be *seen*. One must queue, be held at arm's length behind cordons, be unable to touch or feel – every step a test of intent.

Inside the staff hall I'm met by the curator's assistant, Valerie, hair flicking around her like subtext. Easily distracted, it takes me several minutes to understand what she's saying. Dr Vanetti has been *drawn* into a meeting – an image to my taste; immediately I try to sketch her likeness in my head from what I've gleaned – and is running late. I am commanded, 'Go, look round, be at home. I will find you when she's finished.'

I nod and manage to utter in Italian, 'Yes, I understand.'

She leads me towards the entrance to the public space, where immediately the floor changes to smooth marble. I wander. How else does a person uncover things if they don't get lost? From time to time, my eyes skip, fix, soak up, move on, small object to small object, calmed by tactile things. I don't imagine I'm looking for anything but then I see it. The Bernini. Daphne and Apollo. The sort of pairing that gets taught in art school, only I never paid much attention. What are they doing? Are they dancing? I think they are. The *movement* is incredible. How he made her hair fly like that. Their bodies entwine, both bare chested, bare legged, with odd fragments of rent fabric about Daphne's legs. I'd forgotten it was here – what luck to have found it. I stare, rapt at the detail, the skill that went into making this piece. I can't seem to respond as a spectator any more. I've been staring so long I'm dry-eyed and my lower back has started to ache. I rub it. I've lost track of time. How typical of me. I've always been more at ease around statues than people.

Just then I get jostled aside by a visiting group. Unable to see clearly, I move to read a nearby blurb explaining the myth behind the work. I'm not sure I ever knew this. It says Apollo and Cupid were teasing each other until Apollo went too far, and out of pique Cupid fired an enchanted arrow at Apollo. I stop reading and look back at Daphne with a sudden acceleration of my heartbeat. I remember now. Under this enchantment Apollo falls in love with Daphne and pursues her relentlessly. Unable to escape, Daphne appeals to her father – her father! – Peneus, a minor water god, begging him to save her.

My gaze stutters.

I blink several times.

It says he turns her into a laurel tree. How is that saving her?

Heart beating fast, I see what I missed. Bernini chose for Daphne her point of transition: it's not rent fabric but bark encasing her legs, her outstretched fingers are becoming leaves. This isn't a dance then, but a rape. An attempted rape.

My skin's grown clammy. I want to wipe my face with my hand but my palms are damp and I'm shaking right down to my knees.

Get out of here, Lydia.

I can't focus. Where's the door? Is that green blur the light above the exit? Turning towards it, I collide with a stranger and go down hard on the floor. 'Here,' a voice reaches me. 'Please, take my hand. Are you OK?'

The stranger holds out his hand to help me up but, too cruel, I inhale his scent, bergamot, which is what *He* wore.

Breathe, Lydia. Breathe. The sense of sickness and dizzy disorientation feels like I've been spun round and round blindfolded. Someone puts me in a cab. A woman's voice apologises for her lateness. She keeps saying she's cleared her diary and that she'll come to my hotel in the morning. The cab slips westward but I'm turned too far inward to see the city. I could be in a dark room. I can only think of Daphne and the pointlessness of fathers. Of rape turned into art by men. How dare any man take a moment of brutality against a woman and render it beautiful? If there is any truth in art then a moment of rape should never be beautiful. Nothing about rape is beautiful.

Back in my hotel room I sit on the bed. Deep inside myself, an idea is forming. I want to refashion the Daphne I *saw* into the Daphne I *felt myself become*. It's not a memory. Memories stay where you leave them. This is present. Here with me. So that while I'm sitting on this bed at the same time I'm on another bed, and *He's* here with me, the man my father told me to befriend, *as a favour*, crushing my ribs with his weight, the flat of his hand on my mouth. Since then I've lived in two places at once.

I start sketching, scribbling over what scraps of paper I find on the desk. You're coming out, Daphne, breathing air, smelling scents, seeing colour, and you'll never need to pray to men to save you again.

DELWAR HUSSAIN

Delwar Hussain is a social anthropologist who has published in a number of different publications including *The Guardian*. He writes contemporary fiction about London. His first novel is about a family and their neighbours in Spitalfields. Delwar is the recipient of the 2019-2020 UEA Crowdfunded BAME Writer's Scholarship.

Delwar_h@hotmail.com

All The Man That I Need
An excerpt of a novel

Ma notices that I'm not wearing the Undies she's been putting out for me. They're briefs, with a tight, scalloped elasticised belt, and semicircles where my legs go. She buys them from the Rasta in Petticoat Lane Market, two packs of three, one grey, one blue and one white. Three for me, three for my brother. Ma snips out their 'Made in China' labels so they don't itch our backs. She tells me to put them on. I say no, I don't want to.

'You have no choice,' she says.

'I don't like the feel of 'em, they're too tight.'

'I'll buy you a bigger size.'

'I don't want a bigger size. I just don't want to wear Undies.'

'The lady at number fifty-three has a Littlewoods catalogue. I'll ask her to order some that you do like.'

I shake my head.

'They're more expensive than the Rasta's, but I can pay for them in instalments.'

She isn't listening.

'Why waste money on 'em,' I say. 'And anyway, what are they really for?'

Undies don't make any sense to me. I usually wear jeans, and then shorts in the summer, so I can't understand why I need an extra layer down there. She looks puzzled by this and, for a moment, it looks like they stop making sense to her as well. Not for long though, as she goes back to badgering me about wearing them.

Ma talks to the Arabic teacher. She tells him that she is concerned about me not wearing Undies, and isn't it right that Allah wants me to, as I won't want Him getting cross. It's the second time she's asked him to intervene like this. Yusuf *chacha*, the Arabic teacher that is. The first time was when I found the leather jacket in a Woolworths bag behind the boiler. I started wearing it everywhere I went. Ma tried stopping me, finally hiding it under her bed. It didn't take long to find it again. When kids started teasing me about the jacket, and mothers at the school gate complained to Ma that I was encouraging my own bullying which their children were getting detentions for, she eventually told Yusuf *chacha* to tell me to take it off.

'It comes down to your ankles,' he said. 'It's for a grown-up adult.'

'I know that,' I said, 'but I'll eventually grow into it.' It's what Ma says whenever she makes or buys something too big for us.

'You don't need to wear it every day. Sometimes, things feel more special when you resist temptation.'

On that occasion I reasoned that he, they, were right and I stopped wearing the jacket to bed.

Ma asks Yusuf *chacha* to get involved in these matters because he's the only Man who comes to our house and has, by default, found himself being the Man Of The House. I don't have a Baba. I mean, I do, it's not like I was the Immaculate Conception or anything. He isn't dead either. He left us. So, I don't have a Baba for Ma to get me to do things, so she has to ask Yusuf *chacha*. That's what she is now doing with the Undies. Yusuf *chacha* looks at her and then at me.

'The Prophet, Peace Be Upon Him, said that Heaven lies under the feet of your mother,' Yusuf *chacha* says. 'She is the most important person in your life. So, you have to do what she tells you to do, Mohammed.'

'I do *do* what she says, but I don't know what Undies are for and so I'm not going to wear 'em.' As I say this I wonder whether the Prophet had to wear Undies.

Yusuf *chacha* looks at me, and at her, embarrassed. He's thinking this is not his fight. 'Knickers are important for when you are older,' he says half-heartedly, trying to bolster up the adult's reasoned line of argument.

'I'm not older,' I say, 'I'm ten. Anyway, what will happen to me when I'm older that I need to wear Undies?'

Yusuf *chacha* is embarrassed again. 'Things happen to you when you are an older Man and knickers,' he coughs, 'help with those things.'

I grin at his use of knickers because I know that's what girls wear, but I still have no idea what he is talking about and my mother too seems uncertain. Knowing I am not getting it, Yusuf *chacha* looks at me with his big black eyes, like he is trying to pump information from his brain to mine through his eyeballs. I open my eyes wide, wanting to take in what he is sending me. But nothing happens.

Eventually, Ma and he agree that Yusuf *chacha* will become my Knickers-Minder. When he comes to teach us Arabic he will check whether I am wearing Undies or not. If I'm not, the agreement is that they will shout at me. I decide to go along with it. Ultimately adults are the ones with power, and also, by then, I'm feeling fed up with the whole fuss.

Before the Arabic class starts the following weekend, Yusuf *chacha* takes me into the hallway. He gives me a stare that says this is beyond his job responsibility. All he wants to do is to get me and my brother and sister through the *Qaida*, *Sifara* and the *Quran*, but now that he has found himself having to, he will do it. I unzip my jeans. Just before he arrived, I had put on one of the new larger Undies Ma had bought me. Once he's done looking, I zip myself back up, but as there is much more material in this pair than my jeans can hold, have to leave it open. Jibrael and Nooria hide giggles behind their *sifara*. Once the class is over, I run to my room, pull the Undies off and hide them under my pillow. I do the same the following day and on consecutive weekends after that.

A month goes by. Yusuf *chacha* begins to slack in Knickers-Mindership duties and isn't checking, so I stop wearing them. Then, one Saturday morning, he does a surprise check. He finds me un-Undied. Instead of the telling off I'm expecting, Yusuf *chacha* goes off to find Ma as fast as his walking stick and old Man's limp will allow. She is in the room upstairs where she works on her Singer machine, stitching together the satin lining for leather jackets for Singh and Son's Factory. Jibrael and Nooria join me on the staircase. The sound of the Singer stops and we can hear voices. It isn't long before Yusuf *chacha* returns and the three of us run back into the sitting room and finish the class like nothing has happened. He doesn't raise the subject again. All the while I'm thinking that maybe Ma and he have decided to be adult about this and to allow me to wear what I want or not.

That evening, Ma turns the TV down and tells me to take the leather jacket off so that she can see my face. Nooria and I start shouting, we are in the middle of dancing to Whitney Houston's *All The Man That I Need*. Ma has an announcement to make.

'The summer holiday is coming up in a few weeks,' she says.

'You taking us to Butlins?' Jibrael laughs.

Ma loses her train of thought. 'All I need to make you go flying Jibrael Miah is one tight slap,' she tells him off.

Nooria and I laugh, still doing Whitney's moves.

'At the start of the summer we're going to have a *dawath*. We are inviting the neighbours, your cousins and aunts. There will be lots of food and presents.'

'It's not our birthdays,' Nooria says, narrowing her eyes at Ma like she is talking to an idiot who can't remember our birth dates. She is seven and at that age.

Ma ignores her.

'It is time,' she begins. 'Silly of me to have forgotten... not to have noticed... it should have been done years earlier... before Mohammed had turned ten, but what with your... then again, it's never too late... but it's already late... it's good of Yusuf *chacha* to have noticed.'

'What is it, Ma?' I ask.

'In the summer holiday,' Ma composes herself, 'Mohammed and Jibrael will be Circumcised.'

The news comes as a jolt. I have attended the Circumcisions of lots of boys we know, but it never once occurred to me that I would have to have one too. For some reason, I don't know why, I thought I was exempt.

'Do I have to?' I protest feebly.

'Yes you do,' Ma says.

Had I worn the Undies, Yusuf *chacha* would not have seen that I wasn't Circumcised and we would not be having this conversation. I feel annoyed with myself, zipping the jacket up over me and hiding inside. Jibrael is eight and hasn't got the same concerns as me. He's been bought out by the presents. Idiot.

'What are you getting me, Ma?' I hear him ask from the darkness of the leather.

'Whatever you like,' she says. From her tone, I know she's trying to get through to me too.

'I want a bike,' he says. 'A new pair of trainers, a cap and a car. Can I have a car, Ma?'

'I want to be circumcised,' Nooria says.

Ma tells her to keep quiet or she will go flying.

'So unfair,' she says. 'Why not?'

'Girls don't get Circumcised,' Ma says.

'Why not?'

'Because girls are made differently. They don't have what boys have, and boys don't have what girls have.'

'But why?'

'Well, boys have to do it so they can become Muslim.'

'Don't girls have to become Muslim too?'

'I don't know the answer to that. Maybe all girls are already born Muslim.'

'Miss Hartley-Ogden isn't a Muslim,' Nooria says. 'She's an atheist anarchist feminist. In class she told us that Allah is as real as the Easter bunny.'

Jibrael elbows her in the ribs to shut her up. 'Ma, can I have a gun?'

That night in bed I lie awake thinking. The vibration of the Singer helps me to relax. The whole Circumcision thing made me nervous. For a start, I'm not sure what a Circumcision is exactly. I know that it concerns my willy. I'm not an idiot. What I don't know is did the entire thing get cut off so it then looks like girls' bits? Or just a part? If so, which part? And who got to choose? When the brothers at number fifty-six had it done last summer, they walked around in bedsheets afterwards, holding it in front of them so that it didn't touch the bandage. Every time I went over to look, they called me a sissy and pushed me out of the way, so I never got the chance to see for myself. What's really weird is that I'm excited too. It's the prospect of the present – I know what I'm asking for. But also, I'm to go through something that all the boys have had done.

As sleep overtakes me, Jibrael, whose bed is on the other side of the room, calls me.

'Mo... Mo.'

'What?' I eventually say.

'Do you think Baba will come to the *dawath*?'

He has never asked about Baba before. 'I don't know,' I say.

'When the boys next door did it, do you remember, it was their Baba who took 'em into the room. Who do you think will take us in?'

'I don't know,' I say, turning over and falling asleep.

MAIRÉAD KIERNAN

Mairéad Kiernan is an American writer. She graduated from Tulane University with a BSc in Economics and French. She has lived in Berlin, Paris, and Montpellier. She is currently working on a collection of short stories and a novel.

maikiernan@gmail.com

A Million Pop Rocks
An excerpt from a novel

March 21st 2009. He, Brian Kelly, was coming over at five.

It was raining outside and fresh green was budding everywhere. My mom was downstairs in her office even though it was a Saturday. She was always working back then – freelance editing, substitute teaching, bartending.

I was fifteen.

My mom was home, and Brian Kelly was coming over to do it.

Brian Kelly and I had made out a few times when we were drunk in the woods with our friends. On some occasions, while sitting on rocks and leaning against tree trunks, he touched my bare breasts. On the last occasion, March 13th, hidden in the depths of blossoming trees, I touched his penis, and he dared to stick his hand down my underwear even though all the boys said vaginas were gross and smelled like rotten fish. He didn't really touch my vagina, more like grazed the pubic hair, but still.

I thought by that point he was supposed to be my boyfriend, but he wasn't. Julie said it was because we were copies of each other in the way leaves were – we looked the same from far away, but when examined up close, it was clear we were leaves from extremely different trees.

He liked baseball, chugging beers with his boys, wearing hats backwards.

I liked comics, baking bread, co-ordinating the color of my socks to my outfits.

His friends called people fags and sluts.

My friends called people dorks and babies.

His parents were married lawyers. His mother dealt with botched plastic surgery, and his father with car accidents.

My parents were divorced. My mom, as I've already explained, did many things for money. My dad, I'd never met.

March 21st 2009. I was dressed in a baby pink cami and low-cut Abercrombie jeans with pink flowers on the back pockets. Underneath, I had on a push-up bra and my only thong, which I wore on special occasions like school dances and Thanksgiving.

My mom came into my bedroom while I was tweezing my upper lip.

'Are you excited for your date with Brian Kelly?' Her voice crescendoed when she said 'Kelly' in the most obnoxious way.

'Mom, how many times do I have to tell you? We're working on a biology project.' That was what we were supposed to be doing anyway.

'Whatever you say. You look cute though, even with that hint of a mustache.'

'Mom.' I pushed her out of my room and shut the door.

'If you need any help getting ready, let me know,' she yelled through the wall.

I didn't answer. Instead, I sprayed vanilla bean perfume all over myself, including a squirt between my legs, and swallowed my birth control pill.

I was ready.

Julie's older sister, Megan, told us it was like eating a million pop rocks all at once. Like MDMA times one thousand. Like fireworks shooting in your stomach. Like achieving Nirvana without even having to meditate. She said it was like nothing we'd ever experienced before, and she would know because she'd done it like a thousand times with her boyfriend.

My mom answered the door when he rang the bell. 'Why hello, Brian Kelly,' she said. 'Welcome! It's so nice to meet you.'

I ran downstairs, embarrassed she had used his full name.

'Hi,' he said. He was wearing a backwards Red Sox cap, a white Ralph Lauren T-shirt, and blue jeans. I could smell his cologne even though I was standing on the stairs and he was by the front door.

My mom lingered, watching us not make eye contact or speak to each other.

'Mom,' I said, raising my eyebrows.

'All right,' she said, holding up her hands and backing away.

We went upstairs to my bedroom.

March 21st 2009. Push-up bra. Plaid boxers. Pink skin.

He left right after, as if his mom was waiting outside for him. Or he might've had a friend out there – he was sixteen, so some of his friends could drive.

'That was quick,' my mom said after he slammed the front door.

I shrugged. 'We finished early.'

'Uh-huh.'

In the bathroom, I stared at myself in the mirror. I pulled my eyes open as wide as they'd go. I slapped my cheeks.

'You just had sex,' I said. 'You are no longer a virgin.'

My reflection was the same as the day before: three pimples between my eyebrows, mouth too far to the right, one eye higher than the other.

Julie's sister was a liar. The penis wasn't a magical device that could trigger the sensation of a million pop rocks – it was a large tampon with a latex suit on.

Sitting on the edge of the bath, I widened my legs and pulled my vulva apart.

'How are you? Any different?'

Everything was the same. I was the same. Fifteen. No boyfriend. Three friends. One mother. At the very least I expected my vagina would have something to show for it. Where was this hymen everyone was talking about? I hadn't even bled.

My mom knocked on the door. 'You OK in there?'

'Fine.'

'Can I come in?'

I pulled up my jeans. 'Sure.'

She held me in her arms and rocked me back and forth. 'I love you,' she said.

I breathed in her smell – woody apples and hairspray. 'I love you too.'

March 21st 2009. Non-virgin. I watched the sun set over the sprouting garden in our backyard from my bedroom window. Most of the plants were just beginning to poke their heads out of the dirt. However, the daffodils were shooting out of the ground.

Earlier today, a penis shot into a condom while inside my body.

I lay on my bed and stared at the ceiling.

March 21st 2009. Brian Kelly's penis shot into a condom while inside my body.

I woke up the next day and forgot about it until I sat down at the kitchen table with a bowl of Cocoa Puffs. A single brown banana lay in the fruit bowl at the center of the table.

Yesterday, a penis entered my body.

My mom walked into the kitchen. 'Morning, Rara.'

'Morning, Mom.'

She sat down next to me. 'You OK?'

'Fine.'

She crossed her arms and tilted her chin down. 'Rara?'

'Brian didn't help me with the project yesterday, so now I have to do it by myself.'

'That's men for you,' she said. I leaned my head on her shoulder, and she rubbed my back. 'But you'll get it done.' She kissed the top of my head. 'I've gotta get to work, let me know if you need any help, OK?'

'OK.'

I worked on the project, tidied my room, looked at myself in the mirror, finished the rest of my homework, checked my vulva, but nothing had changed except the date. No pop rocks. No MDMA. No fireworks. No Nirvana. Just March 22nd 2009.

PEGGY LEE

Peggy Lee has worked as an editorial assistant for Three Hares publishing house and the trade magazine *New Electronics*. She is a social media editor for The Word Factory. Her novel *Goodbye Happiness* is set in South-West France during one hot, tragic summer. Think *Call Me By Your Name* meets *Bonjour Tristesse*.

@PeggyRLee
peggy.lee21@outlook.fr

Goodbye Happiness
The opening of a novel

Noémie shut her eyes.

She could hear the hiss of the pool cleaner, the *chachacha* of the cicadas strumming their legs in the afternoon heat, and the hum of the bees and wasps on the lavender bushes – bursts of angry buzzing followed by contented silence once they'd landed on a stalk.

Her nose prickled with chlorine and the chalky sharpness of hot cement.

She could almost have fallen asleep. Almost. If she hadn't been afraid of falling off the lilo into the water and if she hadn't been drifting to the ripples caused by the automatic cleaner.

It wasn't the movement that kept her from sleeping but the shade and sun moving across her face caused by the far-reaching branches of the Albizia tree. Maman complained about the straggly flowers clogging up the pool's filters, but Noémie loved their dusty pinkness. She also loved how the passion flower, whose leafy fronds smothered the stone pool hut, had crept up the Albizia's nearest branches, encircling them like a spider might cocoon a fly. It made her feel as though she were somewhere more exotic than the south of France.

The chink of glass or china floated across the garden. Someone had woken from their siesta and was emptying the dishwasher. A telephone rang.

She hadn't wanted to come, but Grand-mère had insisted. 'Darling,' she'd said. 'If you're going to quit your job you might as well pay your mother a visit.'

When Noémie had protested, Grand-mère had said: 'When was the last time you went home?'

The question made Noémie stop and think. Not because she didn't know the answer, it had been two summers ago. Last summer she'd been too busy with an internship to visit, and Maman always came to Paris for Christmas. It was the way Grand-mère had phrased it. Home. Was Cajarc home?

She'd thought about this on the train ride down. Grand-mère had fallen asleep, her head tilted sideways. Her mouth was slightly open and with each exhalation a tiny whine emitted from her nose. None of the fellow passengers had noticed over the drone of the tracks. The June sun hit the window, warming the carriage to an unbearable heat. Noémie stared out of the window, watching the familiar greyness of the G*are d'Austerlitz* become the fields of Centre-Val-de-Loire, until the flatness gave way to undulating hills and the hills to bigger hills which hid the peaks of the *Massif Central* that she spotted in the gaps made by the valleys. She imagined a giant fist landing in the centre of France, the power of the blow rippling the earth as far as the *Lot* hundreds of kilometres away.

Paris had become her home. Paris with its long boulevards and café-bars under whose plastic awnings she'd sit and smoke with friends, and drink strong Belgian *Chouffe*. Home was the Sorbonne, sitting in the library watching the passers-by on the street below. Home was Grand-mère's flat with its high ceilings and lack of double glazing and creaky floorboards. Seven years. Seven years since she'd packed her bags and left this invisible place, its main claim to history having been the home to Françoise Sagan, more famous abroad than in France, whose grave lay forgotten among peasant families in a tiny, walled cemetery in the valley. And secondly, for having been used in a sketch by Coluche, who'd once stood for President and shortly after been killed in a motorcycle accident – suspiciously, it was said – and who chose Cajarc as a setting for its very insignificance.

And yet, as she'd watched the landscape change from flat fields to undulating forests, cavernous valleys with deep winding rivers and fields of vines or rippling *mais*; from houses of yellow plaster to brick and then stone; she had felt a sense of returning. There was a magic here, a vividness to the summer Paris didn't have.

This had changed when she'd stepped onto the platform at the station. For a second, she felt something like panic.

Maman was waiting for them and she helped carry their suitcases down the train steps. Maman also seemed nervous; she'd been clutching her hands before she spotted them further down the platform and her movements were tense. The straw hat she was wearing was too big for her and she had to hold it with one hand when she bent over. Noémie saw a man higher up the platform watching their reunion and imagined they must paint a charming *tableau*: Beautiful Maman in a pretty dress kissing them each on both cheeks; Grand-mère with her permed red hair and sunglasses; herself, a carnation pinned behind her ear, picked fresh from a flowerpot in front of the station that morning.

She turned away from him. Little does he know, she thought, what this *tableau* is really hiding.

The feeling of familiarity returned on the journey back to the house. While Maman and Grand-mère chatted in the front, she watched the streets slide by undisturbed. The shops, the pharmacy on the corner, the fountain in the square were all as she'd left it. There was a new restaurant, she noticed, with purple awning.

Walking through the front door she smelled the odour of her childhood: coffee, old shoes, warm rugs and the pine cleaning spray Maman used. She tried to ignore that Papa's favourite armchair had been relegated to a dark corner of the living room, and that the print of *Ophelia* that had once hung in the corridor had disappeared. Papa had loved the Pre-Raphaelites.

She took her bags up to her old room. Pushkin had left a round indent on her bed, black fur and muddy paw prints. The collection of CDs was in the same place; in the small space where the stone wall met the low-sloping ceiling – Linkin Park, Tryo, Superbus and Green Day – and on her desk, the clock she'd made in primary school, broken now, with pink plastic jewels she'd glued on wonkily, and an old school agenda she'd kept because friends had written little notes inside. There was her dark-blue dressing gown on the back of the door with the burn in the sleeve, and the tailor dummy in one corner. A summer hat balanced on the knob of wood that protruded from its neck and she'd pinned photos to its torso in a way she now found ghoulish. How young she looked in the photos (how spotty!), arms around school friends, or a younger Pushkin. The wardrobe was full of heavy, woollen jumpers she'd never wear in Paris.

That evening, they'd lit citronella candles and ate dinner on the terrace. Noémie was reminded of the days when her parents would invite guests and they'd sit out and drink wine by candlelight. She'd try to stay up but would fall asleep, her head on the table, and wake up in bed later in the night to hear the crunch of car tyres on gravel and the calls of farewell from porch to car window.

'I'm rather chilly,' Grand-mère said, rubbing her arms. 'It was so warm today I forgot the season. I'm going to fetch a cardigan. Do either of you want one?'

They both agreed they did.

There was a silence in her absence and Noémie shivered in the cool night air.

'Noémie...' Maman said, and for a second, Noémie feared she'd be interrogated as to why she quit her job. 'Pushkin has got used to sleeping on your bed. You might want to shut your bedroom door to keep him out.'

Safe territory. 'I don't mind him being there.'

'He's a rather restless night companion.'

'I'll give him three chances.'

Grand-mère came back with their cardigans. 'I've had a thought,' she said. 'It's the *fête de la musique* soon. Do you celebrate it around here?'

'Oh yes,' Maman said. 'It's very popular.'

'So Cajarc puts something on?'

'They do, but actually the best event is held in a little village not far from here. Beauregard. Noémie will remember, don't you?'

'Yes.'

'It's quite rustic but the decorations are fabulous, aren't they darling?'

'Yes.'

'They have a fancy dress competition every year, and Noémie went once, do you remember? What were you?'

'Algae.'

Grand-mère failed to hide a smile. 'Algae?'

'The theme was "underwater."' Grand-mère's smile was contagious.

'Do you remember the man dressed as a policeman?' Maman asked. Her lips were stained purple from the wine, but it looked pretty like lipstick. 'Everyone thought he was a real policeman supervising the parade and we were all so well behaved, and then it turned out to be someone wearing a costume. What a nasty trick to play.'

They laughed, and Noémie noticed their cheeks were slightly flushed and their eyes sparkled. She hadn't seen either of them this relaxed in a long time. Pushkin came to sit on her lap, and Maman surprised her with her favourite cake, chocolate fondant. Noémie could feel herself letting her guard down. Mellowing. Maybe Maman had changed. Maybe things would be different.

The sun was bothering her: she should have worn her sunglasses. They were lying in a pile with her towel and a book on one of the sunloungers. But she was completely dry now and her skin was so warm that she knew the water would be a shock. It felt good. She didn't want to move from the lilo.

The back door creaked open and Noémie heard Maman's bare feet cross the broken slabs – a heavier tread than Grand-mère's – and the soft rustle of her long, white shirt brushing against the lavender.

She kept her eyes shut, pretending to sleep. There was the squeak of a sunbed, and then nothing. Any minute now, she expected Maman to say something like: 'you really shouldn't be out there alone, *ma puce,*' or 'Please don't get in the water when Grand-mère and I are both asleep,' and this waiting for it meant she couldn't relax. Sullenly, she sat up on the lilo to look. The movement created an indent into which some water slipped, and she flinched. She could almost hear her skin sizzle.

Maman wasn't looking at Noémie at all, but sat on the sunbed very upright, looking out over the valley. Noémie recognised the tautness of her back, the pinched look about her eyes. Her breath quickened.

'What is it?' Noémie asked, and her voice sounded rough and unpleasant in the warm summer air.

Maman blinked as if she'd completely forgotten Noémie was there. 'Something very sad has happened.'

Noémie's chest tightened. 'What?'

'Jean's died.'

There was a pause.

'Jean?' Noémie replied. 'Which Jean?'

'Jean. Neighbour Jean.'

'Ah. Oh dear.'

Noémie felt a pinch of regret. Not because she'd ever felt much for him, but because he'd always been there and now he wasn't. He probably hadn't wanted to go because he wasn't old and could have lived another twenty years or more. She knew what it would mean for Agathe and Julien and Louis and Anne to find themselves alone, without parents, and she couldn't not be reminded of Papa. She understood the grief and denial they must, right that second, have been experiencing, and what they would feel over the course of the summer. It wasn't something she wanted to remember.

'How did he die?' she asked.

'Heart attack. Second one this year.'

'And last.'

'He was a drunk. He brought it on himself.'

Maman had never approved of Jean, but even so, Noémie was startled by the venom in her voice. 'And when's the funeral?'

'Tuesday.' A pause. 'I suppose we'll have to go.'

'Really?'

Maman ignored her. 'Have you spoken recently?'

'With Agathe? No. It's been a while.'

They sat in silence for a bit, looking at the view.

'What will they do?' Noémie asked.

Maman shook her head. 'They're so young.'

'How old is Anne?'

'You'd know better than me.'

Noémie frowned. 'I'm not sure. Seventeen, I would think.'

'So young.'

'What will happen to her?'

Maman sighed softly. 'What will happen to Anne?' she repeated. The question hovered, unanswered, in the still, afternoon air, quivering like waves of heat above hot tarmac.

JOSEPHINE LISTER

Josephine Lister grew up in Oxfordshire and obtained her BA in English Literature with Creative Writing from UEA. Alongside writing novels, she has worked as an education editor in Finland and had a short story published by Mardi Books. She currently lives in London with her dog Meeko.

josephineklister@gmail.com

Little Yellow Teeth
The opening of a novel

It is late at the party and Emilie has taken off her shoes. She walks through the living room in bare feet. Around her everything has started to decay, the peak of the party has passed. People are talking too loudly, pointing at each other in aggressive ways that makes it difficult to decipher from a distance whether they're arguing or joshing with each other.

Across the room, through a sea of heads, Chris is dancing with a girl Emilie used to do ballet with, Arabella. From where Emilie's standing she can't tell that the glossy shine of Arabella's hair is because they're extensions rather than good genes. Emilie fixates on the way Arabella's body is curved towards Chris's lean frame with her arms dangling from his neck delicately. Her body positioning gives the impression that she's weak and fragile, like he's the one holding her up, his hands on the small of her back.

Chris's hair is cut shorter than is deemed fashionable in Emilie's private school crowd and it makes his cheekbones stand out prominently. His clothes are too big for him, though Emilie can't figure out if this was done intentionally or not, and his shoes are a knock-off of a famous sports brand. None of this matters though, she doesn't care what he's wearing. It's the hands on Arabella's back and the way he is smiling at her that has her full attention.

Emilie swallows down the discomfort in her throat, caught there like a fish bone, but can't make herself look away. She's not even sure why she's looking. He's just an old friend, the oldest. They lived on the same road for most of their childhood. I was your best friend, she thinks to herself as she watches him. The thought has a weight to it that she doesn't know what to do with.

When he catches her staring at him, she quickly looks away and walks through the heat of the living room to the kitchen. She is relieved to find the room empty. The door closes behind her and the voices are shut out. She waits to see if Chris will come after her. She imagines him making a joke of the fact she was staring at him and she tries to think of a witty reply, but he doesn't come and the room settles around her, still and static. Above her the light is yellow and weak, casting the whole room into a sickly pallor.

All the alcohol is lined up on the kitchen countertop. Bottles of different colours and levels of liquid face her. She lifts up one bottle and then another, trying to find the drink she brought with her. She finds her bottle of vodka and as she lifts it she sees that it's empty, of course. She puts it back down and looks at the remaining drinks. All the vodka is gone, all that remains is gin and a few brightly coloured alcopops. She wonders who brings gin to a party like this, but decides it's better than having a blue tongue for the rest of the evening.

She pulls a cup from the plastic stack, selecting the one underneath the top one, and starts to mix her own drink. She remembers concocting potions with Chris when they were three, pouring her mum's expensive bathroom products into the sink. It feels lonely now to be making her own drink in the emptiness of the kitchen, and she reminds herself that it's nearly time. Soon she will be out of this town. University will be a melting pot, each individual's history erased, so she can decide who she wants to be. A chance to start over without the baggage of school names or postcodes or reputations. Or so she hopes.

In front of her is the kitchen window and as she glances up she notices some of the guys from her current school outside, the ends of their cigarettes looking like fireflies in the black. She regrets inviting them – Archie, Jacob and Mikhail. They don't know anyone here. Emilie herself was only invited because she used to go to primary school with the guy whose house it is. The boys are all gathered together looking uncomfortable and out of place. They're wearing polo shirts and chinos, and their hair and skin is bleached from the sun they've seen on their Easter holidays. She watches as they take it in turns to push their hair from one side to the other as they bark loudly at each other's jokes.

Then the sliding door opens and Owen, one of Chris's close mates, steps into the garden. Owen's easiness falters as he sees the garden is occupied and chooses to smoke close to the house. The guys from her current school notice him looking over, and Emilie can feel the awkwardness stretching through the glass towards her. Archie offers his lighter and after a moment of no one moving, Owen moves over just enough to reach it.

She turns away from the window and drinks deeply from her plastic cup, feeling it cracking gently under her grip. The cup is nearly empty so she pours herself another and then hops up onto the counter and gets out her phone. After a while, just as she's considering making the trek home, Owen comes into the kitchen.

'Hey Owen, how's it going?'

'Yeah, I was just catching up with some of your mates outside actually.'
The way he says *mates* rings tinnily in her ears.

Emilie glances outside the window and sees that the boys are standing alone once more. They're all positioned in the same way, relaxed and full of confidence, a straight parallel line elongating across their collar bones, extending from one pronounced shoulder to the other. She looks down into her glass and watches the pearlised alcohol swirling in the mixer.

'They're not really my mates, I mean, I know them and all but it's not like we hang out that much.'

'That's not what I've heard.'

Emilie gets down from the counter and looks at him properly, her head throbbing with the newly consumed gin. He has the shaved hairstyle that he's had since they were little kids. He's wearing a Chelsea football shirt that she always sees him in whenever they bump into each other in town, and around his neck is a link-chain that she knows he got for Christmas from his older half-sister who works at the shop it came from on the high street. The zirconia stud in his ear, attempting to replicate a diamond, sparkles dully in the lemon-coloured light. The only jewellery the guys at her school wear are signet rings with their initials engraved on them.

'And what have you heard, Owen?'

There's a stark change in his demeanour. A dark energy bounces in his eyes as if he's found the trouble he'd been hoping to find tonight. Emilie can practically feel him buzzing like a wasp that's been provoked. He passes his tongue over his teeth, tiny squares of stained porcelain that Emilie has always thought are too small for his mouth.

'Just that you're a bit of a good time.'

His hands are in his pockets and he rocks forward on his feet. Emilie feels a sinking within herself and stops breathing. She holds herself very still to try and make it appear that his words have had no effect on her whatsoever. She shifts on her feet and pretends the conversation is boring her.

'Well you know me, Owen, am I a good time?'

'I don't know you like that.'

'Like how?'

Owen doesn't answer, he just keeps grinning at her in that snide, dangerous way with those little yellow teeth. He comes over closer to her. She feels her heart beat fast in her chest as he approaches. She doesn't like the look in his eye, she knows what it means.

He is right in front of her, looking down into her eyes and she's aware that from that angle he can see down her dress too. She wishes she hadn't worn a V-neck dress, the plunged neckline flattering and exposing. Owen's eyes linger and then he reaches past her and picks up a bottle containing the bright blue liquid that she'd dismissed earlier.

'You going to France this summer?' she asks, attempting to change the conversation, shifting her weight onto her other foot to create a little distance between their bodies. She hopes he'll say no but it doesn't matter too much anyway, she'll not be going down for long this summer what with uni coming up.

Both her and Chris's parents have houses round the same lake in South-West France. Her parents bought a house there first and encouraged his parents to do the same when Chris's dad's company had been doing well for a few years in a row. That was back when they spent all their time together. Emilie gets the impression now that her mum regrets it. They can't escape their town even when they're away.

'Yeah, think Chris mentioned something,' he says, stepping back from her, but he's still too close.

Emilie nods and though she's not done with her drink she pours more into her glass to give her hands something to do and her mind something to focus on. 'That'll be fun.'

'You're going down, are you?'

'Yeah, I mean, for a bit. I've got a lot to sort out for when I come back to go to uni.' She says it off-handedly and doesn't notice the shift in Owen's eyes until she looks back at him. 'You all right?'

Owen doesn't reply. Emilie tries to think of something to say to break the painful ring of silence. A loud yell comes up from the room next door as a new song starts to play, a crowd-pleaser. The bassline is heavy and dirty, the vibration causing the glass in the window frame to shake. Emilie casts a look outside, willing one of the guys to see her looking uncomfortable and to come and give her an out. Owen follows her gaze, looking out at the garden and then back at Emilie's pained face. He repositions himself and places a strong hand on her waist, squeezing it tightly. Emilie shrinks and tries to back away from him but he holds her in place.

'So are you gonna put out or do you save yourself for private school wankers these days?'

She's disturbed by his question and blinks hard as her breath catches in her throat. She tries to find something to say but then he's smiling those tiny pointed teeth at her again and she feels herself freezing. She wills her body to do something, to walk out of the room and take her somewhere safer, but it won't respond. Owen lets go of her, as if knowing that she won't move whether he holds her there physically or not, and raises the bottle to his lips.

Emilie watches the blue liquid wash into his mouth. She imagines the sugar coating his teeth, thick and frosty. He keeps his eyes on her the entire time in a way that pins her where she is. She thinks of butterflies pinned to corkboards in science museums. Owen swallows the liquid down thickly and then wipes the back of his hand over his mouth. She gets the impression that he's enjoying this, like he can sense the fear cascading through her veins, rushing into every corner of her body. He smirks and she closes her eyes for a beat too long. She's sure he inhales deeply as if he's smelling her and then she feels him move away. She opens her eyes and sees that he's stepped back so that there's space for air between them again.

MARGARET MEYER

Margaret Meyer writes contemporary and historical fiction. Her stories and essays have been published in numerous UK and international anthologies. Her novel-in-progress, *The Cleftwater Poppet*, portrays the devastation wrought by the 1645 East Anglian witch hunt. Martha, a midwife, tries to avert disaster by making a wax 'witching doll' – the Cleftwater poppet – with shocking and unforeseeable consequences.

margaret@margaret-meyer.com

The Cleftwater Poppet
Opening chapter of a novel

ST MATTHEW'S FEAST DAY, SEPTEMBER 1645

She was in the front garden at first light. There were herbs to cut, rosemary for the roast meat, mallow and mint for her cough. The house and the street and the hill beyond it were dim under a thick, flame-coloured haze. A single magpie winged from it, and as she crossed the grass she saw how the vapour veiled the morning star. Two bad omens. The mallow grew full and fierce at the street's margin. She crouched and cut handfuls.

Over her left shoulder she saw three men coming. She stood up. The men faltered and fell back, as though they had seen some brute, fearful creature rear up. That thing was her. When they recovered they came on apace, up to the house. Then she knew them – Hesketh's lads from the smithy at the far end of the village, and Martin Long from the gaol. She made for the door and was halfway through it when they reached her. They had the blunt look of men uneasy with their task and their shame told itself in needless force. They shoved her aside and she went down like scythed barley, lying over the threshold while her lungs pumped noise like punctured bellows. They stepped over her and went on into the house. She turned her head sideways and saw Simon come from his bed under the stairs with his hands raised: part greeting, mostly alarm. They struck him in his face and ribs with their staves, and then turned for the kitchen. She pushed herself onto her knees and crawled after them, trying to call Master's name. The curtain rail splintered as they wrenched it. Cloth poured onto the floor. Prissy had been shelling peas into a dish. Martha heard it break, the hail of green beads, Prissy's animal wail. Curses she had not heard before coming from the men's throats. They left with Prissy roped between them like a heifer bound for market.

She got to her feet to watch them go. The front door was ajar and the haze seemed to clot and press in as if to veil what had happened.

Simon came to stand by her. 'It were only time,' he said thickly. He was bleeding from a split lip and the red ran into his mouth. 'For our turn,' he said. 'In Cleftwater.' His eyes were huge and dark with a strange fixed stare in them. They looked at each other in silence.

She made a wide circling gesture, to the kitchen, the house, their village.

'Right enough,' Simon said. His voice was flat with fear. 'Nothing's safe now. Nothing.' All the black of the world rose then, blotting her wits. Simon grasped her elbow and righted her and brought her to the kitchen stool, making her sit while he went to tell Master. His steps flustered away over the tiles to the stairs. Droplets of blood marked his route. She heard his hesitant knock on the bedchamber door and Master Kit's voice, deep with the husk on it that it always had in the first of the morning. And then Mistress Alyse's also, growing high with alarm.

Gone Prissy. Taken Prissy. They had wrenched her from here so roughly, from her hearth and her home, Prissy's prized places. Everywhere there were traces of her. Risen bread dough in a bowl in the hearth embers. Gold hairs, glinting from the floor rushes.

She forced her legs to move, hauled herself upright, pulled back the kitchen shutter. Meagre light seeped in and by it she found the jug and drank straight from it, so fast that water runnelled from both sides of her mouth. The fire was all but out. She remade it, coaxing the embers by blowing on them. Her breath was short and the flames took a long time to catch and were weak until she fed them, pine cones and a piece of salt-wood from one of the wrecked ships on the beach. She sat on the stool again. The sun wrote strips of light on the wall and she studied them, unsure of their message. Her cheek was smarting where she had fallen, the skin split and puffing up on either side like lips. It felt bad, like a judgement, to be marked in such a way. Through the kitchen window she could see the backyard's dark beginning to thin, and through it came the faint repeating pulse of the sea, regular as breathing. She listened to it until her heart began to slow.

Maybe she dozed or maybe it was just that her eyes closed and the tide of her thoughts took her, as they too often did. She did not like to be in them. Why Prissy, and not her? And what of the other taken women, from the string of villages south of Cleftwater? Women in Salt Dyke – nine of them, it was said. Some of them dead already of gaol fever and some still to die, if the judge willed it so. In Sandgrave, Rebecca Blosse and her daughter among seven taken. More in Holleswycke, not a half-mile from here. How many? Four? Five? They had sent for the judge to come from Toll Bridge to try them, a man known to have taken coin from the witch-hunter. God help them all. God help Prissy if that judge were called to Cleftwater. Her thoughts were dark and running, coming always to the same question: would they come for her?

A touch – a hand – reached through the dark tide, with an anchoring grip. She opened her eyes. Kit, with concern written on his face; his frown made deep welts of shadow around his eyes.

'How do you, Martha?' he said.

She looked at him, then at her hands. They must talk for her. Inside her were unvoiced words, too many, that shoved and bobbed in her head and chest like trapped birds. That could not be sounded because of the thing in her throat – a thick shape, that stole her voice and used her breath for its own. Something lived in it: a serpent, a worm. All her life it had been there. The herbs she took damped the coughing but did not stop its work. It hurt to talk. Because of it she rarely spoke. Now her hands drew the shapes of their language, soundless signs and gestures made up between them in Kit's childhood, that was their way of speaking to each other.

Well enough.

He put some fingers lightly under her chin and tilted her cheek to the light. *I will bring the doctor,* he shaped back.

Nay, she motioned. *I have my herbs.*

He brought the jug and a beaker and poured more water and squatted beside her while she drank. 'What did they say? When they came. What reason did they give?'

She shook her head. *None.*

'They must have reason to enter a house – any house – like this.'

Her cheek throbbed. She could not look at him. Her life with him had gone along of its own accord, she had lived it more or less content, had never thought to question it. Or be questioned, in her turn.

'Martha?'

She let out a breath she hadn't known she was holding. He was a good man and a kind one. He had rescued Prissy – their buxom, golden-haired cook – from a life of whoring on Salt Dyke docks. The same with her, Martha. She had been his boyhood nurse, and he had kept her on, given her the dignity of work and a home. It was impossible to lie to him. She made her hand into horns and brought it to her forehead.

'They said... what? That she is of the Devil?'

Aye. His servant. She circled her ring finger. *Devil's bride.*

He looked uncertainly at her, then past her. Then his expression hardened, decided itself. 'Rest here a while,' he said. 'Alyse is still abed. Simon and I will see about Prissy.'

He pressed her shoulder and went. She tried to stand but all her strength had drained away. She leant against the kitchen bench. The house was quiet except for familiar sounds; the constant, breathy soughing of the waves and over it, the grunt of the hogs, beginning their day's foraging in the baked, unyielding dirt of the yard. The window showed the wash house and her physick garden and the far flint wall, with its gate that opened onto Back Lane. Beyond it was the sea: listless; the colour of polished pewter. With Prissy gone, there would be more to do. Water to be fetched. Food to prepare. Mistress Alyse would soon rise and want help getting dressed. There was a ringing numbness on one side of her head, and she lowered herself to the stool and sat for a time without moving, trying to find herself among the kitchen's stolid clutter: battered pans, baskets of wizening apples, a rope of drying onions. The kettles hissed over the fire and their noise mingled with the ripe waft of the slops bucket, setting off a sick, seething current running from the base of her throat to her guts. A single thought came and went and nudged again. If they came for her – when they came – what then? Nothing then; she would be nothing. She would be tainted, stateless, like the others who had been taken. She was Cleftwater-born and knew many things, but not the nature of this new terror that had, until today, been safely distant; a rumour only. Now it had come here – a vicious, heedless mechanism that could be neither slowed nor halted.

Fear drove her to her feet, made her movements clumsy. This morning was a check, a warning. What time there was she must put to good use.

She went to the window. A fly on its back spun frantically against the casement and she watched it without really seeing before pulling the shutters closed. Prissy's apron with its map of stains hung from its peg and she put it around her neck. On the over-mantel was the basket of old candle stubs. She took the longest and fattest. Prissy's battered skillet swung from its beam and she lifted it down and put it on the trivet and lit the big candle beneath it. The copper warmed and flushed; the air above it wavered with heat. She pressed the used candle to the pan's base and almost immediately the wax gave, thinning and spreading out as if in surrender. She took the pan off the trivet and fished out the wick with her parings knife. When the wax was doughy, she scraped it into her palm, rolling it into a ball that became a bulb and then a torso with sprouting buds that she shaped into a head and two arms. With a fingernail, she made three notches: two eyes, a grinning sickle mouth.

Her body felt vacant, empty. But in her head and all around it were noises – prayers and pleas and shrieked protests of the other taken women – coming to her in a new, treacherous vapour in which she must now move and breathe. From her palm, the doll gazed steadily out. Already it was cooling, regaining colour, firming its purpose. Still, it was not quite ready. She held its nether end over the heat until the wax quickened again. Then took it to the table and pressed the blade tip in and cut it partway up, leaving a nub of wax at the join. Now it had legs. A grin, and a groin. She propped it against the water jug. Wax doll; witching doll. Poppet. What was its power? Excitement and fear jostled in her chest. She pressed her hands together, as in prayer. Petals of wax flaked from her fingers. Careful now, go careful: for Prissy, for the women. For our lives. She took a pin from her sleeve and drove it into its throat, to stop it mouthing poison.

LAUREN MOONEY

Lauren Mooney works as a theatre producer and dramaturg. She co-runs award-winning theatre company Kandinsky (credits include the Royal Exchange, Manchester and Schaubühne, Berlin) and attends UEA part-time on the David Higham Scholarship. She writes for both adults and children. This extract is from *Tank*, a novel-in-progress for middle-grade readers.

lauren.cmooney@gmail.com

Tank
An extract from a novel for children

At the crossroads, Freya saw them again. The kids from yesterday. The girl who'd taken the mickey, the skinny girl and the boy. Like they were waiting for her.

All three were in school uniform, but they didn't seem to be in a hurry to go home. The girls were standing around in the road up to Freya's uncle's house, talking, while the boy grubbed about in the hedgerows behind them. As Freya reached them, the mouthy girl stepped out into her path.

'Password?' she said.

'What password?' said Freya.

'Well if you don't know it, I guess you can't go through,' said the girl, shrugging, like she was just doing her job.

Freya tried to laugh – how silly and childish, like a treehouse club – but it got stuck in her throat. There were three of them, after all, and only one of her.

'Don't be a baby,' said Freya, and moved to go around them. The skinny girl stepped back to let her, but the other reached out and grabbed Freya's arm.

'I told you!'

'Let me go,' said Freya, trying to pull away. 'I live up there.'

'Liar. You'd go to school with us.'

'I don't go to school,' said Freya, which really was a lie, but so what. She didn't have to explain herself to these idiots.

The boy at the back looked up for the first time and said, 'Why not?' But before Freya could answer, the mouthy girl shook her arm like a maraca.

'Go away,' she said. 'What don't you understand? You can't. Come. This. Way.'

'Oh, come *on*,' said Freya, exasperated, and then with one good hard yank she pulled her arm free. She seized her chance, shoved the surprised-looking girl out of the way and got past. Then, as she began to walk off up the hill towards her uncle's, something hit the back of her head, hard.

'Emma!' said somebody.

The girl who'd grabbed her, Emma, must have thrown something, maybe a stone. It hurt. Without making any conscious decision, Freya turned, retraced her steps and smacked Emma back so hard that it stung her hand. Emma hit the ground, holding her face.

For a moment they all stood there in the road, dust rising in a cloud from where Emma had fallen. The sound had been so loud, Freya was sure she could still hear it echoing – or perhaps that was just her own breath in her ears, the pounding of her heart. She was still outnumbered, but she didn't feel afraid anymore.

The skinny girl and the boy looked at each other, Emma panting on the road between them like she was going to cry. Suddenly the boy laughed high in his throat. 'She's all right,' he said.

Freya realised that this meant her: *she* was all right, deserved to be left alone.

'Yeah,' said the other girl, speaking for the first time. There was something watchful about her, like a deer. 'I'm Bec,' she went on. 'Emma you've met. And that's Tom. We have to take him out because he's my brother.'

'Shut up,' said Tom.

Freya looked at them both, then at Emma, still sat in the road. 'All right,' she said, and turned away, up the road towards the house.

None of them called after her. She'd half-expected them to do something else, follow her, but it didn't happen. Nothing did.

—

Freya set out after lunch on Saturday to find the lake. She'd had glimpses of it since she arrived, but nothing definite; sometimes, when the light was right, she thought she could see water from the top floor of her uncle's house, the light of it at the bottom of the valley. If she walked in that direction, sooner or later, she would find it.

Freya decided it was best to ignore the roads and go in a straight line through the fields. It was easy enough – there was a public footpath sign and stiles over the fences in just the direction she wanted to go – but after ten minutes or so of walking, she reached a little forest and, with no path to guide her, she began to worry about getting back.

Then she saw a deep blue-black between the trees, there one minute and gone as she moved. Water.

Freya pushed through the forest, bracken crunching underfoot, and suddenly it was spread out before her like a blanket: a huge lake, inviting in the sunshine but with the shadows of dark hills on every side. Seeing it, she felt a warmth that was something like relief, like this was a good place, the right place to be. And then she saw them – three figures down at the water's edge. Two girls and a boy.

Freya's stomach plummeted. Didn't anyone else live in this village? She wondered if she ought to turn back before they saw her, but Bec was already looking in her direction. As Freya stood wondering what to do, Bec lifted her hand, slowly, in a wave.

That settled it. After all, she could hardly run away. Freya went over.

'Hi,' she said.

'Hi,' said Bec.

'All right?' said Tom, without looking round. He tossed a stone into the lake where it sank with a soft *thunk*.

Emma said nothing.

'We're waiting for it to get hot enough to swim,' said Bec, glancing at her watch. 'Do you want to come in?'

'You're going to swim in the lake?'

'It's a *reservoir*,' said Emma, as though this was very obvious.

'But we're allowed to swim in it?'

They all stared at Freya like she was mad.

'Everyone does,' said Bec.

'Bec,' said her brother. 'It's hot enough. Come *on*.'

'Fine,' said Bec, standing up.

Without any further discussion, the three of them began to pull off T-shirts and shorts to reveal bathing suits underneath. Freya, who had nothing to swim in, stayed put. Like she knew what Freya was thinking, Bec looked up and smiled. It was a kind smile that crinkled her nose up, and Freya thought: I like her.

'Don't worry about it,' said Bec. 'Just swim in your clothes. But take your jeans off. Not safe. Tom, turn around, let her change.'

'Wouldn't look anyway,' he said, then took a running jump and bombed into the reservoir with his arms round his legs. The water, which had been like a sheet of black glass, came alive when he hit it.

'Oi!' Bec dropped her clothes and followed, reaching the water's edge just as Tom broke the surface, laughing and looking, with his dark hair plastered flat to his head, like a little otter. 'What did I say? You're not allowed in without me. Mum'll kill me if you drown.'

Only Emma and Freya were left on the grass now, Emma tugging the straps of her swimming costume and Freya still in her jeans. Freya was watching the siblings, but she could feel Emma's eyes on her. She braced herself for whatever came next, but Emma just said, 'Don't be scared. It's safe.'

Freya looked around. Emma had pale hair in a ponytail and a small mouth. They were about the same size and weight, but Emma looked strong, like her bones were made of something thicker, harder. She seemed like somebody who always did just as she pleased. Then she smiled, a sour little smile that didn't reach her eyes.

'Except it's haunted,' she said, and followed the others into the water.

Alone on the grass, Freya felt a strange feeling; a rustling, like there were leaves in her stomach. When she'd first seen the water from the trees, she'd been relieved. A feeling like she was finally doing the only thing she'd really wanted ever since she got up here. Or, no – not quite like that. Like she'd been keeping somebody waiting, and now she didn't have to feel guilty anymore. But ghosts didn't ask you to visit them.

'And anyway, they aren't real,' Freya muttered, feeling silly. She tugged off her T-shirt and pushed down the thought she no longer wanted to think. (If it was safe to swim, and summer, and hot, and Saturday, where was everybody else?).

In her vest and pants, shivering a little, Freya followed the others into the water. It was so cold that her feet went numb immediately, a numbness that spread as she waded in, up her ankles and into her shins, her knees. She made herself keep going and then launched forwards, slamming into the surface harder than she meant to.

For a moment the cold was everywhere, pushing all other thoughts aside, and Freya panicked that she wouldn't be able to swim. But her arms and legs were already moving on instinct, treading water, and soon she began to front crawl, passing the others, who were floating and talking not far from the edge.

'Thought you were scared,' said Tom.

'No chance,' said Freya.

She was swimming towards the centre, leaving them behind. But she hadn't gone more than a few metres when Bec called, 'Don't go too far. The water gets colder out there.'

Freya lifted her arm, to show she'd heard, and carried on. Bec was right – the cold was already changing, becoming a weight on her chest – but it was so still and peaceful that she wanted to go a little further than was sensible.

Freya stopped when she could no longer hear the others chatting. Far enough. She turned onto her back and let the water carry her. She was good at floating, and the sun was warmer on her cold skin than before, heat on her face, her tummy where her vest had ridden up from swimming. The sky was huge and cloudless.

She was so peaceful floating there that, when something brushed against her back, she felt the shock like a jolt in every nerve ending and jumped half out of the water.

It must be a fish – just that. Freya laughed at herself and decided she wanted to see it. She turned onto her front, floating with her face underwater. It was freezing, but she counted to three and then opened her eyes.

Here, just below the surface, everything was golden, stirred-up silt moving in the light like motes of dust. She couldn't see anything until – yes – barely in reach of the sunlight, something moved. Something big. Freya's stomach turned over, thinking of sharks, but she knew that was silly. Who was ever scared of a fish? She'd lost sight as quick as she spotted it and swam down deeper, one stroke, two.

And then, under the water, with her eyes adjusting to the dark, Freya saw it. It seemed miles off, like looking far into the distance – like trying to see all the way here from her bedroom at Uncle Neil's house. Not movement. Not a fish. A light. A pale, green light, unblinking in the water.

A hand closed round Freya's ankle. She gasped, filling her lungs with water, and kicked out, beating her way back to the surface; as the air hit her face she started coughing, her throat full of freezing cold water. Bec, who must've grabbed her, was bobbing beside her, red in the face.

'You idiot! We thought you were dead!'

'Sorry,' Freya said, or tried to, between coughs.

'What were you doing?'

'Did you see it?'

All the anger on Bec's face slipped away. 'See what?' she said.

Freya thought of the green light, how pale and lonely it had seemed, and wondered how to describe it. 'It was…' she began, but something held her back.

With her dark, wet hair plastered to her head, Bec looked just like her brother, another little otter. 'It was what?' she said, impatient.

'Nothing. It was nothing. Sorry.' Freya smiled and turned onto her front, ready to swim. 'Shall we head back to the others?'

HANNAH MURPHY

Hannah Murphy graduated from the University of Reading in 2018. She studied English Literature and Creative Writing and was awarded the English Literature Department's 'Best Dissertation Prize' and the 'Rosalind Laker Prize for Creative Writing'.

hannahmurphy803@gmail.com

Galatea of Gretton Road
A short story

After seeing each other for six months, Callum and Erin moved in together. But Erin always made it clear that it was Callum's flat first.

One afternoon at the beginning of August, she walked down Callum's street, past the row of red-brick Victorian terraces dissected into bedsits. She followed Callum through Callum's gate and up Callum's concrete yard, littered with cigarette butts and crisp packets left by Callum's neighbours.

Erin struggled with a box that *was* hers, digging into the cardboard with her fingernails. The sharp edges had started off small pink scratch marks against her forearms. They became hers too.

But then Callum swooped in and took the box from her arms. He set it down on the front step and touched Erin's wrist.

'Look, look here.'

Callum led Erin towards the window of the basement flat. It rose to the lower part of their bare legs. 'Look and see,' said Callum again.

Ducking her head, Erin did look: a set of blinds was half-closed; there was yellow light from the ceiling lamp, plastic floorboards, a braided rug and a folded futon by the far wall. At the centre, standing sideways in front of the window, was a woman.

Her hair was blonde, there were pearls around her neck and shiny black heels on her feet. She was bent over an upright vacuum cleaner, and, except for a frilly apron tied around her waist, she was nude. But she was not a living person.

Callum and Erin had met at art school. They both knew the difference between drawing an object with straight lines and the sweeping, gestural forms meant to signify something organic. This woman had a stiff back, her joints jutted out at angles and her placid face was fixed in silicone.

'Look at the vacuum cord,' Callum told Erin. A hushed reverence crept into his voice and his arm crept around her waist. The cord was coiled – with great care and attention – around the fingers of one smooth hand. It was being played with, absent-mindedly, by a thing that had no mind at all.

But whoever had posed her had neglected to pick the apron strings from out of her crack. They hung down, dangling right against the crevice of a thick, pert, practically pointed set of buttocks.

Erin felt her own crack begin to itch. Somewhere at the base of her tailbone, several ants wandered in circles underneath her skin. She held off on scratching it while Callum's arm was still draped around her waist.

Unpacking Erin's things into Callum's flat on the first floor took up the rest of the day and most of the evening. Space had been made for her on the left side of Callum's wardrobe. She had the top two drawers of Callum's bureau and one side of Callum's work table.

Erin set up her easel, stained with gouache, next to Callum's expensive electronic drawing tablet. While helping Erin with the screws, he offered up everything he knew so far.

The man in the basement flat was small, round, and seldom seen. The box had appeared in the basement stairwell about ten days before: long and tall like a coffin, leaning against the wall. Then Callum had spotted the doll through the blinds, coming back from his Sunday shift at the pub: on hands and knees, posed to sweep up dirt with a dustpan and brush, its bare buttocks raised up like a baboon in heat; it was impossible to miss the intricate craftsmanship of the doll's undercarriage.

'I took a picture,' Callum said. 'But it wasn't the same. It's the kind of thing a person has to see for themselves.'

Erin snapped canvases over her knees or scribbled over paintings with black strokes when she didn't like them, but Callum was easier about owning up to his mistakes. He let her keep the photo.

She agreed that there was something spoiled by seeing her second hand. The problem was the medium: the phone screen nullified the eerie sheen of the doll's skin, it made her less obviously unreal. In a photograph everything was still, so the idiosyncratic stillness was absent: it needed the sound of traffic going up Gretton Road, the crisp packets blowing in the wind, the brush of Callum's fingers on her denim shorts, and the itch in Erin's crack that she refused to scratch.

'It's always the hoover, or the dustpan and brush,' Callum continued. 'And he always puts pearls on it. Weird, 1950s, Norman Rockwell stuff. Only, you know, dirty.'

'Every day?'

'Every day. Right by that window. But I've never seen him get at it.'

'So maybe he doesn't "get at" her?'

'But then,' Callum asked, 'what is it for?'

In the night, Erin found it hard to settle. She palmed at Callum's sheets and threw off Callum's duvet cover. Across the room her T-shirts bulged out from the top drawer of Callum's bureau. He turned over and tried to fold his arms around her and hold her still. Instead, she wriggled, flickered nervy kisses against his neck, got on top of him and got at him.

Over the next few months, Callum and Erin looked into the basement flat every time they left the house. The doll was always dressed in lingerie and frilly aprons; she aired out the braided rug, dusted the window sill, ironed clothes. On Halloween the doll made a special effort, dressing up in a red bustier, fishnets and plastic red horns. Then the days got darker and it was deep into November: Erin still couldn't get her clothes to fit in the bureau, and they would notice the doll in the same pose two or three days in a row. Her outfits started to look less neat, her hair started to look more unkempt. Erin still hadn't seen the man from the basement flat.

'Can I borrow your hand?' Callum asked her.

It was only four, but it was already dark and Callum was working on a commission: £50 for a portrait of some video game character, ordered by a stranger on the internet. Callum's painting had big eyes, a puckered pink mouth and a boxy scribble where her hand should be.

'For how long?' said Erin. She had her own painting to finish: a still life, for practice rather than profit.

'I just need the left one. You'll still be able to do what you're doing.'

Erin offered up her hand and Callum adjusted her fingers. She tried to get on and forget about her left hand but after a while her elbow felt heavy and her fingers wanted to twitch.

'Did you see what he did to the doll today?'

'Same as yesterday,' Callum said, not taking his eyes off his work.

The doll had done nothing the day before, not even a repeat of one of the old poses. She had been propped, quite without care, against the futon. Erin watched Callum's rendering of her hand take shape and noted how he elongated her fingers to suit his particular style.

'Do you think she's letting herself go?'

Callum squinted at his drawing tablet.

'The doll,' Erin clarified.

Callum shrugged. 'Maybe he's just busy with something else. Probably takes a lot of work, coming up with poses, picking outfits, and flushing out rubber vaginas.'

When he got his commission money Callum treated Erin to a takeaway.

Coming back from the corner shop with the beers, he found Erin hovering outside of the basement flat. Hanging down in one limp hand was a loaded bin bag. The other one was closed around her throat.

'Erin?'

She just kept looking through the window. The doll had been posed again. It lay flat upon the floor, legs up in the air, bound at the wrists, the ankles, the throat and the waist. Erin squeezed her neck tighter, then pulled it away and shook out her wrist.

Callum raised his eyebrow, let out a breath and tried to laugh.

'Damn, he's a dirty dog.'

Erin didn't make a sound. Callum toed at a cigarette butt and mumbled, 'This is getting a bit weird now, isn't it?'

It was only then that she looked up at him, blinking.

'What?'

'Us. Maybe we should stop perving in on his business?'

Erin raised no objections. But that night, with the smell of lamb pasanda in the close air of the flat, Erin stripped off her clothes with mechanical efficiency, lay back on the bed and pulled Callum down on top of her.

She didn't wriggle or squirm about on the sheets. She didn't go in for her nervy, restless kisses. She simply lay there, still and silent.

It was a draining sort of affair, trying to be something one was not, trying to make someone what they were not. Callum fell back onto his pillow, excessively sweaty to the touch with his mouth set into a grim line. Erin felt a similar perspiration sinking into her bones as she looked up at the ceiling and said:

'He's going to get rid of her. Any day now. You watch.'

Her suspicions were confirmed when, one night, Callum heard the sound of a door closing. Erin watched him get up from the bed and cross over to the window, looking down at the street below.

'It's him!' he hissed. 'It's him! Quick!'

Erin slid out of bed. Outside, Gretton Road was hazy with December mist, and she saw a dark shape emerging from the basement flat. It was hard to pick out his features, but his figure was thick and fleshy and his lines were all curved, and he carried something awkwardly. He moved silently towards the wheelie bins, turned his head, looking from left to right, and hoisted a bundle into one of the black bins before striding away.

'So, he finally did it,' said Erin gravely.

'He's just binning it! I thought those things were supposed to cost thousands of pounds.'

'He didn't want her. What else was he going to do with her?'

'Sell it?' Callum suggested. 'Stick it on eBay, stick it on Freecycle, have someone come get it?'

Erin merely shrugged. The finality of things had made her feel calm.

But then Callum was slipping on his shoes in a hurry. 'I know what to do,' he muttered as he exited the flat.

From the window Erin saw Callum stride down the concrete yard. He stopped by the bin and opened the lid. For one moment, Callum seemed very still to Erin, looking down at something in the wheelie bin, just as she was looking down at him. The smudges on the windowpane and the mist-wrapped glow of the street lights softened out his features into something almost unreal. Then he dived into the bin, head first, and went rummaging around like a fox inside it. After a series of muffled curses, the sounds of tearing and grinding, Callum came up, triumphant, waving his prize.

'That's disgusting,' Erin told him when he got back in the flat. Not because it had been in a bin, and not because it had been who-knows-where and done who-knows-what in that basement flat, but because in his hand, lying limp in his grasp, was the severed hand of the doll.

'No it's not, it's a gift,' Callum countered. 'Maybe we can put some bleach on her tomorrow?'

For the time being, he put it on the desk and it occurred to Erin that this was the first joint acquisition of the flat: the kind of thing that a couple would struggle to allocate if they ever broke up. But sitting flat on its palm between Erin's easel and Callum's computer tablet, she could appreciate the way it tied the two sides together. Like a silicone, almost fleshy, bridge of sorts. The way that two sets of real fingers will do when they intertwine.

ZAINAB OMAKI

Zainab Omaki is a Nigerian prose and screenwriter. She was selected by Chimamanda Adichie for the Purple Hibiscus Writing Workshop. She is the recipient of the 2019/2020 Miles Morland African Writer's scholarship. She is working on a novel.

zainabomaki@gmail.com

I Promise These Many Fights Will Make Us
The opening of a novel

Mariam, today sun is yellow in sky like picture of canary diamond you show me in magazine many months ago. I stand in middle of construction site, looking up at it while other construction workers move around me – pushing wheelbarrows, driving cranes back and forth, slapping each other backs while they heads go back in deep-chest laughter. I can no look away from sky. Something about yellow nestle in white remind me of you.

Nine months, twenty days, seven hours have pass since me and Adam arrive in Ghana. It have be many more months before that since my eyes last see you. Where is you? What is you doing? What does your life resemble now? I no know. You sit under my skin, hearing my entire life as I tell you, but I am block from yours, no able to see or hear anything. In my imagination, at this very minute, you is looking at sky same as me. Or you is thinking about me while in back of car being drive to your French class. Or you is in bedroom, perch on window edge, reading book which make happiness spider web through your chest. In my imagination, you is happy, always happy, even though it mean you is happy while apart from me.

This is way it is. Even in middle of workday you is able to arrest me. Even after what just happen – fight which have my heart beating hard under cage of my rib, which have laugh and words pouring out of my mouth at same time to Adam, which have my two feet firmly plant in present moment. All it take is one look at sun for you to come back to me.

Four hours ago, I cross expanse of construction site envelope in shadow of high-rise that we is building. It is lunch time. I am going to join Adam and Ghanaian Boys in corner between break-down, sky-blue crane and fence which separate us from site next door. My mama tell me everywhere I go, I should look for home. If I no look for home, I will constant-constant be looking over my back into past – for last place that is home. For long time I think this mean physical place. Place to lay pillow at night that you also love. But in Kaduna, when I meet you and Adam, I realise it can be person too. When I am in Kaduna, I look for home and find it with you and Adam.

Here in Accra, I find it in one room me and Adam rent and with our friend, Danladi. At construction site, it is corner where we eat lunch and play whot card game every day.

Usually, me and Adam go to corner together but today time run away from me. Foreman assign me to section on second floor with silver hair man, Slow Kofi. From his name alone, you know what doing work with him is like. How he move like snail: he will pick one cement block from pile on wheelbarrow between us then lay it gently down. He will pick second one and lay it gently down again. Ha! But I am no late because Kofi is slow. It is because halfway into morning, he start to sing Burna Boy song – I no know it name – in voice that is smooth like honey. From bottom of my stomach, as if it have mind of it own, my own voice come out and begin to sing with him. Before you know it, I am dancing as well as singing. Time run away.

By time I make it outside to go to corner, Adam and Ghanaian Boys have already be there for much time. Sun burn back of my neck as I make my way across. Ground is uneven plenty. It dip down and climb up like wave. Magic rest in air. In way sparks from tip of welders' instruments fall from top of building, and men seem to move in step and sound of metal on other metal is music beat. From distance, I spot Adam back, half cover as it is in tight, white singlet and his ass perch on standing cement block. Though I can no see them, I know Ghanaian Boys is sitting same way as him – on blocks arrange into circle. It is what they do every day.

Have I ever tell you why we call them Ghanaian Boys? What I have tell you and what fall through cracks is something I am struggling to hold on to. Like way I have tell Adam, my best friend, all stories that is funny and important to me but when object catch my eye that remind me of same story, I will give recitation of it all over again until he cut me irritation eye and say in Hausa – he refuse to speak to me in English even though it will improve our English talk – 'How many times are you going to tell me that?'

Ghanaian Boys is call Ghanaian Boys because they is Ghana Buzu. Very different from our Nigeria Buzu. They is three. Isa, Nuhu and Ladan. On surface they look same same as us. They is all fair and thin with curly hair – though some is long and some is short and some is crop to scalp like my own. We all speak Arabic and Hausa, but they own is Ghana Hausa, fake one and ours is Nigeria Hausa, real one. Difference between Ghana Buzu and Nigeria Buzu is difference between ordinary Ghana people and Nigeria people. First is calm like small town, while second is big and rowdy, like big city.

I am near Adam and Ghanaian Boys when Adam voice begin to go up, colour by excitement. 'Hold on, hold on, pick two, pick three, general market, last card and check!' He shoot up to feet with his hand pump up in sky and start to dance, wiggling his wide shoulders, wiggling his waist. Adam will never be dancer.

I hear Ghanaian Boys before I see them. 'Lies! You had like twenty cards, you couldn't have won,' Isa say. I arrive at corner just in time to see him sifting through cards that is on ground in middle of them to find truth. He sift then swipe cards aside in frustration at what he find. They go up before they flutter to ground like baby bird. He jump to his feet too and get in Adam face.

'You cheated.'

Adam snort. 'Why would I need to cheat when I am obviously better than you?'

'It's impossible for you to keep winning! At least once you would have lost.'

'Is it my fault there's nothing rattling around in your skull? I've been trying to teach you for months. Where is my money?'

'I am not giving you one cedi.'

Adam become angry at that. 'You agreed. We had a deal. Where is my money?'

'What deal? Did we sign an agreement? Did anyone hear us make this deal?' He glance back at Nuhu and Ladan who is hanging back like soft liver man who only follow leader. They both shake head, turn aside.

'You bloody bastard,' Adam say.

'Son of a whore,' Isa counter.

I step in then, Mariam. Getting in between they bodies and holding up my hand to separate them. 'Boys, boys, you're brothers,' I say. They is no really – no in sense that me and Adam is – but it is type of thing to say to get everybody to calm down. It work. Isa hiss and grab silver plate that hold leftover of his food and push off with other two boys trailing after they master.

When it is just me and Adam, I tell him, 'You have to stop picking fight. Every time, every time, fight.'

Adam hiss and wave it aside, plopping down on block again. 'Please speak in Hausa,' he say. 'Stop twisting your tongue.'

I sit on block next to him. In silence, I think again that site is very beautiful. Those sparks is still falling. Men is still laughing and doing friendship thing – talking, helping one another carry beam into building.

'I was going to send that money to my mother,' Adam say suddenly.

'You know she called and said there is nothing to eat. My father's health won't let him work. I was going to send the money to her.' He turn his head, meeting my eyes.

Adam is always person who will take care of me, Mariam. You know this. If I fall and break leg, I know he will carry me. If I have empty pocket, he is person who will bring me food. When what happen with us happen, he is one who nurse me through it. When things become too hard in Kaduna, he is one who say we should come here for fresh start. What have I ever do for him, I wonder?

Before I can do plenty thinking, I bound to my feet and hurry across site, ignoring Adam call of my name, and his ask of where I am going. Within building is dark and have dampness. I call Isa name. As he turn, I punch him in face to confuse him. He stagger back and other two boys is in shock. I dig into front pocket of his jeans, grabbing squeeze notes.

'What are you doing?' He push me off.

I grab him again and go for second pocket. Isa push me off again. His clench fist connect with my stomach. Much pain explode and spread. We begin to struggle for money that I collect from him. Other two Ghanaian Boys try to pull me away from him to force my fist open. I no know when Adam arrive. He jump into fight, taking on Nuhu and Ladan. Dust rise from ground around us as fellow workers gather us and begin cheering and hooting, 'Fight him! Get him!'

At end of it, me and Adam emerge from building with wad up notes still in my hand. Sweet air pour onto my bruise face. Adam laugh, hooking arm around my neck. 'Nafiu, I didn't know you had it in you. All these years you're telling me you could actually fight?' Even in my pain, I smile, I laugh. Words bubble out of my mouth. I glance up at sky then. It is only split second action, but everything fall away. Like shedding cloth after long day, I am strip bare. Only you remain.

JYOTI PATEL

Jyoti Patel was born in Paris to British Indian parents. She grew up in London and has a BA in English Literature with Creative Writing from UEA. She has worked as a content manager for several years and is currently writing her first novel.

jyotipatel616@gmail.com

Six of One
An extract from a novel

It's the warmest day of the year so far. Pools of light stretch over the vinyl floors of Hammersmith Hospital. By late morning, the scent of the building takes on a new quality in the heat – disinfectant mingled with warmed pollen. It makes Nik wrinkle his nose as he weaves through the hospital corridors. The closer he gets to his granddad's ward the faster he walks, as though he's racing against some invisible clock whose tick grows quicker, teasing him, telling him today is the day that he'll be just a little too late. His free hand nervously runs through his hair. He can still feel the morning sun in it. His other hand clutches a one-litre thermos flask filled with masala chai, brewed himself an hour earlier.

When he reaches the ward, he stops in the doorway and exhales in quiet relief. He lingers there and takes in the image of his granddad, whose arms are thrown back over his pillow to form an arc above his head. His face rests at an angle towards the open window as if it's reaching for the morning sun. Nik watches his granddad's chest move under the white cotton gown he's been dressed in for weeks now and marries his breathing with its rise and fall.

The ward is quiet today. Hassan, who's in the bed closest to the door, is fast asleep. Nik senses Clark, the patient who's in the bed opposite Rohan's, watching him. Clark ignores Nik's wave, mutters something about visiting hours, and lifts his newspaper higher over his eyes.

Nik takes a seat in the chair next to his granddad. He digs out a couple of enamel camping mugs from his backpack and pours two cups of chai.

'Too bloody hot for tea,' Clark says, turning the page of his newspaper.

'Sure you don't want to try it again?' Nik asks. 'I've gone easy on the ginger today.'

'Not with all those extra spices in there. Scratches the old throat.' Clark tilts his head so he can watch Nik from over the top of his newspaper.

'Well you let me know if you change your mind.'

'Nikhil, beta?'

Nik looks up to see that his granddad's awake, smiling quietly at him.

'All right, Bapu?' Nik holds out a half-filled mug which Rohan accepts without a sound. 'Look what I made this morning.' Nik digs further into his backpack and pulls out an old ice-cream tub filled with chocolate flapjacks. Dark chocolate spills over the top of each square, still slightly sticky from a morning in the oven.

'Now you're talking.' Clark folds his newspaper and reaches for a handkerchief.

'Not too hot for flapjacks then?' Nik tries to keep a straight face as he gets to his feet.

'Never,' Clark says, picking out a large slice. 'Ta very much, lad.' He raises the square of oats to his lips, handkerchief forgotten.

Rohan seems dazed as he moves to his chair by the window, assisted by Nik and his favourite nurse. He doesn't say much but sips his chai and chews on pieces of flapjack, blinking sleepily. They sit together in silence, listening to whirring buses through the open window. Every few minutes a nurse shuffles past the room or Clark mutters and turns the page of his newspaper.

'Where's Avani, beta?' Rohan asks.

'She'll be here soon. She's got the day off to come visit you.'

Nik's index finger runs along the veins of his granddad's right hand absent-mindedly. He feels his throat clam up when his granddad takes his hand. It's a regular occurrence but something feels different today. His granddad's holding on tighter than usual, and it contrasts with his languid air. It reminds Nik of how, when he was younger, his granddad's fingers would curl around his hand when they approached a pedestrian crossing. Nik grips back wordlessly, feeling a rising pressure in his nose and around his eyes.

'I'll go home today,' Rohan says. His eyes are focused on a fixed point outside the window. His voice is so husky and quiet that if Nik hadn't been watching his granddad's lips he would have missed it.

Nik clears his throat before speaking: 'Not today, Bapu. They still want to keep you for a bit longer.'

'Today, beta,' Rohan corrects softly. Nik watches his granddad smile gently at him, drinking in his face, as if he's seeing him for the first time. Nik can't help but grin back and reaches for his granddad's other hand. They sit this way, hand in hand, drenched in warm silence, content just to be close to one another, until morning fades.

—

'It's just me and you now, Nikhu,' Avani whispers. They've just arrived home from the hospital for the last time and are standing in the hallway. Neither seems as though they're ready to proceed further into their home. Their shoes are still on and the lights are off. Darkness envelops them. Nik's been dreading this moment; it seems absurd for them simply to go home and pick up where they left off. But just as his mum's words settle into the air around them, he hears the grumble of a car pulling up outside. There's a knock on the front door. Their home is filled with relatives.

Over the next few days relatives and family friends whom Nik sees only at weddings and Diwali appear in their masses, each depositing their shoes by the front door and a bowl of food on the kitchen counter. They have more bouquets of lilies than vases available. Three bunches end up in a pressure cooker pot filled with water. The fridge that's been almost empty for most of the summer is suddenly full and their cupboards are bursting with deep-fried Indian snacks. A pot of vegetable rice or pan of bateta shak seems to simmer constantly on their stove. A photo of Rohan appears in a large frame on their mantel. A garland of brownish flowers that Nik can't name is placed over it. Later, he discovers that what he thought were flowers are actually twirly wood-chippings. Avani calls it sandalwood.

At some point during this time, Nik's best mates Will and Ken come to visit. He takes them up to his room and finds an auntie he's never met before sitting on his bed, rubbing moisturiser into her feet, as she speaks a quick stream of Gujarati into a tiny mobile phone. She smiles at him as if to let him know his interruption is forgiven.

There's a constant buzz around the house; knocks on the front door like clockwork, the neat clacking of glasses of water being placed on slate coasters, Sanskrit prayers being recited in a corner of the lounge which has turned into a makeshift mandir, the rustling of another bag of ganthiya or sev mamra being opened every few hours, murmuring voices, windows being opened and closed, and even the more frequent flushing of their upstairs loo. Their home has come alive.

Nik's told, by some random uncle whose breath smells of peanuts, that he mustn't shave for the next twelve days. He does his best to hold it together but finds himself stifling the urge to throw something at a wall whenever he hears the word 'expired' used to describe his granddad. Instead, he wakes up early each day, looking for jobs to occupy his mind before the mourners arrive. No matter how many times he loops around their home in the small hours, searching for a task that'll distract him, he always ends up ironing the white salwar kameez that Avani puts on each morning and throws into the washing machine each night. In the evenings, he hoovers up crumbs, grains of uncooked rice, sequins and petals from their wooden floors, sometimes navigating the head of the vacuum around the saris of lingering grannies who, in his opinion, are overstaying their welcome.

Each time he feels the loss, loneliness and panic rising up inside of him, he changes direction. He retreats to the kitchen to wash some dishes. He goes outside to clean his mum's car. He checks they have enough milk for the never-ending stream of chai they seem to be brewing. Even if there is enough, he often pops out to pick up another pint, just in case. The trick, he finds, is always moving.

Death is something Nik thought he knew all too well. Both his father and grandmother died before he was born. But he begins to realise that, although he has grown up very aware of the vacant space those he's lost have left behind, he's never actually experienced loss himself. He hasn't watched death snatch someone away who meant everything to him. In his naivety, he assumed that loss was simply an absence, not a presence. But now he realises that it's very much the latter. This loss of Rohan is always with him, like a child has suddenly been thrust upon him. When it isn't howling in the night, it's gently tugging at his sleeve, reminding him it's there, exercising its right to his attention. In the rare moments when he's completely distracted, like when he's able to fall into happy dreams, his granddad's death hits him sharp in the face, as though it's punishment for being occupied by another thought. He wakes, panicked, clutching at empty fistfuls of air, reaching desperately for what was once in its place. It's easier when grief plays the tugging child, he decides, when it's there constantly – a throbbing dull ache behind every movement and breath.

ABHISHEK PRASAD

Abhishek Prasad worked as a copywriter for over a decade in New Delhi, Mumbai and Singapore. He now lives in London with his partner. His novel is about the scars of India's partition, the rise of Hindu fundamentalism in the 1990s, and the enduring struggle to keep imagination alive.

ab@abhishekprasad.com

Bloody Child
The opening of a novel

1. IT WAS A BIRD, A BIG ONE – A VULTURE?

He was the last one left in the park again, and the light was seeping out of the sky. The match had ended when both teams had stormed off in opposite directions, shaking heads and grumbling gaalis. Now, even the little kids on the swings and slides at the far end of the park had been dragged home. There was only a lost-looking dog, the same colour as the sunbaked grass, sniffing in the bushes for treats. He clicked a button on his Casio and it glowed blue-green, bright as a daydream, but the time was still stuck. Ma had still not shown up.

He climbed onto a concrete pillar along the rusty green fence and sat with one eye on the park gates and the other on the dog. There was no way a dog could jump that high, but it was best to be safe.

She was late sometimes, it was no big deal. He just had to be patient. He just had to sit still, like his father always told him to – like his father himself could, unblinking, unthinking, before some never-ending Test match on TV. Maybe his body would obey now, he thought, away from any scrutinising gaze. He straightened his back, joined his hands on his lap, and took a deep, long breath. Instantly, he began to feel things moving inside him, things growling and rumbling and twitching and stretching, things that he didn't even know could move. He tried holding his breath but it only made things worse – his biceps (such as they were) went stiff, his eyelids began to itch, his heart pounded on the shrinking walls of its cage.

Nope, it couldn't be done. Asking someone to be still was asking them to be dead.

'Man's brain is God's greatest *miracle*,' he mimicked his father's slow, booming voice in his head, making his eyes pop out of their sockets for the right effect. 'What can it *do*? Arré, ask what can it *not* do! In ancient times, learned sadhus could stop their bodies from *ageing*. They could sit naked on snowy mountains and not feel *cold*. All with meditation only. Today we are thinking, "Beh! Impossible. Only stories." Why? Because we have lost all the knowledge of the vedas. It was all stolen by the British, who else? So today, we are not knowing our own mind power, *understand?*'

He shook his head, wet dog-like, and clicked his Casio again.

19:41. At least the time was finally moving.

He managed to count to thirty-four before the blue backlight automatically went off: a new personal record. He had to disqualify it, though; he may have skipped a few numbers in between. They could call him anything – Mickey, Jerry, Paadi, Shaadi, or, worst of all, A-S-S – but nobody could call Adi Shankar Sharma a cheater.

It wasn't fair. Sunny had promised that he would be on the team. 'Pukka promise,' he had said.

It was an important match, he knew that. The Pocket-B boys had beaten them twice in a row and the series was tied at two-each. It was a do-or-die final and the losers had to buy 5-Star bars for the winning team – full-size, not the cheap minis – so, yes, he understood the stakes. He had practised his bat swing the night before and had even worn his new Reebok shoes that had springs inside their soles. But when Pocket-B showed up with one boy missing, his whole team had turned to him. It was like they didn't even have to think about it, like they were actually relieved to cut him out. Sunny promised that he could open the batting the next time. 'Pukka promise.'

He sighed and stretched his legs, flicked a giant black ant crawling up his pillar, and checked his wrist.

19:43.

Plankton glowed in the sea, in some places, in that same Casio shade of blue. Fluorescent plankton, they were called. Or was it luminous? They were like little insects, the ants of the sea, and whales ate them, thousands at a time, just opened their massive jaws and swept them all up like a mug in a bucket. Did it make the whales' tuttee glow in the dark? Was the ocean floor covered in layers of fluorescent poo? Was that what made the sea look blue?

Bio-lumi-nes-cent. *That* was the word. That was the one thing no one could beat him at: spelling. He didn't have to memorise the words, didn't even have to know them sometimes – the letters simply arranged themselves in his head, snap-snap, just like that. It was hard not to call it a superpower, really. At times, he pretended that the really good ones – cantankerous, egregious, phlegmatic, agoraphobic – were magic spells, and if he could look at someone and hold his breath and spell them out fast enough, the person would be cursed to *become* the word. His all-time number one favourite book, obviously, was *Roget's Pocket Thesaurus*. His father had once called it a waste of time, but what did he know? Ma understood. She had studied English Literature in college so she knew almost as many words as him. Way more than his father, hundred per cent, who had once asked her how many l's there were in 'application'. It made no sense that she wasn't the one going to an office and he the one supervising the maid.

19:45.

As he screwed his eyes shut to stifle a yawn, a familiar image flashed on the inside of his eyelids, sharp as an ad in a glossy magazine: Ma standing on a railway platform with two fat suitcases, facing away from him, too far to hear him calling out, and the whole world frozen, utterly still.

'Don't be a baby.' He punched his leg to make it stop. It was nice in the park, all quiet except for the chirping of sparrows in the darkening trees. Why couldn't he sit still for a few minutes?

He sat on his Casio hand, and in the other one, held up an imaginary microphone and cleared his throat to summon Tony Grieg's commentating voice. It was time for the match highlights.

—Welcome to the big final here at The Rectangle, absolutely *electric* atmosphere today. Pocket-A win the toss and choose to bat. Smart move by Captain Sunny on this pitch.

—Here comes the first ball – OH IT'S GONE LIKE A BULLET IT'S OUT OF THE PARK IT'S A SIXXX!

—Through the gap, go and fetch that! The bowler's not happy and who can blame him, this is a *masterclass* in batting.

—And that's another SIX! What a player, what a match.

—There he goes again – oh, he's edged it, it's going straight to the fielder ... CAUGHT! Sunny walks, but the captain's done his job. 119 is the final score. Pocket-A are already celebrating like they can taste the sweet, sticky caramel of victory. But let's not forget, anything's possible in the game of cricket.

—Here we go, first ball for Pocket-B... Oh, it's an edge, it's gone high, it's a CATCH! What a start – wait, it's a NO-BALL! Can you *believe* this? The umpire is pointing to someone – it's Adi Sharma, Pocket-A's twelfth man. They're asking him to judge the no-ball. He's surrounded by both teams now. Wait, has he *confirmed* the no-ball? He has! Oh boy, his team is *not* happy. Going against his team in a match like this, you have to salute the integrity, the courage of this young man. This could cost him his cricketing career but he's not afraid. This is a true sportsman, ladies and gentlemen, *this* is what cricket is all about.

Enough: Adi shook his head to chase away the voice.

It was a stupid, boring, tuttee match. He didn't care about the sixes and the catches and all the childish chik-chik over boundaries and bowling actions. He was glad when his team refused to accept the no-ball and Pocket-B refused to play on, and the match had to be abandoned. Each team had declared moral victory and gone off to different stores to treat themselves to 5-Stars. He didn't care much for 5-Star either, to be honest. He preferred the cloying, creamy Milkybars that melted in the mouth, though he kept that to himself, obviously – milk was for little kids and losers.

What he did care about was that even Sunny, who had always stood up for him, had walked off without once looking back. For the first time ever, Adi closed his eyes and prayed for Lord Shiva to appear before his best friend, his captain, his brother by an oath of fire, and strike him dead.

He took his Casio hand out from under his butt and tried to shake it awake. He was not going to check the time.

The moon had risen above the UFO-shaped water tank that towered over the park. Pressure cookers were whistling in kitchens and he could smell all the dinners being cooked. He could almost see the bright perfumes escaping through window grilles, shooting out of exhaust fans, swirling all over the park in a mouth-watering mist. He could hear his stomach losing its patience.

19:59!

It was the latest he had ever stayed out alone. Nobody knew where he was at that moment, he realised. He could've been anywhere for all they knew – in a hospital, in jail, on the Rajdhani Express to Bombay. Was no one worried about him?

'Know what you should do?' asked A-S-S. 'Go hide on the roof and wait for all hell to break loose.'

He bit down his smile but had to admit, it was a thrilling idea. *Imagine the chaos it would cause.* They'd have to call in the police who would definitely scold Ma and his father for being so careless. They might even force a bribe out of his father's pocket – *that* would make sure they never left him alone again.

Scanning the rooftops around him, scouting for one that would offer the best view over the park, he paused. That's when he saw it for the first time. (It was the second time, technically, but he did not know this yet.) It was just a shadow, a shape darker than the sky, perched on the roof of the block behind him. It looked like an antique pot, a vase of darkness with a snake twisting out of it; a snake with a silver beak that shone in the moonlight. No. It was a bird, a big one – a vulture? – and on its bald head, he could see a single eye gleaming like a lost marble, staring right at him. He had seen vultures before – they usually hung out on the highway, down by the river – but there was something different about this one. The way it stood staring – its head cocked at an angle like a jeweller looking for cracks in a diamond – made it seem as though the vulture had emerged from some shadowy world in search of him. He imagined an invisible wire between them, crackling with a dark energy, and it sent sparks right down to his toes.

He turned around and closed his eyes. Maybe if he could just sit still – if he could count to one hundred, just once, without moving a muscle – maybe then his mind power would get activated and drive the black bird away. He made it to forty-two before he felt the wind rise from the dusty ground and fill his T-shirt like a hot-air balloon, and he opened his eyes, and there she was. Ma. Walking down the park. Smiling. He remembered that he had to play it cool, give her the cold shoulder, etcetera, but it was too late – he was already running towards her, the cool breeze stinging at the edges of his eyes.

Man, why did he have to be such a *child?*

LUCIEN ROSS

Lucien Ross was raised on folklore and a boat. He is writing a lyrical novella about autism and chemotherapy, a collection of strange tales and collaborating on a narrative podcast about queer occultism. When not writing his novel, Lucien makes short films and performs live poetry and flash fiction in Norwich.

lucienross.author@gmail.com

How to Survive a Fairy Tale
An extract from a novel

CHAPTER TWO

In which Helena shares a secret, and Amelia does not.

Helena was silhouetted against the blinding dawn. Young nettles and goosegrass swiped at my legs as I ran after her. The mist was full of shining pinhead rainbows that flashed between my eyelashes. I didn't have to guess where she was going. We'd often taken this narrow path that led from the back gate to the top of the hill when things at home were hard. On those days when Mr Nox would drink too much, that thicket of trees at the crest of the hill which stood between the village and the rolling downs was a place of refuge. Maybe that's why she'd run up towards the hill now, barefoot, in nothing but her pyjamas after finding her father's body missing. I thought about *'finding* someone missing'; it didn't make any sense, the problem with him being missing was that we weren't able to find him.

'Helena!'

She kept running. A cruel thing within my chest began to sprout pale roots. She was supposed to turn around when I called her. She was supposed to come back to me and fly like a startled dove into my arms. She was supposed to say my name *Amelia, Amelia, Amelia,* until our very presence upon this same hill made her whole again.

She didn't turn around.

The fine mist was threatening to condense back into last night's rain if I didn't keep a firm eye on it. As I gained ground, a dark indistinguishable cluster on the horizon splayed out into a fanning sprawl of individual trees that comprised The Nearly Wood[1]. In the centre of The Nearly Wood was Our Oak.

---

1 We had taken to calling it 'The Nearly Wood' as it had too many trees for a grove, however, we felt that a Real Wood should provide the opportunity of getting lost if one so desired, but The Nearly Wood offered no such promises of circumambulation.

It was my firm belief that in any forest left long enough to plant true roots, we would find a tree like this tree. I could not say that they were wise – it wasn't my place to assign homo-sentient attributes to shrubbery as a rule[2] – but I could say that these trees were witnesses. Time is different for plants. One rotation of the earth is a single breath for a tree: a brief inhalation of light, and then as night falls, a single darkening sigh. All trees feel this, but these trees have grown the longest, felt the most rainfalls and the most spinning blinking echoes of the sun, and it has weathered them. Animals have pecked and drilled and burrowed into their bark, and further still into the soft green wood that lies beneath. Lightning has struck. Every true forest has this tree, and we knew that our small thicket of silver birch and blackthorn was blessed to have Our Oak.

Helena was perched on its lowest branch. She pulled her knees up to her chest. The wet moss had left green stains on her pyjama trousers.

'I shouted for you,' I said.

'I know.'

If Helena had been the one calling me, I would never have considered anything other than running right back to her. The world felt so upside down that she might as well have been hanging below the earth at my feet, cradled amongst the roots. I grew hot beneath my skin at this unparalleled betrayal but, I reminded myself, I'd never told Helena about The Man.

'Amelia.' This was not the way she was supposed to say my name. 'Don't lie to me—'

'I can't lie to you,' I lied.

'I wasn't finished.' She went quiet.

The cruel thing in me wanted to dig its roots into her mouth. *Well, finish then,* I didn't let it say.

'Amelia, you're not allowed to hate me.'

'What are you talking about?'

'I need you to promise me it wasn't you.'

'It wasn't!' I said. 'Do you think I just got up in the night and dragged his body up all those stairs by myself, and *what*? Buried it? Burnt it? What could possibly be the point in doing that?'

She said nothing. She suddenly looked very small. In one impossible movement like a picture in a flipbook jumping from one fixed set of lines to another, her face crumpled.

'No! No, don't cry,' I said. 'I'm sorry.'

2 Not in this world at least.

I couldn't make myself touch her. I didn't know how to understand her as both my brilliant friend who never cried no matter what, and this new thing that produced hot animal tears at the hint of a raised voice.

'I know you didn't do it,' Helena said.

'Maybe this is—' I didn't know the word. I ran through terrified clichés like a pack of frantic playing cards – *a silver lining, an opportunity, a new path?*

'Maybe this is a way out,' said Helena.

'We can do anything we like now,' I told her, but what I meant was *you're like me now*. Though I'd been completely alone when I'd met Helena, she hadn't been alone when she'd met me. Mr Nox hadn't been a good father, but that wasn't the same as having no family at all. If anything, it made his presence even larger in our lives, and the fact that he'd nevertheless shown us the odd tender moment of gentleness meant that she never would've let him go.

Helena rested her head against the gnarled bark of Our Oak and let the dandelion-coloured sun soak into her eyelids. The tips of her ginger hair were turning into honey.

'Let's have cake for breakfast every day,' she said.

I knew she was only humouring me, but still, she looked more peaceful. I sat down at the base of the trunk and locked one foot under a thick root that had burrowed out of the earth. If I were younger, I would have called it a fairy bridge.

'We could plant strawberries in the garden,' I said.

'We could turn them into jam.'

'For the breakfast cake.'

'Of course.'

She picked at a tiny hole in the sleeve of her jumper, pulling the wool apart with her thumbnail. 'It's going to be OK, isn't it?'

I wasn't sure if it was a question, a prayer or a direction of her will towards the universe at large. A thick-bodied bumblebee crawled carefully along the side of the tree. I kept very still. I thought about The Man. Earlier, as I'd stared down at the empty gurney in the mortuary where the corpse of Mr Nox ought to have lain, The Man's words from last night had started to resurface, and they were still rumbling in the back of my mind now. '*The body will have to go,*' he'd said, and it had gone, hadn't it? We listened to the blackbirds. I didn't know why I couldn't make myself tell her. I felt like I was concealing the heaviest secret any mouth had ever held.

'It's going to be OK,' I said. With six perfectly segmented furry legs, the bee stepped onto my hand. 'We're going to be better off without him.'

'He's... he was still my dad, Amelia.'

'You hated him.'

'I didn't hate him,' Helena said. 'I just—' The hole in her sleeve was now big enough to fit her thumb through. 'I just wanted him to be my dad.' The sun was rising rapidly, and as she turned to me the dawn spilled from her eyes.

'He was getting better,' she said.

'Hel, he wasn't getting better.'

'Sometimes he'd make us cups of tea.'

'You know that's not enough.'

'The day before he'd—' She couldn't say it. 'The day before yesterday, he was out of bed before lunchtime. It was like he was before we lost Mum.'

'What do you mean?'

'He used to tell me these stories. He was all a bit scrambled really, but he just seemed so... I don't know, real again.'

The bee spread out its little black wings and flew away. My hand still prickled where it'd rested. I needed to tell her about The Man.

I have to tell you something. That's what I was going to say, but I didn't get the chance, because Helena said it instead.

'I have to tell you something.' She couldn't seem to meet my eye. 'I... I think he knew something was going to happen.'

'You think he knew he was going to die?'

'No, it wasn't like that. I don't know. Sorry, it's stupid.'

'It's not stupid to tell me.'

'He thought something was coming to take him away.'

'He wasn't well, Helena.'

'No, no, I know. It wasn't like that though, he was – it was like he was excited. He wanted to go. OK, no, you're right. I can hear how crazy this sounds out loud now.'

I had an imaginary friend who'd possibly kidnapped a cadaver. I didn't have the high ground when it came to 'sounding crazy'.

'It's OK.' I reached up without looking and wrapped my hand around her ankle. I did it impulsively. I couldn't have done it if I'd let myself think. 'You've never spoken to me about your mum before.''

'Dad says – he used to say I look like her.'

I pressed my thumb into the muscle of her calf. I could feel the wispy blonde hairs on the back of her leg.

'I don't even remember seeing Dad drink before we buried Mum. He dug the hole himself and all, wouldn't let anyone else touch the dirt that covered her. I didn't even get to throw the roses.'

I saw Helena in my mind's eye, all in white, throwing roses into a crowd of laughing women. She looked like a princess. I could never get married now. All I'd be able to think about was Helena not throwing roses into a grave I'd never seen.

'Before that, though, he was just my dad. He used to make up stories for me all the time. I think that's why I thought that.'

'Thought what?' I said.

'Thought he was getting better. He started telling the stories again.'

'Was this about the people he thought were going to take him away?'

'Kind of. They were just these fairy stories about this king who lived in a forest – with magic and castles and all that stuff for kids, and sometimes he'd tell it like he knew the king, and sometimes like he was the king and he'd travelled to the real world just to tell me a bedtime story.'

'That sounds lovely.'

'He was,' she said.

The dew on the sunny side of the hill had risen into one long hazy cloud of steam that wrapped around us. I couldn't see the house anymore.

'He always used to end the stories in the same way. He'd say, "*the carnival is coming*".'

'What carnival?'

'I don't know. I used to think he said it to keep me excited for the next story.'

'At least he got to tell you one more before he went.'

'He didn't. I mean, not a whole story. He was just talking about the king again. He really believed he was the king this time. He kept on saying it. He was so excited.'

'Saying he was the king?'

'No, saying it was coming to take him away.'

'What was?'

'The carnival. He was so happy. He hugged me for the first time in years.' She let her calf rest against my shoulder. 'My dad hugged me for the first time since I was nine and he told me that the carnival was coming.'

REX ROWLEY

Rex Rowley is the recipient of the International Excellence Scholarship. The following untitled excerpt is from the middle of the novel he is currently completing. Ray, a young man in Baldwin Village, Los Angeles, describes his experience seeing police killings as he struggles in his final year of high school.

rexrowley22@gmail.com

Untitled
Novel excerpt

Mama was on my case when I missed my college applications. They had been my dream – they were still hers – but since Reggie got sent up north, I'd been hiding in a haze. Mama said my ass would be out her house if I didn't graduate. There was no more closed doors, music and bud. She was a sentinel. I had to come up with something.

I started this thing, just writing my thoughts down about everything I was hearing on the news on a hundred page spiral bound. I titled it Homologue. It took up my time. It also made me look like I was focused on homework, getting back to my schooling.

Door open, studious, Mama even let me put music on again, just none of that shit, according to her – if rap had a genre, it was Shit to Mama, and not That Shit. I got into some stuff I never heard before. Got Heems into it too.

Everyday after school I worked on my spiral bound, changed things I'd written, scratched things out, looked up news reports, wrote ideas in the margins, changed names, changed them back. When I wasn't with Heems, I was writing. It took me a couple months before the notebook was full. I failed every class but gym that semester, but I didn't feel like I wasted my time. The week before report cards came home I transferred my work into a clean notebook so I could read it over. Each entry got its own page even if they were just a couple lines – I didn't feel right about it otherwise:

Deshawn Jones, 34
Hey officer, officer? Officer? Why you ignoring me? Officer? I know you seen me. Imma run over to you, officer? Can you hear me? Can you roll down your window? Hey, officer? Officer? Hey no, officer. Hey.

Judie and Antawnio Small, 56 and 28
When the police arrived in response to a domestic dispute call, Judie was relieved, and angry. The whole building had been hearing that man hitting on his wife for hours – they all knew who it was. She saw the police roll up, hop out, guns unstrapped. She ran out from her apartment to direct

the officers to the right apartment. Angry at the delay, her son Antawnio followed her out. As she approached the officers trained their guns on her. They fired before she could explain. Her son ran to stop them. The officers pivoted their guns to him and ended his life next to the woman who had given it to him.

Andrew Davis, 44
Mr Davis was allegedly caught selling a firearm to a sting operative. Allegedly Mr Davis fled the scene. He was caught by officers and shot on the ground as he allegedly resisted arrest. The part-time reserve deputy claimed he had mistaken, allegedly, his pistol for his taser. Mr Davis was allegedly filmed on a video released on YouTube, telling officers, after being shot: I'm losing my breath, with one officer replying: Fuck your breath.

Benjamin Williams, 35
Police officers took Benjamin Williams into custody to run his name against known suspects in the area. He had been exercising his horse when officers approached him. Benjamin co-operated, knowing that it would be better not to resist. At the police station, Benjamin was checked. He was cleared. However, the police said they wanted to ask him questions. They said that the computers didn't always catch everything. Benjamin began to worry. He said he didn't know why he should be questioned if he hadn't done anything. The police said this was an aggressive response. He denied any hostility and asked simply to be set free. Not before we ask you some questions, the police said, it will only take a minute. Benjamin was escorted to an interrogation room. The police officers began to question Benjamin. He said he was unaware of any of the cases they were describing. Why are you resisting? the police officers asked. I am not, Benjamin replied. The police officers asked him why he was being so unco-operative. Benjamin was afraid. The police officers asked Benjamin if there was anything he was hiding. Benjamin did not reply. Maybe we should take a look, the police officers said. Benjamin resisted but to no avail. Hold him, the police officers said, as they took out a large, police flashlight. Open this boy's mouth, soften him up if you need to, the police officers said. They held Benjamin's mouth open as they forced the flashlight into his mouth. The flashlight was too big for Benjamin's mouth and it broke his teeth as the police officers rammed, repeatedly. The nerve endings dangling from his teeth were pulled apart, waking Benjamin from a non-resisting daze, as the police officers pushed the flashlight deeper, and deeper down his

throat. The flashlight was too big for Benjamin's throat and snapped the rings of cartilage in his windpipe as the police officers hammered, harder. Benjamin lost consciousness from pain and lack of breath and despair.

William Bajidae, 21
Accused of battery by unknown caller. Time of death unknown. Cause of death internal hemorrhaging. Examination of body reveals extensive and prolonged beating while waiting for corroboration of accusation, indicated by several fractured phalanges and metacarpals, fractured sternum, fractured xiphoid process, fractured mandible, torn intercostals between ribs four and five on the right and ribs three, four, seven, and nine on the left, torn lower frenulum, detached cornea in right eye, in addition to some half-dozen burn marks caused by prolonged tasering on the penis and the scrotum.

Terrel Walker, 41
My wife and two girls were in the car when we got pulled over. My wife asked if I was speeding, and I said I didn't think so. Is our registration up? she asked, and I said it was fine. My daughter asked, why they pull us over, Dad? I told everyone it was all right, everything was all right. I didn't know why they pulled me over. My wife looked at me and I know she was scared. I was scared too – we'd seen the news, seen what they been doing all over the country. I watched the officers approaching in the mirror. Their guns were drawn. I looked at my wife. I tried to be calm but I could see the terror in her – I could feel it in me. Please step out of the vehicle sir, the officer said. I looked over my right shoulder and saw another officer approaching slowly on the passenger side. She hadn't got to where my kids could see her yet but I could see her hands clutching her weapon hard. Sir, step out of the vehicle. I looked at my wife, unbuckled my seatbelt and slowly stepped out the car. I didn't do nothing, I told the officer. Sir, I want you to put your hands on the vehicle, he said. I didn't do nothing, I said, my hands raised to the sky. Sir, put your hands on the vehicle. I froze. I couldn't move. I just kept saying, I didn't do nothing, I didn't do nothing. I couldn't think of anything else. The officer raised his gun at me and came around behind me. I kept repeating my phrase as he kneed me to the ground. I heard my girls screaming and crying but I couldn't look. The officer called to his partner. He pinned me down as she handcuffed me. I looked up toward my girls but all I could see was the officer's gun still pointed at me. Oh my God, I said, Oh my God, please don't shoot. They didn't respond and

I felt two shots pass through me. Oh my God, they shot me, oh my God, they shot me, I cried. Not in front of my girls, I thought, not in front of my family. Oh my God, oh God, God, they shot me.

Brian Miller, 29
Unarmed, all of them unarmed. As he was being mauled by a trained police dog, the arresting officer approached, aimed, and ended his life. Unarmed.

Robbie Raymond Tomlinson, 19
The call was for noise but the first police officer there forced entry. Sixteen seconds later seven shots were fired. A second police officer, en route prior to the call, arrived moments later. He saw the first officer turning the body over to administer CPR. As the ambulance arrived, the second officer went down the stairs to help the paramedics bring up the gurney. The first police officer grabbed the body by its ankle and dragged it down the stairs of the apartment to the sidewalk. The four men placed the dead body on the gurney. The news reported that the unidentified person died in the hospital. They also reported that dangerous hallucinogenic drugs were found in his bloodstream. I read all this and didn't see his name once. They erased him. Robbie Raymond Tomlinson. Robbie Raymond Tomlinson. He's a year older than me. How do I know this won't be me too? If I take a button, howl at the moon, how do I know I won't be lying on the ground, face down, when seven slugs slip me away? Will my family see them flip me over, pretend to save my life? I see you Robbie, see them drag you down, limp, lifeless, and I see them drag me down too, feel myself thumping down the stairs. I see their lies Robbie, know you left this life inside your own home. I know you weren't bad Robbie, because I know I'm not bad. I see a thousand ways of dying every day: shot, stabbed, car crash, suicide, overdose, heart attack. I see it all Robbie. But the one I see the most is the one you saw too. I'm afraid Robbie. How do I know when they will come for me? Just promise me one thing, Robbie? If I pray for you, will you pray for me too? If I remember you, will you remember me too? I won't forget you Robbie. Don't forget me.

It took me the entire week to transfer everything over. I'd stay up till one, two in the morning, take my time, write legible like I'd never done. I think Mama was suspicious when she saw me studying hard over the break instead of going out with some boys, playing PlayStation, or whatever. I didn't even roll with Heems that week – he went with some homie I didn't know, Polaroid in hand and backpack with reused water bottles and two or three KitKats as always.

When the report card came in the mail, Mama flipped her shit. She yelled for me and I knew she was in the kitchen, at the table, eyes on fire. I was in the bathroom. I yelled, coming Mama, taking my time with my hands under the tap.

Her eyes shook, tiny vibrations, pouncing from my left eye to my right, back and forth. Bring me that goddamn notebook Ray, right now.

I went back to my room. The notebook was center on my little desk. I took it back out to her. She tore it open and I breathed in audible and she looked like she'd kill me if I said a word. I stood on the metal divider between the kitchen floor and the living room carpet and watched her eyes tear through my pages.

I thought she was going to stop reading, tear it up, get up, hit me. She read through the first page, eyes went back up top, read it again. She turned the page, kept reading. I watched her turn over the pages, watched her face flicker, on fire. When she got to the end she closed the notebook. She didn't look up. She put her hands over her face and for the first time in my life, I watched my Mama cry.

LILY SHAHMOON

Lily Shahmoon is a playwright and novelist from London. Her debut play, *Lipstick*, opened to four-star reviews at the Southwark Playhouse. At UEA she started the process of writing her new novel, *Pas de Deux,* about two ballet dancers locked in a battle of lust, envy and ambition.

Email: lily@shahmoon.com
Twitter: @LilyBlubber

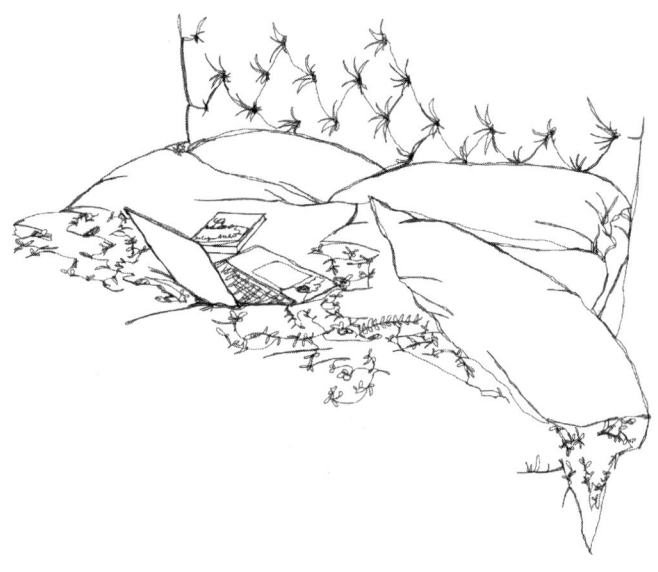

Pas de Deux
The opening of a novel

RAMY

Natalya Annekova is a fucking piece of work but he knew that already, didn't he? He knew it couldn't be him, couldn't be coincidence; not this many times in a row, not with this many dance partners. And still Lorenzo with his *Tali darling*'s and his *Ramy baby*'s, kissing his hand like he was one of his rent boys with the frosted tips, Natalya Annekova with her green juice and her leopard print leggings, *it's the Royal Ballet Tali darling, have some fucking class.*

Lorenzo's still calling him, trying to get him to come back. Like he's gonna stand in that rehearsal room and watch Annekova pull sarcastic faces in the mirror while Lorenzo mispronounces the French names of dance moves and tries to encourage her to forget what she thinks happened. And for what? Miss medium turn out who takes two hours to learn a step? It's not her talent that brought her here, it's that bloodhound manager. Vlad, always standing guard in rehearsals with his meaty frown, how are they supposed to get anything done? *Vlad.* There's something abjectly sexy about single syllable Russian names.

Tomorrow. Tomorrow he'll be back in class bright and early and if he sees Lorenzo he'll say something blasé and forgiving, to assure him that it was *his* fault for not properly containing the problem. Twenty-four hours should give the Russian Princess time to wipe the smacked-arse look off her face.

He turns off the main road and down towards Seven Dials. Neal Street is basically empty this time on a weekday, peppered with shop assistants and rich women with nothing else to do, dressed in the way of rich London women, like they're trying to look like middle-class London women with jeans and knit trainers and Zara puffer jackets. Chanel bags with the buckles turned inwards.

Hagar's flat is above the Birkenstock shop. He rings the doorbell but doesn't hear any sound, so he rings the bells of flats A, C and D, just to be sure.

Someone answers but it's not Hagar, a crackly male voice.
What?
'I'm a friend of Hagar's, her bell is broken.'
Tell her to fucking fix it. It's the middle of the fucking day.
'Then maybe get a fucking job rather than sitting around on your ass answering your neighbour's doorbell.'

The sharp mechanic buzz of the door being unlocked, and through the speaker the man saying *Twat*. Ramy takes the stairs two at a time but his knee starts hurting and he has to slow down. He should have changed back into joggers instead of storming outside in leggings, now the cold has wormed its way into his joint and it hurts like a motherfucker. He stretches it out on the top step before he knocks, tries to fix a smile on his face.

Hagar opens the door in an apron, her hair twisted around a ratty purple scarf. Sometimes she looks so much like his mother, he has to close his eyes and open them again, to stop himself from saying *Maman* and kissing her on both cheeks.

'Wait there,' she says.

She comes back with lit sage and a peacock feather, waving them at his head and all the way down to his feet, so he can see the scarf in her hair and the greys wrapped around it, more of them now than he remembers. She grunts when she stands up.

'Great,' he says, 'I smell like pot.'

'You're not bringing your shit energy into my house.' She beckons him in. 'And wipe that grin off your face, you're scaring me. Why didn't you call? I could have had a client.'

'You don't work on Mondays.'

'*You* work every day. What are you doing here?'

God, she is so like his mother, her arms folded over her breast, her V-neck with the lace sleeves that drapes down to her hips, the way she wears her apron with the tie across the back and knotted at the front. The crease in her brow. Her disappointment.

'I needed to see you,' he says, falling onto the sofa. He's careful to take his shoes off before he lifts his foot onto the coffee table, stretching out his knee again, releasing an angry jolt of pain. He breathes through his teeth until it eases.

Hagar goes back to the oven, clicking it on. There's the smell of burning garlic in the flat, and flour and za'atar.

'It smells of Lebanon in here,' he says, but Hagar doesn't respond as she slides a tray into the oven and flips it closed.

'What happened?' She calls over her shoulder.

'The usual. Annekova.'

'Bolshoi's brightest not tickling your balls the way you like?'

'Said I was harassing her. Commie bitch.'

There are cards out on the coffee table, probably left over from some client she had over the weekend. They're made of heavy, matte card with gilt edges, each with a different image. There are animals and elements, ethereal women with their heads downturned. Oracle cards, he remembers. Hagar hates Tarot.

'I'm heating manaeesh, if you want one.'

'Don't want it in my teeth.'

'I'm making you a tea then.'

Ramy gathers the cards off the table and knocks them against his chest until they fall into place, flipping through to make sure they're all turned the right way. Then he starts to shuffle, the cards slipping over and between each other, raspy little sighs. When Hagar shuffles, the cards jump out at her, freakish, landing upright on the table like they've been compelled to speak. Nothing jumps out at Ramy. He has a go at spreading them out on the coffee table like he's in a casino, picking two out with his left hand the way Hagar sometimes tells him to do.

The life-giver.

Fire.

'What do they say?' Hagar asks, filling the kettle.

'Apparently I'm going to start fucking women again.'

She tuts and brings out a teapot, filling it with loose tea from a round copper tin, dropping something else in it; bark?

'Let me see,' she says, bringing the teapot and two mugs over to the coffee table, leaning over Ramy to put them down without disturbing the cards. The sage smell is strong on her, and under it, lavender. She rubs herself with lavender in the mornings, he's seen her do it, little sprigs she buys from the florist in St Martin's Courtyard.

She narrows her eyes as she peers over the cards, tutting, collecting them all up in her hands and shuffling again.

'If you wanted a reading you should have booked,' she says.

'I just want a friend.'

She is about to retort when two cards jump from her hands and slap upright onto the table. The life-giver again, her sweeping white hair, a hand cradling her swollen stomach. And the healer, with a green circlet and a green stone in her open palm.

Hagar frowns at the cards and gathers them up, shuffling faster this time. Again two cards jump out. The healer, fire.

'I hate it when they do that,' Ramy says, trying to suppress that chill he always gets when the same cards come up more than once. 'They're supposed to be random.'

'Insanity is doing the same thing over and expecting a different result.'

'I don't think that's what that means.'

Hagar folds her hands around the deck and places it back on the table, pouring tea out for both of them. 'You're in pain,' she says. 'You didn't need the cards for that.'

'I'm a ballet dancer, my life is pain.'

Hagar doesn't laugh. 'Is there someone to take care of you at home? Benny?'

'Benny's in Southampton with Eddo and his harem of twinks.'

She frowns at him like she's *this close* to giving him a warning. She's always telling him to be nicer to Benny, even though she also thinks he's an idiot.

'When does he get back?'

'I don't know. We're fighting.'

'One day you're going to run out of people who like you.'

Hagar takes one mug for herself and hands Ramy the other. He can hear his mother in his head, *Such a sensible girl. Why don't you just marry her?*

Maman, she's a Jew. That would shut her up.

'Have you apologised?' She asks.

'To Benny? He's flying sixteen hours a day. If anyone deserves an apology, it's me staying back and working to fund his lifestyle.'

'So it was a planned trip.'

What, she's on *his* side? She's met him once, and he spilled wine on her and then as a way to apologise tipped the rest of the glass over himself, splattering it all over her shoes. So they're fighting, so he hasn't been home in four days. It's not the first time he's upped and fled like a sad-boy teenage runaway. And he posted pictures of Eddo's beach house on Facebook so clearly he wanted Ramy to know he was alive. That's what this is. This is what they do.

'He'll come back.'

'And the Russian girl? What did you do to her?'

'Oh, Annekova?' For a moment Ramy had forgotten all about her. 'She accused me of groping her during a lift.'

'That's bullshit, right?'

'Course it's bullshit, it's a Fish Dive, my hand is supposed to be on her thigh.' Although hands do slip, sometimes, lose the tension and suddenly you're higher on the thigh than you thought, your fingers grazing leotard where there should only be tights. 'Still, it's *ballet*, people touch you, that's the point. Not like Tsarina Natalya hasn't been touched all over.'

'Not this, I beg.'

'I'm not saying the *whole* cast of Spartacus, I'm not, but how many burly Russians do you think it takes to handle her until one of them eventually "handles" her?'

'Who's to say she didn't handle them?'

He thinks again of Vlad, his wide waist, his high forehead. He's probably never spilled a glass of anything in his life. He can probably break glasses just by making a fist around them. Terrifying man. What might he and the Tsarina look like twisted around each other? That thing about the Spartacus men was probably a rumour, but she could actually be doing it with Vlad, frantically in the back of the Lexus he drives her around in, his fingers in her mouth.

Benny should come home soon. Any day now.

'Anyway,' Hagar continues, 'What does it matter if you touched her? You're gay.'

A sudden, sharp twinge in his knee stops him from answering her. He eases it back up onto the coffee table, reaching down to get full extension in the hamstring, pulling against the tension and massaging his kneecap through his leggings. He places his other hand over the massaging fingers, in case she gets a glimpse of the surgical scar through the sheer fabric.

'Bad?' Hagar asks, but he shakes his head. She doesn't have to know everything.

He can feel her watching as he rubs, stretches, tries to touch his nose to it. This isn't the worst it gets. Sometimes he can't get to sleep because of the burning, screaming pain all through his knee and calf and thigh. And then when he gets to sleep he dreams of falling. Or not falling really, *landing*. He dreams of landing on something that isn't his knee. He lands on his arm and his elbow popping out the wrong way, or on his head, tearing all the muscles in his neck. He asked his doctor if the dreams could be a side effect of the medication but he'd said no. He also said he shouldn't be experiencing any pain anymore. He said any pain left over was pain inside his head, that sometimes pain inside your head hurts much worse than the body pain.

'I'm a ballet dancer,' Ramy said to him, 'my life is pain.' He didn't laugh either.

ELEANOR SHEEHAN

Eleanor Sheehan is an American writer who considers many places home, presently California. She obtained her BA in English Literature and Art History from the University of North Carolina, Chapel Hill. Before focusing on fiction, she worked as a journalist and editor. Her writing has appeared in Splinter, *Mother Jones*, Hunker, *Dwell*, and elsewhere.

eleanorsheehan@icloud.com
eleanorsheehan.com

Ghostwriter
This is a piece of speculative fiction

ELEANOR F BOLAND
December 16, 0000 – January 21, 0081
"Don't try." [1]

These things are never easy to compose. They tend to drone on for too long, over-embellishing the dearly departed's successes and sometimes downright fictionalizing his or her influence. Word after word stamped on the screen like gold thread in a brocade. If she were still with us, our beloved Eleanor F Boland (EFB), she might say, "don't waste your breath." Then again, given her mercurial disposition, she might read the ensuing eulogy and ask, "where's the rest of it?" Even so, we have tried our best.

Last cycle, between the shuffling of UBER MOON A7 and TESLA SYNTHOLONY 3, EFB decamped this plane for the next. Not one to shy away from the unspeakable or the topically difficult, EFB would insist that the circumstances surrounding her death be reported accurately and without any prevarication of the details, however gruesome. Consequently, with great discomfort and heavy hearts, we must report that EFB was Dispossessed from our unit by the crushing jaws of a mountain lion. While her wounds suggest that she put up a courageous fight, this rare night creature proved to be a more formidable foe and she succumbed to a fatal neck wound, bleeding out on a sandy geological indent, under the only sagebrush bushel in a two-mile radius. Attempts to recover her remains were delayed by inclement weather. When search and rescue was able to successfully retrieve her body, eighteen hours after the estimated time of attack, carrion crawlers had already begun circling overhead. Her corneas were not spared from their jurassic beaks.

As one of the last remaining plenipotentiaries from the ZEROED years (before the beginning of OURSTORY), EFB's upbringing presents an expository obstacle. We know that she was born in what was once called a state, that she enjoyed a somewhat nomadic lifestyle until quarter age, and that she settled in THE PACIFIC TERRITORY shortly after the CLIMATIC RUIN INCITATION of SUSTENANCE EXIGENCY SUPPRESSION (C.R.I.S.E.S) began unfolding across all of Earth's populated regions.

One of the only childhood anecdotes Eleanor delighted in recounting concerned a particularly unappetizing insect's ingestion. And though it feels strange – perhaps a bit infelicitous – to repeat it here, the synchronistic comparability between EFB's infancy and her culmination is too uncanny to omit. When she was a young girl, no more than three, Eleanor's mother left her

---

1 Indeterminable phrase origins.

alone to play in a shed by their domicile. Her mother's brief absence opened an opportunity for Eleanor to try new things, to experiment, without parental objection. Instinct encouraged little Eleanor to pick up, investigate, and then chew on a large, brown roach. Upon returning, her mother found half the roach hanging from Eleanor's lips and slimy roach effluvia smeared across her cherubic cheeks. We cannot be sure what kind of physiological effects cockroach consumption had on a young EFB, but we are virtually convinced that its occurrence somehow augured her ultimate planetary departure.

Just as she would not want the story of her passing sanitized nor censored, Eleanor would not want her death to be devoid of pedagogical purpose. Therefore, with great emphasis, we must also promulgate that her untimely passing can be attributed to misfortune and misfortune alone. We hope Eleanor's death will serve as a reminder that even in our eon of EXTENDED EXISTENCE, our eon of SUPREME SURVIVAL, and our eon of ALL WATCHED OVER BY MACHINES OF LOVING GRACE, celestial acts of tinkering do still occur. Preparation is no weapon against the wrath of the cosmos. Preparation is no weapon against the adapted mandible of a nearly extinct species. Preparation makes THE GODS laugh.

All evidence considered, nothing, excepting the feline encounter, was unordinary about EFB's day. In fact, she had been quite prepared, if not over-prepared. An avid trekker, she had been hiking in the canyon behind her [MUSK BUNKER] as she typically did at night, before the lethal daytime heat encroached. And, like she usually did, Eleanor had been wearing UV METALLIC FLEXIARMOR, she had been carrying bear mace, she had activated her HYPER-REFLECTIVE LOW DENSITY KINETIC SHIELD. She had climbed up the orange path behind our unit's homestead, the last in THE PACIFIC TERRITORY, up into the mounds, where she walked into THE UNMARKED. Based on the data gleaned from her APPLE SUBDERMAL TICKER, the mortician was able to approximate that she was attacked four miles from the trailhead.

Track marks indicated that the puma, whose range was previously assumed to be farther north, stalked her for at least two miles. With almost inexistent prey and scarce water, experts posit that the lioness had not eaten in weeks, if not months. It is unclear how this once prevalent prowler survived THE (UN)GREAT DROUGHT of the 2060s, though experts have also hypothesized that she somehow evolved under the pressure of meteorological extremity. The mountain lion that killed EFB is believed to be the last living of her kind in THE PACIFIC TERRITORY. Eleanor would be proud to know that she died so another being could thrive for a transitory moment in space-time.

During her years of orbit, EFB was a devoted scribe. She wrote seven manuals, seven reality simulations, and seven treatises. She was awarded several GLOBALIZED LAURELS for her endeavors, however EFB loathed the cupidity of recognition. She abhorred the profligate consumption of fame. Speaking to THE CURRENT WEST SCROLL in 2041, her last interview, she said, "I am no woman, I am no face. I reject the sybaritic offerings of approbation. I reject the identikit bestowed upon me. I am not a writer. I am No Woman."

After THE AQUATIC CONFLICTS of 2053, 2059, and 2063, EFB retreated further and further into obscurity, until she never left her bunker. Though she was urged by members of her unit to provide the public with her once fiery condemnations of CENTRALIZATION and (DE)NATURALIZATION and VERNACULAR UNIFICATION, she no longer felt that her words would resonate – she no longer felt that her words could cut, nor inspire. As such, she devoted herself fully to her familial unit and to her loving life partner, Travis Jean (TJ). Together, they invented novel ways of irrigating sub thermal greenhouses and developed a vehicle through which TJ could [re]experience his lost passion for wave combing (a phenomenon that disappeared during THE RECALIBRATION of 2048).

In 2077, TJ transmitted his consciousness to our unit's network before choosing to depart from his flesh suit in 2078. After his bodily exodus, EFB struggled to reclaim the joys that once flowed through her. Each day after his decampment, she seemed more and more moribund. She wanted to join him in THE ATMOSPHERE, but feared ejecting too soon, before her children and grandchildren were adequately braced. Eventually, she began preparations for this transfer. The procedure would have taken place one week and three days after her unanticipated death. Since her consciousness was not recovered in the accident, EFB will unfortunately not breathe on in THE DIGIPLEXUS with her adored Travis Jean as she and he had intended. Eleanor would at least be comforted to know that she died the way we used to die: permanently and without predestination.

Elements of EFB's spirit will live on in her progeny, Persephone, Archimedes, and Cleopatra; their children, Clarice, Oedipa M, Pythagorus, Townes, Hank (Charles B), and Polly Jean (PJ). She is also survived by one great great grand-progeny, Ozymandias.

ELLISON SKINNER

Ellison Skinner is a London-based writer with a BA in English Literature and Creative Writing from Warwick. They have a keen interest in mythology, folklore, magical realism and horror. Their current projects include *They Seem Hospitable Here,* an unconventional murder mystery, and *Ghostless,* a fantasy novel about grief and the transformative power of storytelling.

ellison_skinner@outlook.com

The Teakettler
A short story

When I was a child, I took the tram into town every weekend to visit the zoo. It was my favourite place in all the world. They had a creature there that was something like a dog and something like a kettle, which walked around backwards and made whistling noises when it was distressed. Sometimes steam would come out of its ears, and when this happened its keepers brought it tea in a fine silver pot, along with a cup of bone china. It drank obediently but showed no pleasure in the act. There was a sad look in its eyes. It never tried to escape, but you could tell it didn't want to be there.

One Saturday – I always went on Saturdays – I had the idea of bringing some exotic teabags for it as a special treat. We had some at home, kept in a small patterned box with a hinged lid, and each one was a different flavour: lemon and ginger, cardamom, clove, mint, hibiscus, and more. I brought them all to the zoo, and the keepers allowed me to place one in each cup so that the teakettler might choose what flavour it liked. It chose the lemon and ginger. I filled the cup with hot water and watched with delight as the creature drank deeply, its dog-like snout buried in the teacup, drinking and drinking as though it were dying of thirst. Back then, I never thought it odd that a kettle would want to drink tea. At school, my science teacher had explained that humans were sixty per cent water – and yet we still needed to drink water every day in order to stay alive, didn't we? The teakettler drained the cup with a rattling sound. Then it ambled up to me. We looked at one another through the bars. For the first time it spoke, in a voice that hissed and whined terribly.

'Little boy,' it said, 'you mustn't think I don't appreciate this, but I have to ask. Why bring me this gift? No one has ever brought me a gift before.'

'You don't seem like you enjoy what the keepers give you,' I said.

'I don't enjoy it. You're right there. Tell me, little boy, what is it that you want?'

I thought about this for some time. Just as nobody had ever given the teakettler a gift before, nobody had ever asked me what I wanted and meant it.

'Well,' I said, 'I'd really like a new bicycle. My old one was stolen ages ago and my parents never got me a new one.'

'Go home,' said the teakettler. 'It is waiting in the hall for you.'

I went on home, and there was the bike, gleaming and new. When I tried it out, it was even better than I'd hoped; its gears never needed oiling, and its leather seat was the perfect height for someone of my size. It was painted electric blue. I rode it every day after that, even Saturdays, all the way around town. It was a few weeks before I realised I hadn't said thank you to the teakettler, nor had I been back to the zoo since my last visit. It was too far to cycle there, so I took the tram. (Eleven, my parents said, was old enough for a boy to take the tram on his own.) As a thank-you gift, I brought the teakettler some sugar cubes. It dropped them into its cup one by one, and we both watched as the golden-brown icebergs dissolved in a boiling sea.

'Delicious,' said the teakettler, finishing its tea and licking its lips with a long tubular tongue. 'Tell me, boy, how have you been keeping?' It looked tired today. There was a heavy slouch to its shoulders and its tail drooped, like a flower that hadn't been watered in a while.

'Pretty well,' I told it. 'But I'm starting to feel cooped up, lately. My bedroom is so small. There's no space in it for my things, and my parents keep going on at me to tidy it, but once I pick things up off the floor there's nowhere to put them. I wish I had a bigger room.'

'Go home,' said the teakettler. 'You'll find it's grown six times in size.'

I went on home, and my bedroom had become a chamber fit for a king, with damask covers on the bed and a Turkish rug on the floor. An en suite bathroom led off one side. It had gilded taps and there were mosaics of sea serpents on the walls. When I examined the cupboards and shelves in the main chamber, I found they were filled with everything that an eleven-year-old boy could possibly want: a rocking horse that neighed and pawed at the ground, a miniature dragon that spat out real flames, a toy car big enough for me to drive around in. If I grew bored of an object, it vanished and was replaced by a new one, even more exciting than the first.

I was so engrossed in trying out all these new curiosities that I forgot to go back to the zoo for two whole months. My parents, though impressed by my new room, quickly tired of my inability to put anything away. The rug was often covered in scorch marks from the dragon's mouth. However, the bedroom itself was so large that I could hide virtually anywhere and know they would never find me. Being sent to my room was no longer a punishment, but a privilege. When they berated me, I simply retreated into my newfound wonderland, barring the door with heaps of toys and games. No one could reach me in there. I was safe.

Eventually, though, I knew it was time to go back to the zoo. Guilt had started to eat away at me, like a vulture picking scraps off a corpse. I took the tram into town and went to see the teakettler. I brought with me a silver spoon, which I had filched from my grandmother's cutlery drawer.

The creature looked worse than before. Its fur had fallen out in clumps, exposing pink goose-pimpled skin, and the flesh around its eyes sagged. When it saw me, it brightened. 'Little boy! It's been so long.'

'Yes,' I said. I dropped the spoon in front of it. Before it could thank me, I rushed on: 'Listen, could you do me a favour? My parents are really starting to get on my nerves. Is there any way you could make them back off a little?'

'Go home,' said the teakettler. 'It's done.'

I went on home, and true enough, my parents no longer noticed when I made a mess. In fact, they didn't seem to notice me at all. Often, I had to remind my father to lay a place for me at the table, and even when he did, I might as well have eaten in my room. The conversation passed me by as if I weren't even there. When I tried to join in, my mother would give a vague, uncertain sort of smile, as if I'd said something very rude and she wasn't sure how to respond to it, and would carry on talking.

After a few weeks of this, I grew tired of being ignored. If the teakettler was capable of changing my parents' behaviour towards me, I reasoned, perhaps it could also be altered for the better. As the tram rattled towards the zoo, visions exploded in my head: presents every day, breakfast in bed, no school, unlimited attention and unconditional love. But even in the privacy of my own mind, I was forced to admit that no creature, no matter how powerful, could manufacture love when none existed. No matter. I could make them worship me, make them respect me. That was close enough to love. There was no gift this time – I'd forgotten to bring one. It didn't matter. We had an understanding, the teakettler and me.

It looked really terrible, this time. Its ears drooped low. Mites were jumping in and out of what was left of its fur. It shook its head slowly from side to side, as though it couldn't control its own movements, and a strong smell – like sour milk – came off it. I ignored all this and came to a stop in front of the bars. It looked up with rheumy eyes.

'You made a mistake,' I said to it. 'That last wish – it's not what I wanted.'

'How so,' said the teakettler, after a moment.

'My parents treat me like I'm not even there,' I said. 'It's not right. It's worse than before. Why don't you make me someone important? A king, maybe? Or an emperor. Then they'd have to take notice.' I imagined it again: blind adoration, embraces whenever I wanted them. 'You must,' I said, 'you must, you must.'

'What will you give me in return?' said the teakettler.

'I've already brought you teabags, and sugar cubes, and my grandmother's best silver spoon – what more do you want?'

'I want to get out of this cage,' the teakettler said.

'You must be crazy,' I said. 'What – let you out, so you can run away and break our deal? I'd never see you again. No. Ask for something else.'

The teakettler gazed at me for a long moment. Then it sighed. With that sigh, its body seemed to dissolve. First what was left of its fur became translucent, then its ears disintegrated, and then it was gone. It became steam and wisp and blew away on the breeze.

I stood there and looked at the empty cage for a long time. Then I took the tram back to my house and went inside.

The bicycle was gone. I knew before I went upstairs that my new bedroom would be gone, too, along with all the things inside it. My old room with its bare floorboards and sagging mattress was back and my parents were behaving like themselves again, which is to say that they bawled me out as soon as I got home for tracking mud all over the house. My mother made me scrub it out of the stair carpet with a wire brush. My father banged his fist on the hall table and shouted about awareness and responsibility as I scrubbed, my hands turning raw from the soap, the mud getting under my nails.

I went back to the zoo a few more times after that, but I never saw the teakettler again. Its cage stood empty for a month, until it was replaced by another creature. This new occupant was a two-headed black pig with eyes like wheels that revolved continually, so that you never knew which way it was looking. I tried to talk to it from time to time, but it never responded – only stood there with its two heads swaying and its eyes turning in its skull, around and around and around.

ROBERT F W SMITH

Robert F W Smith writes about cultural and religious conflict and the British past. His current project is *The Puritan's Wife*, a novel set in southwest England during the Wars of the Three Kingdoms. His doctorate in early modern history was awarded by the University of Southampton.

rfws2001@gmail.com

Halcyon Days
Extracted from The Puritan's Wife, *a novel*

Christina Godsell woke early. Normally so did Jeremiah, but he slept long this morning, and she lay quietly till he stirred, giving thanks for the unaccustomed leisure. Eventually thirst and the call of the privy provoked her to rise, and this woke her husband in turn. Jeremiah groaned as he rose, joints snapping, and then groaned again, differently, as he dressed after their prayers at rising. As he donned his hose, Christina noticed the bruised lump on his left knee, and the delicate and awkward way he tied his points, as though his hands were lame. She took them in hers, and perceived the soreness and blistering.

'Jeremiah, what ails thee?'

'Yesterday was harder manual labour than I am accustomed to. The flesh is weak!' he said, with good cheer.

'Let me,' Christina said, and helped him finish dressing. 'There is a doctor of physic in the market by Penket.'

'These are but small ailments, they will heal in time. Naught to what many men suffer uncomplainingly. Besides, most doctors of physic are mountebanks, this thou knowest.'

'Nay, visit him for an unguent or salve of some sort, I pray thee. I saw thee flinching at a little touch.'

'Aye, very well. Thou'rt right, there's no virtue in suffering needlessly.'

'Good,' Christina smiled. 'Since thou art going into town...'

'... might I engage a serving man, and a maid to help thee? I bethought me of that.'

'This house is so great, and now that thy revenues will stretch to it, I see no reason not to engage help for us.'

'So, so.'

'It really were best done today, or as soon as may be.'

'Certainly, yes,' said Jeremiah with a hint of irritation. 'It will be.'

'And then there are the broken things left over from thy work of yesterday – really it will not do for them all to lie in the yard like that, for all to see; they should be taken away or burned.'

'I know!' Jeremiah exclaimed. 'Heaven above, Christina, I am not a simpleton!'

'I did not mean to scold,' said Christina, abashed.

'Set to thy daily work and be comforted. I shall return straight when all is done.'

As soon as he went and stillness descended, the strange immensity of the house became unsettling. She found herself walking slowly and softly through the rooms, trying to make no noise, as if she feared that some beast might leap out at her – which was nonsense, of course. She only realised she was doing this once the bang of an unfastened upstairs shutter in a gust of wind made her jump and exclaim out loud, and her voice startled her with its very ordinariness. She told herself that once the place had been cleaned and furnished as she liked it, the sense of intrusion and watchfulness would disappear. With that prospect in view, she knuckled down to housework.

Slicks of old grease, dust, soot marks and cobwebs waxed thick throughout the rectory, especially in the kitchens. The wife of the late Dr Brymer had been slatternly – or perhaps merely afflicted with idle and dishonest servants, Christina said to herself charitably. It seemed worse because all the moveable goods were gone, disbursed by the previous minister's executors, save for a gigantic lead cistern in the yard which must have been judged too heavy to move. The cistern was quite dry, of course. Unfortunately, the well was nearly dry, too; Christina drew water for the cleaning, and it came up muddy. Nevertheless, cleaning took all morning, and the fire made the already close atmosphere scarcely tolerable. She scrubbed the flagstones and basins until they foamed, and sweat stung her eyes more than she could bear.

Inevitably, she soon became thirsty; but there was little to drink, as yet. While walking the previous day she had noticed a brewer's house nearby. She went out for two firkins of small beer to tide them over until the morrow. It was only a walk of five minutes to the place. A few thin, dirty men of middle age were loitering outside the brewer's, probably the same from yesterday. She resisted the impulse to clasp her hand around the purse in her pocket. At her arrival, they exchanged murmurs in the dialect of the West Country, accentuating its thickness, so that she struggled to understand exactly what was said. One tipped his hat in her direction, flashing her a wide yellow grin, though the most derelict of them did not seem to see her at all. The alewife was a flabby old woman with grey curls plastered to her temples by sweat, who addressed Christina as 'my dearie' at first, but changed to 'Mistress' after she identified herself.

Christina lugged the heavy firkins home, taking rather longer than five minutes this time. Once back in the house – which, being windless, seemed even hotter and closer than the street – she found a moderately shady place to sit, and then drank deeply of the oaty brew. Soon she felt uncomfortable; her underlinens had soaked with perspiration during the morning, especially the journey back from the alewife's house; and now that she was indoors, they had started giving her cold pinches when she moved. Her frock was stained in various ways, as well, from sweat and dust and other things.

Vain though it might be considered, Christina decided that she would put on fresh linen with something cooler over it. Besides, her mother had told her before she married Jeremiah that cleanliness and tidiness of dress were no less important for a wife just because she happened to be wedded to a minister. She went upstairs and changed into a new smock and petticoat, and selected the lightest gown she could find, a brown one of fine merino wool.

Through the half-open shutter of the chamber she could hear women's voices in the street outside.

'There's trouble for somebody.'

'I'll wager we can expect more than a pinch of gunpowder on the sabbath.'

'Aye, gunpowder and treason!'

'Sh! Say not so, not in the street.'

The women passed on, returning home from market. Christina sighed. Jeremiah would have to clear the debris from the yard as soon as may be. His poor hands would suffer; he was not framed for a mechanical's labour, that was certain. But it could not be helped. There it would stay until he hired a man to help.

It was noon, or thereabouts, so to cheer herself, she fetched a little bread and beer, sat by the window, out of sight from the road, and took up her midday recreation, one of the few she permitted herself: her needlework. She had been embroidering a verse of Scripture onto a square of white satin with red and yellow threads. She was not skilful, but quickly improved at things she turned her hand to, as her father had told Jeremiah once, soon after their first meeting. The work would be a pretty thing when finished, she knew; perhaps a cover for a cushion? She would find something suitable to do with it.

The verse she had selected was Ecclesiastes 4:11: *If two lie together, then they have heat: but how can one be warm alone?* Marriage was ordained for that reason, among others, she knew: that the wolf of loneliness should be kept from the fold. She hoped her husband would be pleased by her thoughtfulness.

Elsewhere, Markham Whitelady and his horse rounded the curve in the Whitechester road, coming out of the shade of the High Wood which climbed from the fringe of Verwood all the way to the hillcrest of St Martin – only a country mile as the crow flew, but a long, dry, dusty mile as the morning wore on to noon. He had not the heart to spur Arion, who was becoming long in the tooth, to anything faster than a stroll in such heat; and besides, the afternoon's business promised to be as tedious as the morning's.

The sunlight struck him with new vehemence as they emerged onto the ridge, past the five mile stone at the bridge, above a streamlet reduced these last two months to a trickle of stagnant water. Markham delved into his saddlebag for his flask and took a long swig of beer. His guts griped uncomfortably afterwards, and he cursed the alewife he had heard evidence against that morning, whose sour drink had affected three villagers in ways Markham would not ordinarily care to hear described in such detail. Now he would make himself sick, he knew it; it was his way of old. He never could stand to hear of sickness. But what else was there to hear of? Nothing of glory, of grandeur or divinity – old crones and verminous barley. Nothing was fit for poetry any more.

He gazed with a jaundiced eye at the Whitechester cathedral tower, jutting up from the murk above the town in the middle distance. For as far as he could see, the patchwork fields and dry green copses were indistinct with haze; but something atop the tower gleamed gold, winking occasionally. The loop of the Tetch below Whitechester where its New Mills stood blazed like liquid metal in a smelter's furnace. Above it all was heaven, where only a small scatter of clouds, whiter than fulled broadcloth and seeming no bigger than a man's hand, drifted across the blue. Surely soon the weather would break?

A dust-cloud hanging above a hummock down the slope declared the presence of traffic on the fork of the road which came up from the town. Within minutes, hoofbeats could be heard. A lone horse was trotting up the ridge; Markham pitied the beast.

Its rider, when he appeared to Markham's view from behind the knoll, was a small man in a light riding cape stained white with dust. He had a few bags and a satchel, which was thickly stuffed, but evidently weighed little, or the animal could not possibly make such speed. A post-rider, then. Markham felt a sudden unaccountable hollowness under his heart.

Seeing him ahead in the narrow lane, the rider slowed his horse to a walk as the distance closed.

'What news?' Markham shouted as he passed.

'The king will raise an army against the Covenanters!' came the call back.

'Is it certain?'

'Rumoured, universally rumoured, sir.'

The rider spurred on, and disappeared in the dust.

As he guided Arion down the road's left fork, the track that led along the ridge to Crofthouse, Markham felt the sword at his side begin to weigh a little heavier.

REBECCA SOLLOM

Rebecca Sollom moved to the UK from Australia to earn her PhD in astrophysics from the University of Cambridge. A recipient of UEA's Seth Donaldson Memorial Bursary and an Escalator award (National Centre for Writing), she is currently at work on a speculative novel about Australia's climate crisis.

becsollom@gmail.com

The Fireman
An extract from a short story

INTROIT

The wiring rig doesn't work first time. Matti spends his whole shift waiting, callout after callout for automatic alarm calls and minor car wrecks, and the damn thing doesn't catch. He has to go back before his shift the following night, his bike light in his teeth and his hood up against a dump of late season snow, and rig the set-up again. The electrics box isn't protected with a lock or anything. It's just a little flap at the rear of the building that opens right out. When he's done, he closes it neatly back up again.

It's not until the third time – a whole week later – that what he's wired up actually does what he intends for it to do.

INVOCATION

Matti first saw the boy at a 12:45 p.m. Sunday showing of *Avengers: Endgame*. The weather was decent – for early spring this far north in Finland anyway – so maybe you could say that the cinema was a bad idea, but they worked four-on, four-off at Oulu fire station and it was the first of his four days off. Plus it wasn't like he had other plans, so he let himself do what he wanted. Snacks were overpriced but that day he was thirsty. Matti joined the queue to get a Coke, and that was when he saw him.

The boy was one in a group of six or seven kids, all of them in wheelchairs. All the wheelchairs and all the kids were different, a mix of headrests and armrests and wheels, bright snow jackets and mittens and arms and legs. There were carers, too, all women, pushing a kid each, joking around and chatting. They came up in batches out of the lift, while Matti watched. They were the kind of people you weren't supposed to look at, but he did look. He found it compelling, the way some of the kids wriggled and jerked inside their bodies and held their heads in positions that didn't seem right. And also: this one kid.

He was different because he looked more or less normal – in a wheelchair like the rest of them, maybe, but otherwise physically fine – and because he looked wiser than the others in some way Matti couldn't pin down. Not happy or angry or sad or bored. Matti thought that he looked *peaceful*. Also, there was something about his eyes and his lips and his hair and his neck that Matti found thrilling in a way he knew he shouldn't but which he had absolutely no control over. It was the same with movies: can you help being a person who loves supernatural horror, or who only ever watches screwball comedies? Of course you can't, was Matti's feeling about that, no matter how much you might have tried to fight your preferences, or for how long. To him, this kid had a lit-up-from-the-inside kind of beauty.

Matti couldn't stop looking at this one boy.

Once he had his drink in his hand, he hung back. He'd already decided he'd follow the group into whatever movie they were planning to see, but as he stood there scuffing his big shoes and scrolling on his phone, he figured out their tickets must be for *Avengers: Endgame* too. This made Matti smile, because it made him feel close to the God idea he used to love so much. He'd fallen hard for God at one point, back when he'd been a kid himself. He'd even gone so far as to sneak into three or four services at the big Lutheran church in the centre of town, but people at home rained down so much shit on him about it, he swore he'd never go back. It was sad to think about, because he'd been all but convinced back then that God was the best thing he'd ever come across.

The carers took the kids to the front of the movie theatre, close by the screen. Matti sat three rows behind, right over next to the wall, and watched the whole movie play out in the lights on this boy's face. Sometimes the kid laughed when he, Matti, didn't, and other times it went the other way. Occasionally the kid chatted to the carer sitting next to him, his appointed girl for that outing, and Matti wondered what it was like to have an appointed girl like that. He kind of envied the kid having an appointed girl.

Something strange and sweet began to flower in his chest. Already it felt like his life was drawing into a point, approaching one of those places in a movie where everything finally changes. Afterwards, he drove close but not too close behind their bus. His fingers drummed on the steering wheel, tapping out what seemed to him a kind of blessing.

CONFESSION

'Of course a single person can adopt,' the social worker said, polite and friendly. 'The process isn't short. There are many interviews. But if you're approved, we aim to make the best match that we can, both for children and prospective guardians.'

Matti had cycled to the Children's Services building, and his knees still jigged up and down as he sat in the social worker's office on the very edge of his chair, which was too small for him. The woman was tiny too, with a red nose and a blue pen that she kept stroking between her fingers.

'What if I have a child in mind already?' Matti asked.

'A relative?'

'No,' he said. 'A boy I met.'

Matti knew as soon as he said it that he shouldn't have. Her whole face changed right in front of him. Her body too: the way she leaned back. She tried to hide it, sure, but that made no difference. He put on his best smile and looked her in the eye as squarely as he could.

'I'd be good at looking after him,' he said. 'I watch a lot of movies. I've seen *About a Boy* and *Wonder* and *Lorenzo's Oil,* and lots of others too.'

The woman put down her pen; she looked over her shoulder, off to the left, as if searching for somebody to speak to. There was nobody there, though. Just a picture on the wall. A painting of a woman and a child and a man linked together, holding hands, walking through a field of yellow flowers.

Matti thought his voice sounded deeper than it ever had before; deeper, maybe, than a decent voice had any right to be. 'I wanted to volunteer to spend time with him first,' he said.

'As I explained,' said the social worker, 'we have a comprehensive vetting process.' Her face was rigid now, he noticed, upright and alert. 'You'll need to register.'

She handed him some forms on a clipboard, her blue pen now tucked up for him inside the clip. But when he went to write his name his hand kept catching on itself, stuck in a loop like when a movie wouldn't stream right and the circle on the screen kept turning round and round. He felt sick; he felt like she could see right inside that part of his head where he kept all his private thoughts about the boy. Like, for example, his image of the two of them together, watching movies. Matti doubted that the boy – being twelve, or maybe thirteen, at the most – had seen all the earlier *Avengers* films, so that was where they'd start. During downtimes on his shifts recently, while he lifted weights and listened to everyone else's chatter roll around the bunkhouse, that'd been all he could think about. That, and how the kid wouldn't even need the wheelchair most of the time they were together because Matti could just carry him around. He figured the boy probably weighed less than a midsize carbon extinguisher.

Matti put the clipboard down on the desk. He left the building quickly, skimming down the fire stairs four at a time. Then he cycled back to his flat and sat in the dark with his curtains shut, coming to terms with what it was really going to take.

KYRIE

When the alert comes in, at 10:39 p.m., he is laying up wet hoses with Mika and Alex and Emil. Mika is telling them about a reality TV show he likes. 'And then, the pair of them start fucking underneath the covers,' Mika says. 'Can you believe it? Right there, on the screen!' Emil and Alex laugh, and he laughs too, but a beat behind, like always. They know it, and he knows it too, and it's been years since he tried to fix it or make it any different.

Immediately they drop the hoses, move for their gear, mount up. They're driving out of the station before the watch leader gives his brief.

'A children's home,' he says. 'Single-storey dwelling. Full of kids in wheelchairs.'

The watch leader rubs at his sweating forehead under his helmet. They'd had a fry burn in a takeaway in Välivainio an hour back; nobody on the shift is fresh. They don't need to be fresh, though, Matti knows. The crew will do what needs doing whether they're tired or not.

'Seven in total, plus two adults,' he continues. 'All to be brought A-side after extraction. Thermal blankets, but you can't assume the kids can wrap themselves. Understand?'

They nod that they do, and that's when Matti's chest gives way inside itself. Shivers run in his hands and feet and up behind his eyes. He shakes them out. It's dark inside the truck and nobody sees. If he knew how to pray, he'd pray for mercy – over and over again. He takes a slow, deep breath, and watches the blue lights throb and play across the parked cars that they pass.

And then, there is the building: brilliant and bright. Even in the snow, the blaze has taken quickly.

Alex jimmies open the double front doors and right away, even as he's slammed by the heat and noise and all but blinded by the thick, dark, bargain-basement insulation smoke, Matti feels the presence of God surrounding him. He's been to plenty of burns in his life, but he's never felt this before. He has to stand still a moment to take the feeling in, to make sense of it, and as he does the others elbow past and disappear inside. He could be watching himself through a camera placed high above his head, he thinks, with spotlights blazing all around to light his way. He could be an actor in a film, with God as his director. What he feels is *peaceful.*

Matti follows the others into the building's wide main corridor. A few metres in, over to his left, one of the crew wedges open a door, and another comes through it, carrying a girl with long, dark hair. Further on and to the right, a third – Emil? – peels off into a smaller hallway. Matti keeps on walking straight ahead. Towards the rear of the building the fire is more intense. It roars, like fires always do. He's guided only by his instinct, or by God's. One room, two rooms, empty. The walls have posters and children's drawings stuck along them. A bathroom, then a cupboard. Maybe this was not the way, is what he thinks.

But then – around a corner to the right, a final door.

Smoke or not, he'd know this one boy anywhere. He's lying down, head on the carpet. A good boy, breathing low to the ground and clean like he's supposed to. He's wearing pyjamas and a soft, blue hooded robe. A miracle from God. Matti kneels down.

'Breathe through your robe,' he tells the boy, and he does.

Matti lifts him, and the boy is just as light as he imagined.

STEPHANIE Y TAM

Stephanie Y Tam hails from New York. A writer, researcher, and podcast producer, she's worked for Freakonomics and Radiolab. Previously, she explored her love for storytelling and social sciences at the University of Oxford on the Daniel M Sachs Scholarship. She's writing a short fiction collection and an intergenerational novel inspired by family stories, oral history, and the lives of immigrants.

stephanie.y.tam@gmail.com

An Inheritance of Flight
An extract from a novel

CHAPTER ONE – DISAPPEARANCES

New York, 1997. The first time my father disappeared, my mother started seeing the world in symbols. It began that night in June, on the cusp of the Hong Kong handover. Sweating in our Bronx sublet, windows flung open to disperse the humidity that hulked through the walls. Two global cities on either side of the world, streets sweltering on the brink of boil. My mother woke up just past midnight to find my father's side of the bed empty. Her hand instinctively reached out, but her fingers closed on air. Where he usually slept, the sheets retained the inverted contours of his body, but none of its heat.

A tremor ran through the ground. Beside her, the glass on the bedside table quivered and sang, the water vibrating ripples. Her mind churned through the past few days, searching, searching – what had she missed, how could she have been so blindsided? As the ground shuddered underneath, she tried to sift through the sliding layers, find something that would make sense of his disappearance. Her failure to predict this latest shock. While the foundations of our family gave way, she flung open the closets: empty hangers rocked back and forth. She ransacked the drawers and crawled under the bed, looking for a note or explanation – something, anything left behind. But there were no traces of him: her husband, my father.

The vibrations slowed, then ceased. In the glass by the bed, the rings on the water disappeared. The surface seamless once again.

'There are always signs,' my mother told me. 'I should have known. The problem is that I recognised them too late.' She began to train me to read for symbols that could organise the past, signs that could predict the future. Anchors within a world constantly shifting underfoot.

'In your father's ancestral village, there was a temple. Within that temple, there was a scroll. To the undiscerning, like you or your sister, it would simply appear to be a piece of paper with some classical calligraphy scrawled on it.' Her eyes slid towards mine. 'When I first saw it, I too missed its significance, blinded by love for your father. I know now it in fact harboured a demon: one that was intended to bring prosperity and power to his family, but instead enslaved them to the principalities of the underworld. Generations of opium-eaters. It was their family's curse.'

Shintoism, she then whispered, which confused me. My father's family practised a blend of folk Buddhism and ancestor veneration. Wasn't Shintoism Japanese? Why would my father's family have anything to do with a Japanese religion? But Ma just nodded gravely, as though that said it all: of course, they invoked Japanese demons. Of course, her mother-in-law was herself a demon.

Through signs, she structured the chaos of my father's disappearance into meaningful sequences. A piece of paper revealed an ancestral curse. A burst of sparrows prophesied their flight from China. An empty OxyContin bottle released the demons of her husband's past. When he left without warning, when the ground gave way, there were talismans that served as footholds to climb back up to the surface. For what else are words on paper, but symbols thrown against an absence, an abyss?

In the *Sailor Moon* comics that my sister and I used to read, there was a character, Rei Hino, who flung strips of paper with words written on them as weapons. We had always been puzzled by such a flimsy form of attack; surely, the lamest superpower of all. None of us wanted to be Rei when we played Sailor Scouts. And yet the tools of her rage were powerful; her words fluttered on a wind of their own, labels slapped onto the foreheads of demons. A way of categorising, then mastering, pandemonium. Time and again, she exploded her enemies.

For my part, it wasn't just my father who went missing; it was also the memories. I don't remember how many times he left, or how long he was gone each time, or just his absence.

'How can you not remember—' Eve presses me, when we speak on the phone.

'I just don't,' I retort. 'I'd rather focus on the times he was back.'

But my sister has always been persistent. 'The studio across the street. The trash bags, the bathroom light? Just after your sixth birthday; you were still wearing that silly paper crown.'

And then the memories wash up. Ma, heaving past the trash bags blockading the door. Ba, his mouth contorted, backing away until his hip rammed the dining table. Empty OxyContin bottles cascaded onto the floor, the plastic containers glowing a familiar, fluorescent orange.

There was a slight noise, and we all turned to the bathroom. A light shone underneath the door – a single line of light.

'Who's in there?' Ma's voice was brittle.

The knob turned, a copper click. I don't recall her face, or anything else about her.

Eve tells me, 'She looked at Ma, and then she looked at us. And she said—'

'I'm sorry you had to see this,' the faceless woman said to me and Eve. She did not address our father, or mother, just us.

Ma stayed behind but sent us away. Eve and I held each other's hand tightly as we walked back across the street, as though we knew even then that one of us might also disappear if the other let go.

—

Now that we are scattering across the world, I struggle to sleep. Last year, Eve moved to Los Angeles. Ma threatens to return to Hong Kong, though my grandparents still won't speak to her. Ba has vanished again. But everyone – even my grandparents – has promised to attend my college graduation next month. It will be a first for us in the United States of America. A family reunion: our only one in over a decade, even as we accelerate further apart.

Sometimes, when I'm lying awake at night, I try to weave together the voices of my estranged parents, grandparents, and sister into a narrative that will bring us all home: a counterspell against the forces breaking us away from each other. I start with my parents, try to imagine them in love. It scares me, to think that love can leave so little trace on your heart. That after a decade or two its imprint can be wiped out, a palimpsest already fading by the time I was born. When did the waves start washing us to separate shores?

When I asked my mother for stories as a child, she gave me boiled tea eggs.

'Here,' she said, rapping one on the countertop. Fractures spread across the stained shell. She picked at the broken crater. Flicked a piece of shell away. 'This was my childhood. Poh-poh would give me this when it was my birthday. Once a year, a single egg.'

It was beautiful, in its way – a mottled spiderweb of tea-coloured cracks where the liquid had seeped into flesh. Yet something about the intricate patterns sent a shiver down my spine. It looked diseased, like the age spots on Poh-poh's hands.

'A boiled egg for your birthday?' I creased my nose. Eve and I had eggs every weekend.

'Yes.' A curt nod. 'We were always so grateful.'

I rolled the tea egg she gave me between my palms, meditating on my mother's childhood. The egg left a sticky residue, the faint smell of star anise and soy sauce.

'It's true,' she said. 'My childhood was not like yours. Better off forgetting.'

'But you must remember more than a single egg?'

'I remember very little these days,' Ma said, 'and even that's too much.'

Over the years she dropped traces of her early years. I gathered them carefully, curiously. Reassembled the shards, eggshell-thin, that she cast off. Piecing together an explanation for her silences; for where she went, when she disappeared while sitting right in front of me, eyes glazing with distance. Was it to her childhood in Hong Kong, where my grandparents still lived? Or further back, to the place of her birth, the village compound in Guangzhou? As my mother shivered and stepped out onto a sea of broken glass, I trailed her across the waters. Three generations. Two continents. A stretch of open ocean across which dreams were lost.

Sometimes, if I lie awake long enough, I find my parents on the other side of the waters. A solitary boy picking through damp streets running with trash. A young girl with a long braid slipping into the gap between two walls. At twenty-one, I've come to understand that the past has a call for my parents as strong as that of their own daughter: a pull that only strengthens with time.

Hong Kong, 1961. My nine-year-old mother slept in a bunk bed with her grandmother, my Bak-bak. Tossed by turbulent dreams. The lap and lick of water against the hull of a fisherman's boat. Crash and coil, crash and recoil. The creak and groan of wood bracing itself. She moaned until Bak-bak shook her awake, and she surfaced gasping for breath.

Baby Girl, wake up! Bak-bak's knuckles rapped her shoulders. You're safe. We made it.

The boat, she gulped. I dreamed of the boat, our escape. Waves, endless waves.

Her grandmother stroked the nape of the girl's neck, where the hairs were feather soft. Waves are not evil things, she said. If you listen carefully, they can be music for the soul, mirror the rhythms of the body. They can draw sleep to you, instead of chasing it away.

Bak-bak tried to teach the girl to breathe to the rhythm of a slow tide.

Instead, the girl timed her breath to her grandmother's. As she listened to each rattling intake, then shuddering exhale, she spread her arms and let herself be towed to sleep by her elder.

But there were nights when Bak-bak was gone, the bottom bunk empty. Every few months, she secretly travelled back to Guangzhou to bring groceries to an impoverished aunt, who languished in China after the rest of our family had fled. I inherited their stories about the aftermath of the Four Pests Campaign.

Sparrows, the Chairman had declared three years earlier, are the public enemies of capitalism! They steal from hard-working peasants. Down with the birds, down with the pests!

Everywhere, peasants rose up and shot the little creatures out of the sky. The air thickened with the frenzy of wings. When the birds landed on trees, dedicated Communists beat gongs and pans until they fell out of the branches, dead of exhaustion. When the avian refugees fled to foreign embassies, crowds circled the perimeters and pounded drums. By the end of the second day, Polish embassy workers had to remove the feathered corpses by the shovelful. Nowhere to fly, nowhere to land.

The air hung with a heavy stillness. Then, at the end of two years, a low vibration rose from the earth. Locusts. With no birds to keep the insects in check, their hungry, clicking mouths devoured swathes of farmland, down to the very straw that lined the villagers' roofs. Millions of men, women, and children began to starve, their cries flailing heavenward.

In the days of the Great Famine, my mother told me, disappearances were common. When you said goodbye to your father, you never knew if it might be the last time you saw him. An elderly couple, rumoured to have hidden grain, vanished from their bed; an uncle discovered the hut pillaged, the earthen floor dug up. A three-year-old cousin went missing; a flutter of yellow cotton on brambles was all her parents ever found of her. My mother was no longer allowed to play outside, though she did not understand why. She only knew what Bak-bak told her: Never trust your neighbours. Never open the door on your own. You don't know who – or what – is outside. My grandparents started to whisper of flight across the waters, even as all around them friends and relatives dropped to the dust in the fields, the roads, the village. Nowhere to fly, nowhere to land.

OMER TENNENHAUS

Omer Tennenhaus writes literary fiction. Born in Israel as one of a set of triplets, he found his niche in arts, and began writing fan fiction in primary school. He graduated summa cum laude in a multidisciplinary degree course in humanities and arts from Tel-Aviv University. He will continue his studies with a PhD in Creative-Critical at UEA.

omertennenhaus@gmail.com

The Sticking Point
The opening of a novel

Once there was a universe.
　Any time / no time.
　Any where / no where.
　Any how / no how.
The universe existed for billions of years. Then came the birth of a consciousness separate from it.
　Cosmic dust gathers to form an embryo as black and twinkling as the space around it. The embryo begins to develop, starting with a spinal cord that gives it shape. A heart begins to beat, and a brain begins to think. A face sticks out over a neck, and ears pop out on each side. Arms extend as organs sprout, and eyes see a nose protrude beneath them. A mouth opens and inhales vacuum into lungs. Legs kick, hands wave. Skin thickens all over. Nipples and genitals, hair and nails grow, until the baby with the consciousness is free to move.
　The baby flies across space, growing as the universe expands. When it passes a star of hot plasma, a twinkle on its pure black skin blooms into a spot of hot plasma. When it passes a brown star encompassed by multiple rings, another twinkle blossoms into a brown spot encompassed by rings. Thus the twinkles on the baby's skin transform into spots of endless variety, mirroring the universe: a spot of ice that burns at the same time; a spot of water that raises steam; a spot that absorbs light. When one twinkle turns blue and germinates green patches, the baby decides to inspect the planet that caused it. So it hovers in front of Earth and views images from all times at once.
　A bumblebee drinks nectar. Waves crash on promontories. Orange leaves travel on the wind. A cloak of shadows engulfs every tree and building that stands on the ground.
　Raindrops splash against mud, causing flowers to collapse. Birds swoop away and moles dig into the ground. Dinosaurs race against a hurricane as humans ride on their backs.
　The baby sees air and lava, canary yellow and bathtubs. A lion gnawing

at a zebra's belly. The baby sniffs at dusty old parchments and feels its skin tingling, listens to a dinner party full of laughter and chewing, smells an odourless scent. Oceans form and oxygen invades the atmosphere. Glaciers congeal after robots drop temperatures to a new low.

Pyramids levitate upside down and kittens run on sand. Cities float above one supercontinent. The sound of silence diminishes as humans start to dance on the streets and embrace one another; the baby brings its fingers together and feels the friction of touch.

A fish swims alongside strings of DNA while humans gaze at the clouds. A dog chases its tail while a pharaoh takes a picture of their palace and posts it online. Spiders hang off a web and mate while humans make love. Snails and eagles, lizards and gorillas live their lives while humans write books about life.

A vial hovers above a wine glass. The vial empties its transparent liquid onto the red wine, emitting heat but no odour. A spoon materialises, stirring the solution until the poison is ready. The baby then raises the glass to its mouth. It sees humans who part their lips to take a sip – sees itself sitting with them around a table, it will join them, it was always there – they close their lips around the rim of the glass, and so does the baby. When the where becomes the if, and what who why, how—

The blue spot with the green patches sprouts, spreading all over the other spots as the poison streams through the baby's veins, until its entire skin is blue and green. Only its pupils remain black, and they twinkle as its eyes observe its new home. It will walk on the ground and bask in the sun, paint a picture and play the piano, run a marathon and learn languages. It will eat and poop, cook and clean, sleep and breathe; make friends and start a family; laugh so hard it will start crying, and cry so hard it will start laughing. It will love. It will exist as a human, not as a humanoid entity. It will study the cavity that has just fissured its chest open, and seek medicine that will seal this fissure back into flesh.

The baby looks down at its chest. A perfect circle – all black, no twinkling – has pushed the blue and green flesh aside. The baby inserts a hand into the cavity. The hand passes through the cavity and out the back, as though nothing is in the middle of its chest. Then it sees the same hole in the universe: a gap in the vacuum, smaller than an atom, somewhere between Earth and Mars, where the baby is hovering. As the universe continues to expand and the baby continues to grow, so does the cavity and the hole, widening across its chest and space. Humans would call this a slow pace. They would also call this a problem.

The baby tries to stretch its flesh towards the hole to shrink it; tries to fill the hole in the universe with matter, then antimatter. But it cannot devise a way to diminish either gap, for it does not know what caused them. Something has gone, leaving nothingness in its place, and concentrating on this lack only makes the baby realise its lack of knowledge towards this problem, as though another cavity has ruptured in its brain.

What to do next is another thing the baby does not know. Up until the advent of the hole, it knew everything there was to know, could do anything that could be done. What has triggered this deficiency? It was watching Earth, watching time, watching humans—

The baby re-examines the planet, scanning nature and listing every organism, dead or alive. Yet it can no longer perceive all beings at once, and instead detects only six humans from the same city, the same humans it saw sitting around a table, mixing poison into a glass of wine. Scenes of their doings flash from different moments of the same night:

An old couple lying in bed, forcing their eyes to stay open out of fear of falling asleep. With their backs to one another, they hide their wakefulness, each wishing to prevent the other from sharing their fear.

A young person lying in bed wide awake, staring at the ceiling and crying tears of joy. There is no need for sleep – he can see his dreams playing on the ceiling, can see himself ending violence and bringing peace.

A middle-aged adult punching a mirror. He thumps his shattered reflection again and again in an attempt to wake up, even though he knows he is not asleep.

A teenager running through the hallway of an abandoned building, her lighter flickering on and off in the dark. She knows someone is out there, stalking her in the middle of the night, yet she cannot find anyone alive.

Lastly is a medical student who inspects the organs of a dead body that lies on her bedroom floor. She documents her observations in a notebook and wonders whether she should stop early and eliminate the evidence, before her parents return home.

As it probes into the humans' consciousnesses, the baby recognises the same lack in their brain: the medical student cannot answer every question she asks herself about the human body, nor can the hallway runner know who is stalking her. The baby fast-forwards and sees that they will get some information – but never a full picture, never at once. They will experience time passing between the moment of curiosity and the moment of discovery, whether minutes, days, or years; yet even a lifetime would not suffice for some of their questions, and they would die ignorant.

What does it feel like, to wait for knowledge?

The baby sees the old couple crying from their fear of falling asleep, and the mirror puncher removing glass shards from his stinging palm, and realises that these experiences echo the dangers of the cavity in its chest. It touches the edge of its cavity, and its fingers flinch back, as though touching an open wound. Tears well in its eyes, and it cries for the first time. Then it recognises the same reaction in the ceiling watcher, who is waiting for tomorrow to dawn, hoping he can make it better than today.

Hope. The baby cannot find an equivalent to this emotion in itself, for hitherto it has felt no need to improve its being. But now it feels everything the humans do: hope and need, sadness and suffering, ignorance and temporality, existence. And it hopes – no, it knows – that it will find an answer to the gaps that are threatening it and the universe, or a shred of an answer, on Earth. It just wants – no, needs – to understand how these six humans would find this answer, and then, perhaps, it will be able to reverse the expansion of the gaps. The flesh in its chest will heal, and its body will no longer cause itself pain. It will be free to observe all of its creations, and try to live as one of them.

The baby abandons its knowledge and enters the minds of the six humans, inhabiting their bodies while also witnessing them like a ghost floating nearby. It begins to see and hear, smell and touch, taste and know only what they can. It begins to experience what it means to be human.

Rajasree Variyar is an Indian-born Australian writer now based in London. She has a background in financial services and degrees in Arts, Commerce and Psychology. In 2019, she was the runner-up for *Shooter Literary Magazine*'s annual short story competition and her novel-in-progress, *The Wanted Girl*, was shortlisted for Hatchette UK's inaugural Mo Siewcharran Prize.

rajasree.variyar@gmail.com

The Wanted Girl
The opening of a novel

Janani knew, the minute the midwife placed her naked, squalling, soft-as-silk daughter in her arms, that she couldn't lose this one.

An image came to her mind, burying a bundle gone cold and still, in the dirt by the young coconut palm. Her hands drew the hated little body closer.

Tiny limbs moved in fitful pumps as Janani looked down into a face as round and purple as a mangosteen. The baby's mouth moved over the swollen skin of her breast, and her plaintive wail died as she found the nipple and began to feed, her minute fingers resting against the skin over Janani's heart.

Janani watched her in the light of the oil lamp, her eyes trailing along each line of her body, trying to find something that made her less than perfect. '*Rock, my little peacock.*' The lullaby escaped through her lips, the first words she'd managed since that last, pain-riddled push. Hands were fussing around her, tender and papery – Kamala, the old, strong midwife who had delivered Darshan and likely most of the rest of Usilampatti village over what seemed like centuries. Janani barely noticed, until someone spoke.

'Give her to me.' Pain and weariness turned what should have been a familiar voice into a half-recognised echo.

No, Janani tried to say. It stayed a tired whisper in her mind. She wanted to hold this new life for as long as she could. There was a rough fumble, nails scratching against her forearms, and the warmth of newborn, new-drawn skin was gone. Her daughter began to cry again. The noise stuttered into existence like a steam engine's chugs. The door closed, muffling the sound.

Get up, you idiot, Janani thought. She raised herself on to one elbow, then rolled on to the other. Kamala loomed over her, hands on her shoulders, gently urging her back onto the thin pallet. Her wrinkles had reshaped themselves into grim worry. 'Rest now, child.'

Janani's arms were shaking beneath her. She collapsed back on the bed. One hand came down on the mat with an angry thump. She'd lost track of the hours she'd lain here but exhaustion was drifting over her like fog.

Sleep dragged her under, blanketing the shadow of the baby's cries.

Janani woke.

The shutters had been opened, letting bright sunlight and the warmth of the day pour like molten gold through the bars on the window. Light extended in strips over the room, reaching up onto the bed and over her feet. She lifted them away from the burning heat, drawing them up into the shade. The smell of blood and must had dissipated, carried away by fresh air laced with the familiar aromas of the village – chickens, tamarind and tomatoes in simmering *rassam,* ground rice, cow dung, motorbike fuel.

For a moment she lay staring at the roof thatching, disoriented by dreams, blinking in the broken darkness. There was a plastic pitcher of water on the tiny round table by the bed, crowned by an upside-down steel tumbler. It woke her thirst. She sat up, tensed for the sharp shoot of pain she remembered even from that first birth, Lavanika's, five years ago. When there was nothing but a dull ache, she shifted her legs over the side of the bed, the cement floor cool against her feet.

The water was already warm. She drank anyway, cup after cup, until she became aware of the low hum of voices beyond the door. Kamala's bag, with its lotions and powdered herbs and roots, had disappeared. The tiny room was still cramped, but as tidy as ever. Her fading saris were folded and stacked on top of the squat, splintering cupboard that housed her husband's clean lunghis. Her ancient sewing machine sat nestled in a corner. Everything she owned, tucked away in this room.

The straw mat that Lavanika slept on when the heat was unbearable was rolled and leaned against the wall, and Janani felt a deep, desperate yearning for her, to bury her face in her little girl's curls. As always she'd sent Lavanika away from the pain and blood of birth.

The tumbler abandoned, she pushed her fists against the pallet to leverage herself to her feet. A fresh sheet had been laid under her as she slept, and she noticed for the first time that her night shift, sticky with the wetness of fluid and blood and piss, had been changed.

The baby.

The room was empty of her.

It was as though she had never been born.

Janani took a half-step, and when the pain didn't increase, continued towards the door.

A glint in the sunlight caught Janani's eye, drawing it to the gold-framed picture of the goddess Meenakshi Amma that had been her mother-in-law's wedding gift. Janani stopped, her hand on the door latch and her womb throbbing, and stared at the perfect, peaceful face. *It's all OK*, it seemed to promise her. She fought the urge to kick it to the floor, feeling sick.

She pushed the door open to face her husband and mother-in-law.

Darshan and Vandhana stood in the one room that made up the kitchen, living area and the draped-off nook that was Vandhana's bedroom. They'd been speaking in low voices, but both looked up as Janani entered. The midwife had gone.

There was no sign of her baby.

Instead, a few plates painted with the remains of *idli* and coconut chutney were stacked on the step of the open back door, ready to be washed. Janani felt a sudden stab of surprise that her mother-in-law had prepared breakfast. She hadn't had a choice, of course. Vandhana's only exception to her rule of minimal housework was when Janani was barely able to stand. The smells of roasted onion, ground coconut and hot, sweet tea still lingered, and Janani was suddenly aware of the new ache of hunger in her stomach. She thought of her daughter nuzzling for her breast and looked instinctively around the room.

'You should eat,' Vandhana said. 'Go and take a bath first, though. You stink.'

Janani's mouth felt parched again. She took another step forward, craning her head around Vandhana to look in the corner of the room, searching for a small bundle of legs and cloth. 'Where's my baby?' she said.

Vandhana stepped towards her. Her husband remained where he was, head down but eyes on her like a sullen child, his mouth thin and almost hidden by the thick black forest of his moustache.

'You stupid bitch,' her mother-in-law said.

Tiredness had made Janani slow. She blinked.

'The useless thing,' Vandhana said. 'Just like the last one. It's not worth any more thought.'

Darshan looked down and away, and that was enough.

Is it for the best? Janani thought. It was a flash of a thought, hot and grimy and she'd heard the answer a thousand times, but... *No. No, give her back. I want her.*

She couldn't force the words through her lips.

Through watering eyes, she saw Vandhana turn and walk towards the back door.

She couldn't let it be too late. Not again.

Janani took a step forward and then another, her arms outstretched.

'No!' she said. 'Where is she?'

A second later Darshan was a wall in front of her, hands on her shoulders. He manoeuvred her back towards their bedroom. She scrabbled at his arms. Thin though he was, she was still so tired. Before Janani could form a thought, she was half-sitting, half-lying on the unforgiving mattress, Darshan standing over her.

'It's easier,' he said. 'We can't afford another girl, you know it.' Her placid, inert husband sounded as angry as she'd ever heard him. 'What are we going to do? Even if we stopped eating we couldn't pay another damned dowry.'

Janani didn't realise she was crying until she felt the pounding sign of too little breath in her head and dampness on her cheeks. *Dowry.* She thought of the golden jewellery she'd worn on her wedding day, locked away in a chest in the cupboard, out of her reach. From beyond Darshan she could hear water being sloshed from a bucket behind the house – Vandhana, washing the plates as though nothing had happened, as though she hadn't held her new granddaughter hours ago. Janani tried to get up, not caring if he hit her, but Darshan's hands were on her shoulders once more, holding her down.

'Just trust Amma,' he said. 'Rest and I'll bring you some food. You need to build up your strength. Hopefully you can be back working by the end of the week.' At the door, he turned, his face seeming softer in the sunlight. 'You're well enough, aren't you? The next one will be a boy.'

'I don't want the next one!' she said, but the door had closed, muting the sound beyond it into a frustrating wasp's hum. Pushing herself off the bed, Janani stumbled to the door, her stomach muscles groaning in protest. Hard as she pulled, it wouldn't budge.

Maybe it's for the best. Maybe it's easier.

A memory filtered into her mind from another life, of sitting on her father's lap and listening to the low rumble of his voice as he told her the story of the birth of the baby god Krishna. Krishna's mother, Devaki, had seen her brother, the doomed king Kamsa, dash six of her newborn children against stone in front of her eyes, their little skulls smashed like pomegranates trodden underfoot. The seventh, the only girl, had slipped from his grasp as he swung her at the wall by her little feet. She had transformed into the mother Goddess in the sky above his head, and cursed Kamsa, reminding him of the prophecy that Devaki's eighth child would kill him. There was no escaping fate.

Leaning against the door, Janani imagined her baby slipping away into the air, shining in triumph against the stars.

She burrowed her wet face into one arm as she pounded the door with the other, and her breasts cried tears of milk into her nightdress.

J H L WAI

J H L Wai is a writer from Hong Kong and Canada. They graduated from UC Berkeley in 2019, and their work has been awarded the Orwell Society Dystopian Fiction prize. They are currently working on a novel about Cantonese pirates sailing on the South China Sea during the Opium Wars.

waitjayce@gmail.com

Tysami
An extract from a novel

A creaking sound broke through the commotion. The crack of gunshots, frantic shouting, orders relayed, drowned out by the deafening noise of a snapped mast crashing down onto deck. Heart in throat, Ah Sai watched as the junk beside them – one of Ah Bo's larger ships – split in two, the mast burrowed into the cabins beneath, exposed compartments rapidly taking on water. They weren't near enough to board the other junks, so the crew climbed over the gunwales, no time to bother with ropes or boats or ladders, jumping into the frothy mass below. Some weren't quick enough, and they slid along the deck into the water, trapped by scattered parts of the ship. Half the deck was already submerged, and as the ship sunk deeper, a wave swept over their struggling heads.

'Let the ladders down for survivors,' Captain called, and the deck boys ran to the bulwarks. Ah Sai grabbed a musket.

The enormous shadow of the British ship fell over the waters next to them. It was illuminated even at night, just two turns of day to the harvest moon, a cluster of sails silhouetted above. It lit up with gun and cannon fire on both broadsides. The crew scrambled to return it, shooting aimlessly, vision wiped blank by the sudden flashes. Around them, Ah Bo's remaining junks were heaving with movement and clamour and gunfire. Ah Sai could smell the stinkpots, a sharp, rotten stench, like bodies that would wash onto shore. The boy on top of the foremast was young – new to the crew and pimple-faced – but skilled, lighting pots and hurling them across with a practised arm. Ah Sai fed a shot into the musket and swung it towards the ship. Into a rhythm now. Fire, load, fire. But each bullet fell short, dropping into the water like dead flies.

Across the foreign bulk, another of Ah Bo's junks had been reduced to flame and debris, the surviving crew pushing through the water to the other ships. It was ablaze from shot shell, the mainsail now a pyre stretching its orange wings to catch on the other sails. A burning body hurtled overboard. A scream, snuffed out in water. The British ship looked barely touched. The last of the crew who had lost their junks were still swimming when Ah Bo's fleet started drifting away, slow but ripping open space to the rope ladders. There were men and women at the sweeps. Ah Sai felt rage flare in his gut. That Ah Bo, the chief, would abandon the people who stood with him. The survivors from the sunken junk next to them climbed onto deck, dripping and pale with chill, like water ghosts trapped in the world of the living.

In the light of the burning ship and the near-full moon, together almost as bright as morning, Ah Sai saw the British readying the broadsides again. A lascar running onto deck carrying bundles of gunpowder, shots rolled and rammed into the barrels of cannons, officers stood waiting to pull the gunlocks. He could imagine it, Captain's beloved ship bursting into flame, bits of wood blown into the water, expanding, drawing outwards, a cloud of orange and yellow and red, dense acrid smoke, and then everything gone. He let out a shaky exhale and reached out to touch his Captain on the shoulder.

'Captain, we have to go. Ah Bo's ships are moving west.' The sails were trimmed taut, but the winds were too calm.

Captain gritted his teeth. 'Take to the oars.'

They rowed until dawn, their limbs moving in rhythm with the beat of the drum, trying to carve more distance from the British ship. Even Captain had taken an oar opposite Ah Sai. Their muscles cramped, their throats were parched, and when the sky lightened into a silvery blue, the girl on lookout called to them and said, 'the foreigners are about five lei away.' The crew released a collective breath, and the unbroken pulse of the ship eased as the drummer relaxed. Captain rose, gesturing Ah Sai to follow, though he barked at the rest to keep rowing. Ah Sai grabbed a water jug and had it circle around the rowing crew.

The British had fallen behind, no surprises there. Their ship was heavier, and their officers rarely cut their hands on the unpolished wood of the sweeps. They left the rough work to the seamen and lascars and cabin boys. Ah Sai had seen – held – a Navy gentleman's hands before, a night in the city, palms un-calloused, smooth as the handkerchief the officer had tucked in his breast pocket, silken with a small corner embroidered by his wife in England. It had been a stolen fumble, hidden in the alcoves and the dense fog of an opium den.

The morning mist that Ah Bo's fleet was wading into now was cooler than the smoky fog of nights in the city. But it was the mist that made them overlook the other ship until it was too late, puffs of steam merging with the haze. It emerged out of the sea fret like a san, a sea monster that dealt in mirages, that closed in on sailors like a gigantic clam. Their ensign was raised – a stark red cross against white, the Union Jack in the corner – and it was moving without sails to buffet it along. Steamers, Ah Sai knew. They could move even when the winds were still. There were shouts from Ah Bo's main ship, but the steamer passed them without gunfire or warning.

They appeared again, not an hour later. The ship that had been chasing them since yesterday towed by the steamer. No preamble, both ships opened fire. Another of Ah Bo's junks destroyed, the whole broadside littered with shell and shrapnel, tilting slowly into the sea. The crew manning that broadside littered with grapeshot. The survivors dropped into the water and sunk or surfaced, climbing into junks around them.

Fook Jeh took her station at the cannon, packing the shot and the gunpowder in, eased it into course with Ah Sai's help, and let it fly towards the steamer. It seemed like a graze, but the force of it jolted the waves and rocked heavily into the hull of the ship. It puffed steam but didn't move. The steamer's crewmen disappeared below deck, frantic. The first ship, the one with the many sails, had run too close to the shore, and even with all the sails set, it couldn't drift. Was it finally over? Surely the British could not give chase now. He turned to Ah Bo's main ship, to see if the chief would signal where they would go next.

The clang of a grappling hook at the gunwale behind him. Ah Sai spun around. There was a stream of boats paddling swiftly from the two British ships, a river of white and navy. Another grappling hook. He unsheathed his knife and crept aft towards the taffrail. 'We're being boarded,' he yelled. His hands shook. When he looked over into the waters, there was already a mass of boats crowding at the bottom of the stern. He cut the rope from the hook, and a bullet narrowly missed his face. Another hook. He moved to cut it. A smatter of shots from several handguns. He jumped back and ducked.

'There're too many of them,' Captain shouted. 'Get back, Ah Sai.'

The soldiers were firing relentlessly. There was no way to stop them boarding. The first few men climbed over, and they had pistols and revolvers aimed at them, boarding axes in hand, swords swinging. Ah Sai watched with panic as one of the kitchen boys fell with a bullet to the gut. The girl on lookout, bleeding from a sword to the chest. He ducked behind a barrel and saw Captain do the same, grabbing a revolver. Ah Sai's hands were still trembling, and all his rounds missed. Five shots and not one connected. More were boarding, a tidal wave surging over the stern, white and blue flooding the deck. Somehow the soldiers were not falling. There were just more and more and more.

'Abandon ship!' Captain's command pushed through the din of gunfire. Did his voice shake? Ah Sai couldn't tell through the noise. And then they were hauling boats over the bow, climbing past the anchors. Ah Sai took one last look at their ship, so many dead on the deck. The kitchen boy's sister lay next to him, his hand in hers, blood pooled around both of them. The girl on lookout who had joined the crew with the pimple-faced boy, the boy who was kneeling over her body, keening. Ah Sai couldn't pull him away. Fook Jeh's older cousin sprawled face down and unmoving, sword still in hand, a widower who knew how to make paper cranes and lotuses and lanterns. Fat-jai slumped over a crate, the eighth son of an eighth son, so they called him the lucky son, a burly boy who was the arm-wrestling champion of the crew. Felled by an axe, a massive wound that dragged down his spine.

Ah Sai was about to lower himself from the gunwale, Captain on his heels, when a cry shattered the air behind them. The pimple-faced boy had stood up again, a cluster of joss sticks in a fist, a pistol in the other, and the basket of stinkpots in front of him, a mass of gunpowder at his feet. '*Idiot* boy,' Captain yelled, running back onto the ship.

The deck exploded, splinters of wood and flame flying up all around them. The force of it made Ah Sai lose his grip on the rail and stumble into the boat below him. Fire, so much fire. His ears ringing. An officer near the boy flung overboard by the explosion. The waves swept outwards, and the boats with it. The ship started to sink, and Captain didn't appear over the bow again.

—

On the night of the harvest moon, Ah Sai would not celebrate. He would find himself stranded in the mountains, the remnants of Captain's crew ploughing through the dense forest with him, avoiding the villagers whom Ah Bo had blazed out of their homes. Those of Ah Bo's crew who were too exhausted to escape into the mountains would be beaten and killed by the villagers they had once terrorised. From his hideout with a view over the shore, he would see boys barely fifteen wielding sticks and knives, bringing them down and down, and boys barely fifteen bleeding out onto the ground, boys crawling and dropping still on the rocky sands.

On the night of the harvest moon, he would not be splitting a mooncake with Fook Jeh and the Captain, would not be licking lotus paste and lard-grease pastry off his fingers, would not be praying to Seung-Oh, the moon goddess. He would find himself in front of a temple, praying to Tin Hau, goddess of the sea, praying that she would protect the Captain's body where he lay among the wreckage of his ship. He would find himself faint from hunger, Fook Jeh beside him and the crew behind, on their knees in front of the goddess, weak with thirst.

On the night of the harvest moon, he would not be watching the fire dragons dance, the scent of incense wafting through the city streets, globes of joss sticks spinning in the air. Instead he would watch the smoke rise in the next bay east where the last of Ah Bo's fleet had been standing by. He would smell the burning of wood when the wind rushed west. He would hear some time later, in the early hours of the following morning, when the harvest moon still hung ripe and heavy over their heads, that Ah Bo's base had been completely destroyed, but the chief himself was gone.

DANIEL WILES

Daniel Wiles is from Walsall in the West Midlands. His work has been published in the Electric Reads *Young Writers Anthology 2017* and online at *Black Country Arts Foundry*. Excerpted here is the beginning of his novel set during the Industrial Revolution. He is the recipient of the Booker Prize Foundation Scholarship.

yelawan@gmail.com

A Black Country Parable
An excerpt from a novel

CHAPTER ONE

Michael stepped into the cage. It was about ten feet wide and long. He was followed by a dozen other men and women. Squeezed tight. He wore an ashen grey cotton shirt that was once white. Outside the cage men and women moved around the vast sea of black land, down its banks, in and out its wooden offices. He watched them. Women unhooked and hauled skips of coal from the pithead and pushed them down the short banks to be loaded onto waggons. Men moved waggons about the land to be deposited onto slag heaps upon it and onto barges that were in turn loaded by other men and women and piloted along the cut for distribution. The giant pit wheel breathed slow and methodically. Westward groups of gulls laughed. Central to the bank the giant chimney sicked up storm-black smoke and created a lingering baldachin. The steam engines rattled loud and hot, a constant alarm. People shouted. Dead leaves from surrounding woodland carried across the ground by autumnal wind. Rooks and crows amongst the black earth. The thick smell of smoke and soil. He stood as each other man, soldierlike with incarcerated eyes. Waiting.
 Winter soon.
 He looked down at the man who spoke. A fellow hewer. Already half-naked and bearing scars across his chest that lacerated his soot-fogged skin. His stature unusually small. His hands unusually large. Michael recognised him.
 Suppose weem paired up.
 Ows that? the fellow hewer said.
 Lawrence day tell ye?
 Work me stall, car spake to that cunt.
 Neednt bite onds that feed ye.
 Doe bite. Juss doe fancy spakin to im.
 The fellow hewer looked up to him and smiled and his last few teeth were shades of brown. So, what was ye told? he said.
 That om to be paired up wi someone who looks as yow do.

Cain.

Michael.

So yowm new.

Ar.

Where frum?

Brownills, Michael said, turning to Cain who still stood looking at him with that partial smile plugged with chewing tobacco. His face viewed better now and around the mouth a scratched patchy beard dyed with soot and slick with oil. His nose daftly small like a shirt pocket button and stabbing silver eyes that shone oddly bright.

The huge iron chain that held the cage started moving. The sound of mechanical breaks like the cracking of fingerbones. The cage lowered rhythmically. Everyone started to undress to their long johns and held their clothes clutched against their groins. Dark grey light swapped for the hot orange glow of Davy lamps and candles. The heat bathed them slowly from toe to head. The reek of chokedamp, sweat, and manure. The shouts of the colliers and snap of the hewers picking at the walls. As the cage was swallowed into the belly of the earth he looked up and saw a child peering over the lip of the mine. Why Why does this earth take the child Why do we allow it as men and when will it change One child more Almost every week One child more growing underground without sun and plague on their lungs Why does He allow it The mine brings coin and life One child more and we can forget. That's the reason.

He had a child of his own. Four years before. His wife died in childbirth. A friend of the family barren to have her own offered to be the child's minder. They married and raised the child ignorant to his true mother. Sometimes he went fishing with the boy along the canals. There was always something to find, even if the fish that darted along the shallow cut floor were proving evasive. Frogs and toads. Dragon and damselflies. Crickets. Along the farm fields hedgerows that held robins and sparrows, hunting worms and in turn hunted by kestrels. A lone fox springing headfirst into the small embankment.

There was a worry that lived in him. Bored into the centre of his back like a woodlouse. Unreachable. He spoke with his wife about telling the boy of his real mother. She always resisted. I am his real mother, she said. The truth denied by her as if the woman that shared his life and paid with her own did not exist. Nor did she ever exist. The boy himself existing in an unknowing land of creation and revocation for if his true mother never existed then how could he.

The cage hit the floor. Everyone stepped off. The workers replaced by the morning shift oozed lazily from the sump and onto the cage. The cheerful noise they brought with them that could only be described as end of shift jubilation, left with them up the shaft as the cage was lifted again. The wind was gone now. Air stagnant and damp. Michael looked about him whilst the other men spoke to the underground manager.

Ours is five, Cain shouted.

They left their clothes at the sump floor and picked up Davy lamps and walked down the in-bye. Immediately they were met with a young boy who had iron chains around his abdomen. He was pulling a small skip of coal along the narrow track road. The boy was covered in abrasions where the chains rubbed against his skin. He looked up at the men. They moved. He carried on. Michael turned and looked down at him again and noticed burst blisters all about his body that were bleeding from the centre. The boy winced with each step. The only part of his face that was left free of black were the lines around his eyes. He fell to his knees and slowly took his chains off. They dropped to the floor with a dull thud like a chair falling on a rug. He approached the undermanager who presently took a stick that he kept under his wing and started whipping him with it.

Leave the nipper, Michael said.

The undermanager looked at him from up the in-bye, inclined so he had three feet on him. Cain nudged Michael and said, Less goo.

The central pit was about ten squared feet in size, but on the far side there were channels that led to different stalls where men would work. The ground was logged with deep black water that held glowing shapes reflected from the lamplight. Moving and dancing. Men waded through it ignorant of its murk and scum that lacquered the surface. They did also. Wooden beams supporting the ceiling disappeared into the water. They walked past the unsteady fire of a furnace that moved foul gases and smells of the mine haphazardly through an upcast.

Two boys emerged from a small ventilation shaft. They looked unhuman like some blind, bald rodents unearthing themselves in search for scraps of candlelight. This he had saw before, it was he fifteen years ago. Picked up by a man after midnight and worked until sundown the next day. He saw the darkness. He saw the nothing. Sometimes he would go months without seeing the sun. But kids always preferred this job to haulage work. It was frightening and dangerous, but perhaps not as frightening as the pain of iron chains pulling on the skin, the odd shapes that spectred yellow on the wall. The angry men. The ache. The tire. The fear of the undermanager's whip.

He reached into his trouser pocket and lit the candle with his lamp and handed it to the boy. When the child took it he realised it was a girl. She took it like a timid squirrel taking a nut. The two children, stark naked, held the wicked gold carefully between them. Decorated faces blotted with soot. Already it dripped onto their hands and ran down their wrists. They burrowed back into the vein of the mine. He moved into the arteries.

From there the mine took three different directions. Each artery had only enough room for men to crouchwalk. Michael was a tall man and struggled to fit in them at all. Cain moved down the tunnel with ease. He squirmed his way through. His perspired body scratched by the rough walls. Shoals of grey worms earthlodged. He was a giant parasite in the body. At each stall the mine opened up a bit and that's where the men were already at work with pickaxes. The clap of sharp reports. He shouted at them when they swung back and almost hit him. One man on stall three turned and stared at him. He was bald and looked around fifty and had burn scars covering so much of his face so that he looked monstrous and devoid of all facial expressions. When he reached the fifth stall Cain was already busy on it. It was hardly opened up at all. Indented about two feet tunnelside. He placed his Davy lamp on the floor and knelt down and took his boot off and shook the water from it and after doing the same with the other he lifted the pickaxe and struck it against the coal. Then the two of them spoke in between pops of pickaxe.

Why do that. The lad, Cain said.

Any a nipper.

Doe trouble yaself wi it.

Ye got young a yown?

No response. Michael stole a look to his side as they hit the surface at a steady pace.

Boy has a choice to work the mine, Cain said.

Doe know that.

Is yown workin down eeyah?

Ay of age yet. Doe want im down eeyah though. Thass why om workin two mines now so e can goo to school.

Ow old bin e?

Fowah.

So yowm still workin up Brownills?

Ar.

Cain stopped. The blood orange marble from the Davy lamp lit up his wide eyes. Well I doe know if yowm more sense than stupid, he said.

CHAPTER TWO

His shift ended. He and the other men and women were loaded back onto the cage and spewed from the mine. He went to the village and bought a white loaf from the bakery. Got there just before closing. A family should never look upon a loaf a bread as luxury, the baker said, shuffling about behind the counter. The village empty save a few partied crows and pigeons in dead trees that lined the streets and rowdy dregs that hung outside the pub. A shout of accusation. Jeering of a crowd. Towards the south a red glowing skyline. The sun long set. This crude painting the living beast of industry, the chosen child to the earth's breast with its perfect heart beating metronomically throughout the night. He held the loaf under his arm and walked.

Along the cut, desolation of light save the distant glow of the fires and furnaces. He trudged through mucked puddles. Each of his boots stuck for a second before being sucked back out. Nesting coots squeaked from the reeds on the opposite bank. Nocturnal mallards huddled with beaded eyes watching him pass. Clouds of gnats about his head. Swifts swung about screaming from hedgerow to hedgerow. Fork lightning over the horizon. Whitish blue against the red. A figure came. He did not notice it until it was five feet ahead. It was a lad. He was bleeding down his neck and his cream shirt was ripped loose at the arm. Deep gurgling thunder. The lad went past him, head down but looking up at Michael from the corners of his eyes. Turbulent quacks of ducks. He turned around and saw the lad sprinting barefoot down the cut.

He walked until he reached the new iron bridge. He used it to cross the cut and followed a path until he arrived at a small bungalow. From outside a small haven from the smoke and dirt. Warm yellow windowlight. He wiped his boots on a brown bristled mat and opened the door and walked in.

BROCK ZAWILA

Brock Zawila is an author from Victoria, Canada. His fiction appeared in *The Malahat Review*'s 200th issue. From 2014 to 2015 he co-founded a writer's collective that ran events connecting unpublished writers with published authors. In 2017 he received a bachelor's degree from the University of Victoria's prestigious creative writing programme.

zawilabrock@gmail.com

A Dome Within Falling Domes
An excerpt from a novel

CHAPTER ONE

The burned man comes to my door on the third Sunday of each month and asks me to sign a petition. I don't have his name and I don't know if his solicitation is professional or pure lunacy, but he knocks, and I sign as he explains which new local crisis requires my endorsement. A fear of him is understandable since, aside from his scars, the man is much taller than me and his refined posture pits him motionless on my doorstep. I always forget that he arrives on the third Sunday of each month and if I could ever remember his coming, I would without a doubt feign absence. It doesn't help that on Sundays I am a man of the living room and it would be hard for him not to see me through the bay window as he crosses the front lawn of my duplex.

I typically open our encounters by saying, 'Oh, it's you,' as if we were old friends and he will nod and start his spiel. After signing I change my grip on the doorknob as I watch his jawline delta of melted flesh stretch and squish to the slow cadence of his speech. Then I take a small action. I'll scratch the back of my neck and repeat the last words he said to me as a question, or maybe I'll look over my shoulder and furrow my brow at some unseen urgency. Whatever it takes to signal to him that our monthly exchange was slipping away, and he leaves respectfully. He smiles at me as if to let me know that even though I've been short with him, this was an experience he was used to.

To this day I hold two key opinions of my role at the company. These opinions only ever changed in nuance, but the core of them persisted throughout. First, the software was unfortunately good. Second, Sully found me.

In that email she praised an editorial I'd written back when my interests in technology were more enthusiast than advertorial. The writing gave credence to emerging technologies that had a penchant for garnering societal fear. Specifically, how software that engaged in data collection was often warred as a false dichotomy between the benefits of mass information and breaches of privacy.

I rejected the argument. These were simply tools that could be employed in as many amoral ways as they could immoral. An algorithm might be inserting your interests into a bingo cage to spit tailored advertisements at you, or it might be assisting a city planning department pinpoint communities using too much water during a drought. I appealed to history, argued there were few machines, simple or otherwise, that'd been constrained to their utilitarian applications. The printing press allowed knowledge and history to be preserved in a manner that had never been witnessed before, but it also perpetuated mass misinformation. The crop-breeding technologies employed in the green revolution of the 1950s and 60s provided countries with food surpluses. It also led to mass deforestation and an unsustainable rise in population. A hammer could strike a nail or a skull or a nail into a skull or a nail into a beam.

There was a controversy that followed the article and as is the dance of controversy, my work found important eyes. I followed the rhythms of modern success. I managed social media accounts for start-ups. I beat the drum. I was hired by a company that made water management software. I beat the drum. Then for a long time, there was nothing. So, when Sully emailed me to ask if it would be all right if we did the interview at my house, I said yes.

I was either living or hiding in the capital city of British Columbia, Canada. I didn't own my house and my yard was shared with the tenants who lived in the suite next to mine, but I'd been living there for some time and had claimed the space with yellow rhododendrons and white flowering clematis that climbed the banister leading to my back door. I claimed it with sea stones and moon snail shells stolen from nearby beaches, claimed it with rosemary, thyme, and spearmint.

Sully knocked on the gate to my yard while I was watering my garden. I recognized her from the masthead of her company's website. She was short or I was tall. When she came to shake my hand, I had to slouch to meet her eyes. She declined my offer for tea and stood on the summer-brown lawn in a mauve jumpsuit with long lapels. She wore her platinum dyed hair in a topknot. I dragged a pair of folding chairs out from underneath the stairs to my suite and placed them at an angle facing the rhododendrons. As we sat, she turned her chair towards mine and for a moment we shared a silence as she flicked through documents on her phone – the grand second brain. One of these documents was my portfolio.

She sniffed the air. 'My grandmother loved these plants.'

'They're very resilient.'

'I haven't seen one since I was a child in her backyard, and now that I'm reunited?' She bit at something. 'They are beautiful, or nothing else.'

Her eyebrows looked as though they'd been mashed into her forehead. She was at her phone again, scrolling through my document.

'Beautiful or nothing else?'

'I'm saying they have the capacity for colour and growth. That's their thing. I won't deny their claim to prettiness.' She clicked her tongue. 'If I was an idiot, I'd congratulate them.'

'Please don't patronize my flowers.'

'Is there more to this?'

'Does my portfolio not excite you?'

'The ubiquity of "qualified" is a puff of smoke. Speaking of which…' She took a chromatic pen-shaped vaporizer from the breast pocket of her jumpsuit. She uncrossed her legs and sneered at the rhododendrons. 'Do you feel fucked up?'

I chuckled. 'Should I?'

'Depends on who you ask.'

'It also depends on what it is I should feel guilty about.'

'We've all done things we're not proud of.' She inhaled and blew out a small raincloud. 'When I was a teenager, I made cigarettes from butts I took from ashtrays.'

I sighed. 'Yeah?'

'These days, you've got to condense shame. And we do want you. You or someone else.' Her phone made a noise.

'Well, you could show me the product.'

'A moment.'

'You know, I have a theory about phones.'

Sully kept at her device, holding it up as though she were taking a video of me.

'Think about all the different forms of personal record a human being has held throughout existence, how up until the development of modern computers, human beings had one way to remember an experience. We could commit it to a physical object like a photograph or a diary…' I cut my lecture short. Hearing it aloud for the first time made me feel vile. It's gauche to speak of consciousness in such a fragmented manner. One must be prepared to quote greater minds, to weave their observations into greater meaning.

Sully shifted in her seat, still catching me with her lens. 'You stopped.'
'It's stupid.'
'No, come on. I'm interested.'
'Are you filming me?'

A trickle of water snaked its way past our chairs and filled the heel of a footprint I'd left in the garden soil. One of my eyelids fluttered so I placed the tip of my ring finger to the fragile skin. The stream thickened overtop the grass and I realized I'd left the water running. I got up to turn off the hose and asked if Sully wanted anything to drink. She shook her head and followed my movements with the lens of her phone.

I filled a kettle and loaded a teabag with rooibos, watching her crossed leg bob up and down. Browsing the *Hopscotch Security* webpage, I confirmed that the scowling lady with the platinum topknot was the same co-creator of the 'Bernard' security algorithm.

I sat back down with a mug of tea. Sully was looking at the rhododendrons.

'I also have a theory about phones,' she said. 'The way we communicate to each other has been revolutionized. Each of us is a public figure sitting on the fringes of a market, square, or park bench. We gotta understand that each online interaction is communicated facelessly. Let me ask you, Rudy, do you trust what you can't see?' Sully unlocked her phone and handed it to me.

At first, I was looking into a basic camera interface. A dialogue of numbers scrolled vertically on the left-hand side of the screen while an intersecting network of lines adjusted to the different points of my face. I saw myself raise my eyebrows and the crooked gleam of my canine as I smirked. I felt as though something very personal was being placed into a sack of infinite space. The screen froze.

At first, I thought the feedback on Sully's screen was just the camera's output as it lagged behind the phone's processing power, but I soon recognized that I was actually being presented with a series of mesmerizing images. There was my face, spitting out emotions I'd not given. Primary reactions like happiness, anger, sadness, fear and confusion soon gave way to nuanced expressions. I saw myself wistful, bored, and aroused. I saw my mouth change uncannily into shapes only an actor would present as they practised in a dressing room mirror. My eyes and brow furrowed and unravelled, they winced and softened and squinted as if in harsh sunlight.

I saw myself shift into middle age. The lines on my forehead darkened and stretched. My hairline was offered predictions. In what I later learned was a follicle-observing algorithm, the software gave me a sixty percent chance of baldness by age fifty-five, a twenty percent chance that the hair loss would be postponed till I was sixty-five to seventy years old, and another twenty percent that I would keep a distinguished, thin patch of greyish-blond for the majority of my life.

Next, I was dropped into my youth. I saw my features shrink horrifically. The software found pictures my mother had posted of me as a boy on social media and within moments I was looking in real time at a child that could've been me. For a while I sat with her phone in my lap, considering the novelty of having thirty-five years of life reduced to a string of alphanumeric commands.

Sully took her phone back. I noticed then that she was drinking my tea. 'You don't sleep. You go to a café that neighbours a sleep clinic. You clench. Your mouth cramps when you yawn.'

'We could be lovers, knowing what we know.'

'I haven't been flying out to here, there and everywhere just to interview people. It's not my forte.' She scrolled through lines of data. 'Like I said, we want you, but we don't need you.'

How long did I sit in my yard after Sully left? The small grasps of life flickered in front of me. How long was it? It was minutes or an hour. Rhododendron, mint plant, rosemary, moon snail, teacup, and so on. I thought about what she'd said, about my not sleeping. This was a sad truth. How long was it?

Later, after the afternoon had sewn itself to the tree line and plumps of geese flew south, I was eating an unpeeled carrot in a comfortable chair, stealing glances of the scene outside while reading a news article on climate change, when the burned man knocked at my door.

Acknowledgements

This anthology contains work written by the 2020 cohort of UEA's MA and MFA in Creative Writing: Prose Fiction. We are grateful for the support of the UEA School of Literature, Drama and Creative Writing in partnership with Egg Box Publishing, without whom this anthology would not exist.

We would like to thank our course directors Philip Langeskov, Naomi Wood, and Andrew Cowan as well as our other workshop tutors Trezza Azzopardi, Giles Foden, and Jean McNeil for their guidance and insight.

We are thankful to Tash Aw, Julia Blackburn, our visiting UNESCO fellow, and Joe Milan, our David Wong Fellow, for their contributions to this year's Masterclasses and one-on-one tutorials.

Special thanks to Nathan Hamilton and Jasmin Kirkbride at the UEA Publishing Project alongside Emily Benton and Sarah Gooderson for their help designing and proofreading this anthology. And thanks to Roz Edenbrow for allowing us to use her beautiful monoprint on our cover, and to Lucien Ross, Ellison Skinner, and J H L Wai for their elegant line drawings dispersed throughout this anthology.

Thank you to the editorial committee – Christabelle Dilks, Mairéad Kiernan, Josephine Lister, Lucien Ross, Omer Tennenhaus, and J H L Wai – all of whom volunteered their time to create this anthology, and to the meticulous Prose Fiction editors Tanya Banerjee, John Dimitroff, Drew Evans, Alice Franklin, Linden Hibbert, Zainab Omaki, Jyoti Patel, Ellison Skinner, Rajasree Variyar, and Daniel Wiles.

With thanks to all the donors who contribute to the scholarships that support our writers, including the Annabel Abbs Scholarship, the Booker Prize Foundation Scholarship, the Bourne Scholarship, the Curtis Brown Award, the International Bursary, the John Jarrold Scholarship, the John Boyne Scholarship, the Kowitz Scholarship, the Malcolm Bradbury Memorial Scholarship, the Miles Morland Foundation African Writers' Scholarship, the Seth Donaldson Memorial Bursary, and the UEA Crowdfunded BAME Writers' Scholarship.

And last, but certainly not least, a huge thank you to all the students on this course for their camaraderie and perseverance through the ups and downs of this year. Good luck to all of you as you bloom out of this course.

UEA MA Creative Writing Anthologies: Prose Fiction

First published by Egg Box Publishing, 2020
Part of the UEA Publishing Project Ltd.

International © retained by individual authors

This book is sold subject to the condition that it shall not, by way of trade or otherwise, be lent, resold, hired out, stored in a retrieval system, or otherwise circulated without the publisher's prior consent in any form of binding or cover other than that in which it is published and without a similar condition including this condition being imposed on the subsequent purchaser.

A CIP record for this book is available from the British Library
Printed and bound in the UK by Imprint Digital

Designed by Emily Benton Book Design
emilybentonbookdesign.co.uk

Proofread by Sarah Gooderson

Distributed by NBN International
10 Thornbury Road
Plymouth
PL6 7PP
+44 (0)1752 202 301
e.cservs@nbninternational.com

ISBN 978-1-913861-00-1